Emily
Warm Regards
Karen Thurecht

MURDER AT THE DUNWICH ASYLUM

BY
KAREN
THURECHT

Murder at the Dunwich Asylum
Copyright © 2020 by Karen Thurecht.

The author would like to acknowledge the Quandamooka people, and thank the traditional owners, past, present and future for their custodianship of the beautiful Island of Minjerribah.

Printed in Australia

First Printing: December 2020
Shawline Publishing Group Pty Ltd

Paperback ISBN- 9781922444301

Ebook ISBN - 9781922444318

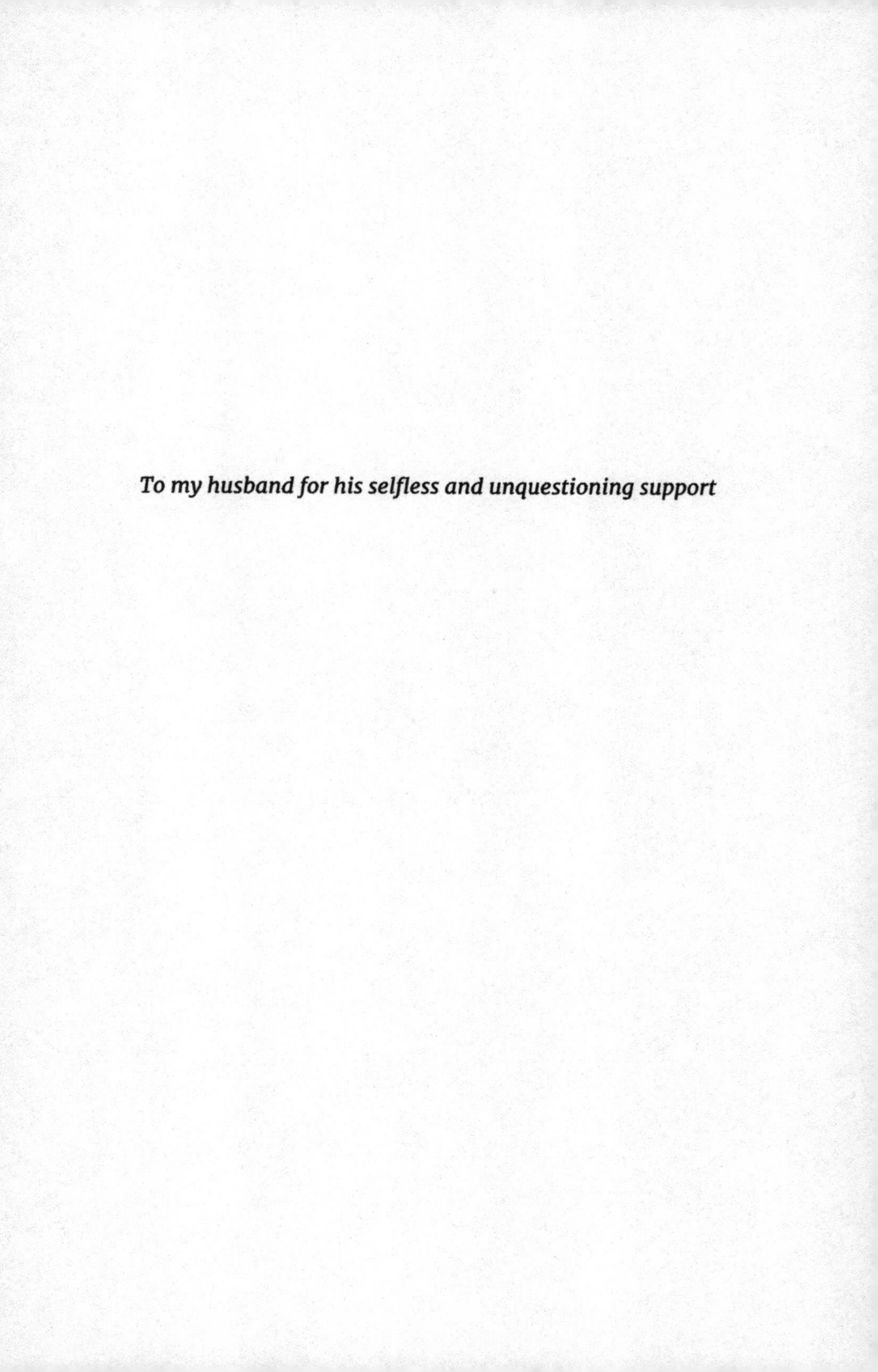

To my husband for his selfless and unquestioning support

CHAPTER ONE

It will not be a matter of surprise to your Honourable House that grave and serious abuses have crept into the administration of the asylum at Dunwich, which demands the immediate attention of the Government. - The Week, Brisbane. Saturday 10 January 1885.

---

23 SEPTEMBER 1884
WALLACE

Wesley Wallace made his way through the bushland behind the asylum, ready to begin the breakfast shift. The morning sun was warm on his head and a thick fog of alcohol-induced confusion crowded his thoughts. The sound of bird calls pierced the fog, threatening to trigger a pain in his head that would mark the rest of his day. He couldn't see well at this time of the morning on his best days, but this particular morning, his sight was the poorer for having lost his glasses. The path he took from the Aboriginal community at Myora to the asylum at Dunwich was well trodden. He traversed it himself at least three times a week. The majority of the people living at Myora also travelled the path regularly, as most of them worked intermittently, if not frequently, at the asylum.

Wallace coughed roughly and spat into the sand. Beyond the trees, clouds were forming over the mainland.

'Blast. Rain coming.'

His hut leaked like a sieve in the rain. Turning his head away from the line of flat land at the other side of the bay, and back to the track, he caught a glimpse of a shape ahead. Something dark swayed back and forth, slowly, just within view, then was gone. The shape was only clear for a second at a time, disappearing as the track wound in and out of thick bush. The untidy tangle of tea-trees interspersed with mangroves rising from the swamp not-withstanding, the shape appeared eerily out of place. As he edged closer, birds stopped screeching. Quietness fell about him. Something troubled him about the atmosphere and the view ahead, but his mind was not yet ready to unravel the mystery.

'Bloody Blacks.' He coughed again. 'Bloody stories would send a man half-mad.'

He kept walking, determined to reach the asylum and a long mug of thick tea before the morning's nausea overwhelmed him. He walked the next few yards, his attention focussed on the dark shadow ahead, still swaying ever so slightly, as it began to form into a reliable shape.

Wallace sucked in his breath. He recognised the shape of boots. Boots swinging from the bottom of two stockinged legs, disappearing into the heavy brown fabric of a woman's skirt. The figure of a woman hung with head falling to one side from the lower branch of a giant fig. Wallace stood below the tree for several seconds, trying to force his brain to tell him what the image meant. As he circled the figure hanging above him, a wave of horror rose in his breast. His breathing quickened and caught in his throat. His hands shot to his face in a feeble attempt to close out the image. Gradually, Wallace released his fingers a little at a time and peered through them. The woman's body swung gently back and forth above him. Birds continued to call, and the sun continued to warm him, while the swinging body of Emily May Baker grew colder.

* * *

'Holloway! Holloway!' Wesley Wallace banged with his fists on the Superintendent's door.

Wallace knew he would come quickly. The cottage only had two rooms. The door opened slightly, and the Superintendent's pale face poked through the opening, the chubby face of his wife directly beneath it. Wallace explained what he had seen in one lengthy breath. Despite his hurried account, Holloway seemed to grasp the salient points.

'Get Vissen,' he said to his wife.

The door closed for a moment while the Superintendent and his wife threw on their day clothes. Then the Superintendent's wife, Brigid, burst through the door and ran directly toward the Stores. Wallace shifted from one leg to the other, it was already warm, and the sweat was pearling across his brow. Maybe he should've gone for Vissen himself. Holloway stepped through the door wearing his red woollen jacket and military pants tucked into high leather boots. How could he bear the heat in that costume? It was only a matter of seconds before Brigid, and the Storeman and second in charge at the asylum, Cornelius Vissen joined them. Within five minutes they were hurrying along the sandy track that joined Dunwich and Myora, toward the hanging site.

Wallace stopped a few yards from the Moreton Bay Fig and pointed. He was out of breath, the pain in his chest worsening. The group stood gasping for several seconds.

'Vissen, have her taken down at once,' Holloway shouted.

Wallace watched Vissen's expression change. He couldn't imagine in his wildest dreams Vissen climbing the tree to release a body. He watched and waited as Vissen wiped beads of sweat from his brow. How long was everyone going to wait while Vissen stared with that look of panic on his face? When it seemed impossible that they could stand there glaring in shock any longer, as Emily swayed gently above them, two Aboriginal men appeared around the bend in the track. They stopped and joined the group, staring up at the grizzly image.

Vissen shouted at the two workers, 'Get this body down now!'

The pair didn't hesitate. They climbed up the tree and released the body.

'Have it taken to the hospital,' called Holloway irritably.

The men lowered the woman's body and carried it respectfully between them.

Wallace stepped in to help, tears pricking his eyes.

Wallace held the body in his arms and tried to stop himself crying. In spite of the effort, his face became wet, and he struggled to see. Blinking back the tears, he focussed on the backs of the two men who were now holding the woman's head and shoulders while he supported her legs. He found if he maintained his focus on the muscles rippling in the man's back ahead of him, he could sustain his balance and keep walking. He narrowed his focus to the moisture making tiny channels in the valleys between his muscles.

'God, if I'd only drunk less.' He coughed and spat again.

Bile rose in his throat and he managed to swallow it down.

Hair fell lankly from the body.

'Don't look at her face,' Wallace told himself.

He repeated it several times before his eyes travelled upward toward her face. It barely looked like his Emily at all. He stumbled, and the contents of his stomach rose until, finally, the force was too much for him to control. His entire stomach contents burst from his mouth and nose in a torrent of foul-smelling bile and half-digested food. He set Emily's legs on the ground so he could convulse without dropping her. At last, he stood up, wiped the back of his hand across his mouth and resumed his grasp of the corpse. He was numb.

Wallace and the two men carried Emily's body all the way into Dunwich, stopping several times so that Wallace could adjust his grip. The two men supporting her head and torso didn't utter a sound. The grim little group came into the asylum from behind and made their way directly to the hospital ward where they lay Emily on the long wooden table at the back of the building. Wallace stayed for several moments after the others left, arranging her tunic over her thin legs, wiping her face and stroking her hair back from her forehead. She didn't feel the same as she had when she was alive. Wallace missed the throb of life that should have been pulsing through her body. Emily had always seemed so thoroughly alive. He had difficulty equating the body on the table with the person he knew.

Wallace entered the Superintendent's office just as Holloway settled into his leather chair.

'This is all we need,' Holloway complained. 'While the idiots in Brisbane collect letters of complaint from the inmates about the lack of sufficient cabbage in their diets, one hung herself just outside the grounds.'

Brigid, who is also the Matron at the asylum, was hesitant.

'Is there any way we might prevent the circumstances of her death from reaching Brisbane?' she asked.

Holloway paused for a moment while he considered this, then his face contorted in the way it often did when his wife spoke.

'Don't be ridiculous woman, you couldn't keep gossip like this from reaching Brisbane. In half an hour the community will be buzzing with it. There is a boat due today. I'll wager the crew will know the whole story within five minutes of docking.'

Until that point, they had both ignored Wallace, who was listening in silence.

'Is the body laid out in the hospital?' asked Holloway.

'Yes, it is,' said Wallace. 'It's the inmate Baker,' he said. 'Emily May Baker.'

'Intolerable nuisance of a woman,' barked Holloway.

Wallace gritted his teeth. He was saved from speaking out when Vissen came through the door. He was pale and carried the bearing of a man who had news he would have desperately preferred not to tell.

'The Justice will be here shortly, Sir,' he said.

Holloway lifted his head in surprise.

'Who?' he cried.

'The visiting Justice,' explained Vissen, 'He's arrived on the *Kate*. What will you say to him?'

Holloway examined his hands.

'Well,' he said, 'I imagine I'll tell him the simple truth. The woman was not of sound mind and she wandered off the grounds in the dead of night and hanged herself from a dammed Moreton Bay Fig.'

Holloway turned his head to the side and grimaced.

Vissen said nothing.

'It's not a prison, Vissen,' declared Holloway, snapping his head forward to look directly at the storeman. 'We don't lock the inmates in cells... as a rule,' he added, remembering Ward 10.

Vissen continued to stand still in the doorway.

'Well?' demanded Holloway.

'The dispenser Reeves,' he began, 'caught up with me on his way back from the harbour. The *Kate* is carrying the visiting Justice, as well as another visitor, a young doctor from the hospital. Apparently, he's interested in institutions. He's on something of a sightseeing visit, as far as I can make out.'

'Good Lord!', shouted Holloway as he stood up, disturbing the ink well on his desk. 'This is insufferable! Are we running a zoological sanctuary? I've business to attend. I've neither the time nor the inclination to entertain casual visitors. Vissen, see to it he's informed he's not welcome, and he's not to leave the boat. He can return to Brisbane with the Justice this afternoon. What's his name?'

'Who?' asked Vissen, confused.

'The Justice, for God's sake!'

'Callahan,' said Vissen. 'The visiting Justice is Callahan. He's been here before. But sir, I have to tell you, Justice Callahan and the young doctor are, as we speak, on their way up from the causeway.'

At that moment, Callahan and the young doctor appeared behind Vissen in the doorway of the Superintendent's Office.

Holloway remained standing and immediately lowered his voice to a silky tone, full of welcoming cadences. He thrust his hand forward to take that of Callahan.

'Welcome back,' he said. 'I am so glad to see you again. Our Cook Wallace here will be honoured to prepare a meal for you.'

Holloway made a flourishing gesture toward Wallace at the back of the room.

'Of course, you'll dine with us at midday,' He motioned toward Wallace as though he expected him to leave, but Wallace didn't move.

'I believe you've had some excitement,' said Callahan.

'Heard of it already, have you?' said Holloway.

He breathed heavily through a forced smile. Holloway turned his eye to the younger man standing a pace or two back from Callahan.

'This is Hart,' said Callahan in an off-hand way. 'Doctor Hamish Hart. He's come to view the asylum. Has an interest in places like this, workhouses, asylums... that sort of thing. He's my guest,' he said with emphasis.

'Most welcome, I'm sure,' Holloway grinned unconvincingly. 'I trust you will have a pleasant and informative day with us.'

'Oh no,' said Callahan, 'The doctor's staying a week. He has the permission of the Colonial Secretary. It's all arranged.'

Holloway swallowed hard and managed to croak out an objection,

'Ah, our accommodation,' he began, 'it is... well... we have nothing to offer...'

'That's perfectly all right,' said the doctor. 'I've brought with me a tent and blankets. All I need is a meal once a day and some tea.'

'What would you do to occupy yourself for a week, Sir?'

'I hope to familiarise myself with some of your cases,' Hamish said with all the enthusiasm of youth. 'I'm most interested in institutions such as this. I've been invited to write an article for The Brisbane Courier. There's some very exciting new research coming from England...'

Holloway cut him short.

'I can see your mind is set,' he said. 'There's another boat leaving Thursday. If you find the living harsh, as I expect you will, you can return to the mainland then.

Wallace slipped out unnoticed to prepare lunch for the guests.

CHAPTER TWO

A number of facts in connection with Dunwich have been brought to my notice and are worth mentioning here. It is an extraordinary state of affairs that there is no record kept in the Colonial Secretary's office or any other Department in Brisbane, of the men and women who are sent down to Dunwich. A person entering the Dunwich Asylum does not give in his or her name until he or she reaches this institution itself. Consequently, should any friend who has lost sight of him or her desire to trace the lost one, before such a friend can ascertain whether the missing person is in Dunwich, he or she must charter a steamer and visit the Island itself. - Queensland Figaro, Saturday 9 August 1884

---

23 SEPTEMBER 1884
HAMISH

Doctor Hamish Hart gathered together his things, ready to leave the office. The welcome had not been an entirely enthusiastic one, but he was certain the Superintendent would soon get used to him. He nodded self-consciously as he left, noting that Holloway, his wife and the storeman Vissen, were glaring at him, reluctant to speak again until he'd gone. Hamish was glad to leave them behind.

'Irritable self-absorbed lot,' he thought as he closed the door behind him.

He caught a flurried whisper from inside. 'What on Earth were you thinking...' But he didn't hear any more.

Hamish glanced around at his options. There was a gap between the tents in the gully to the left of the telegraph office and the buildings to the right. He hauled his gear to a site between a tent and a ramshackle hut that was neither tent nor building, more a lean-to type of structure fashioned from roughly hewn wood and sheets of rusted iron.

'This will do,' he said out loud.

The area was flat and green, allowing room for several tents, and it served him a view of the settlement. He laid out the canvas and took up his hammer to bang in the first peg. It slid straight into wet sand. Water was seeping up through the ground, so he moved his canvas to the left a few feet and tried again, finding the same result. He stood up and glanced around at the other tents. The ground seemed drier beneath them.

'Evidently, this space is free because the ground is sodden,' he said, glancing around to see if anyone was near. He wasn't sure if he had spoken his thoughts out loud or not. There was no one to advise him, if he did. He poked around with his boot to test the water seepage in several places, then chose the driest patch of a poor lot and set up, knocking the pegs well into the ground in the hope they'd reach dry earth. Since Holloway had offered him no instruction on where he should pitch his tent, he was confident he wouldn't object to his choice.

Three quarters of an hour later, Hamish stood back to survey the scene before him. A row of low buildings made a line along the ridge, nestled comfortably below a hill that formed the backbone of the Island. A garden of well-tended marigolds, dahlias and cosmos surrounded the house behind the Superintendent's Office. It was a British cottage garden in a scene where the light was too bright, the sky too blue and the air too humid. Hamish wiped the sweat from his brow and dragged his fingers through his damp fringe. He was noticing the heat in the air for the first time since his arrival. Hearing a low hum, Hamish coughed as something flew by his mouth. He waved his arms about instinctively. Bees hovered in front of his face.

Hamish saw thriving beehives scattered around the cottage garden. As a result of the running commentary supplied by Callahan as they drew in on the barge, he knew he was looking at the Superintendent's cottage.

In front of him two timber buildings stood about sixty feet apart and there was another longer one about one hundred yards distant. Then there was a large brick building. According to Callahan, this was the hospital. Various other buildings, stores and offices were scattered along the ridge leading down to the harbour. There was also a series of other poorly built huts and tents to the back of the settlement, which accommodated staff and some of the inmates. Callahan had explained that those inmates who earned special privileges by working for the household of key staff members, were permitted to establish their own tents or build huts along the row called the 'top tents'. Apparently, these inmates enjoyed a level of independence and privacy not accessible to others. Hamish noted many of the top tents had their own fences and gardens.

Hamish was in no hurry to join Holloway and Callahan. It was clear the Superintendent didn't welcome his stay, but the place itself didn't seem unwelcoming. He set himself a log in front of his tent and started a fire to boil water for tea. Sitting on his log, Hamish gazed across the mangroves out into the bay. The mainland shimmered on the horizon, long and low, glistening silver on this sun-drenched morning. Thrown out in strong relief against the sky, was the white strip of beach at Peel Island to one side and the two white sand hills of Moreton Island to the other. According to Callahan's commentary, there was a leper colony on Peel. It would be good to go there as well. A feeling of contentment settled on him, odd in such a place. He had an overwhelming sense of being in the right place at the right time. This sensation punctuated a life that was more or less spent feeling like he didn't belong.

'Of course, I did spend the first seven years of my life in a tent,' he whispered. 'Not so strange that I should feel comfortable here then.'

Hamish smiled at his memories of the Ballarat goldfields. His parents had sailed from England, landing in the Colony of Victoria not long before his birth, setting up their lives in a tent on the bank of the Yarra River. When word of gold in Ballarat reached Melbourne, his mother and father packed up their meagre belongings and their newborn and made their way to the goldfields. It was there that Hamish first felt comfortable in his skin and in his surroundings.

Hamish poked a stick into the coals that kept his billy boiling. He concentrated on the red glow blinking on and off in the coals until a shudder ran through his entire body. He glanced around. Was someone watching him? From where he sat, he had a clear view of the settlement in every direction, to the mudflats and the mangroves on the left, the sweeping coastline to the right and down to the water's edge. There were a few straggling inmates returning from work in the gardens, but they were swatting sand flies from their faces as they walked, taking no notice of him at all. Hamish glanced behind him. There was no one there either. There was anticipation beyond the calm, an underlying foreboding. Something intangible and fearful seemed right behind him, or in front of him. He couldn't tell which.

Hamish finished his tea and used both hands to sweep the hair back from his forehead. It was the colour of sand and he wore it long to cover a scar that ran the full length of his face on the left side. He was forever brushing it back, so the length did little to serve its original purpose. He was aware of the irony. He also knew the foppish look belied his need for order and tidiness, another reason to smooth it back. His skin was pale and freckled. He should be wearing a hat, but he could never remember where he'd last left it.

Hamish had been told he was handsome, if it were not for the scar. His mother's sister made the comment, so he doubted it counted for much. Others had complimented him on his high cheekbones and his eyes that were essentially green but changed colour according to his mood. The scar continued to impact his self-image throughout his life, leading to a tendency to hold his head down rather than look people directly in the eye. He stretched his thin legs, stood up and braced himself. He was taller than most men, and this also contributed to his stoop.

Hamish knew he had to join the tour of the settlement while Callahan was on the Island, because after he left, he imagined the Superintendent would ignore him. He saw Holloway and Callahan emerge from the office, and rushed to join them, catching up as they were entering the female ward. Holloway motioned to a larger woman with strong shoulders and an ample breast to join them. This woman had been in the Superintendent's Office when Hamish first arrived, but they had not introduced her.

'My wife, Brigid Holloway,' Holloway said. 'She's the Matron here at the Dunwich Asylum.'

The woman had a no-nonsense face, the face of a person used to being in charge. Ash hair was captured in a tight bun at the nape of her neck, but wisps were escaping all around her face, revealing a hint of curl that would not be controlled. Brigid explained there were presently twenty-three female inmates at Dunwich. There had been twenty-four until last night. Only one of these women was under the age of forty.

'Of course, that was the Baker woman,' pointed out the Matron, 'The one who committed the final sin. The remaining women are elderly, inebriates, or ill,' she said.

'This small group of women makes up only a tiny proportion of the three hundred and four inmates at the asylum,' said Holloway.

'This particular ward is built to hold thirty,' the Matron explained.

Hamish surveyed the scene, taking in every detail. The timber building was small and rectangular, with iron beds lined up on either side of a narrow space down the middle.

'Most of the inmates are out working at this time of day,' the Matron said. 'They're in the laundry or in the gardens. Of course, there are some who are ill and in hospital.'

Hamish noted the beds were neatly made, and the room was clean, not the clean that he would have preferred, scrubbed and sanitised, but clean, nonetheless. They didn't linger long in the darkness making their way back through the door they had entered.

A couple of elderly inmates sat on the veranda blinking in the sun. Hamish stopped as the group passed them.

'How do you do?' said Hamish to neither woman in particular.

One of the old women, dressed in an alarming number of woollen shawls for a warm September day, gave a rambling account of her ailments. Hamish smiled throughout the account.

'I wish you well,' he said when she finished.

Encouraged by a sympathetic ear, the woman sidled up to Hamish.

'Hear that girl Emily topped 'erself last night?' the woman said nodding conspiratorially.

'Yes, I've heard,' said Hamish, wondering at the rapid rate news travelled at the asylum.

He opened his mouth to ask the woman what more she knew, but Brigid Holloway took his arm and led him on. He followed reluctantly, not wanting to miss his one chance to be shown around.

The group moved on to what Holloway described as the first of the male wards. Once inside, Hamish was shocked to see that forty beds were crammed into a space that would comfortably fit thirty. Iron beds were lined up as they had been in the previous ward. A shaft of silver light filtered through the filthy windows, illuminating a cascade of insects dancing about in the glow. The room was devoid of human life.

'We lock the inmates out of the ward during daylight hours to prevent idleness,' explained Brigid. 'Most of them work to maintain the community; mattress makers, bootmakers, candle makers, gardeners, maintenance workers, tending the animals.'

'Due to its isolation, the asylum runs its own cattle, pigs and sheep,', added Holloway. 'The cattle provide an ongoing milk supply as well as fresh beef. While the soil on the island is poor,' he went on, 'the land being mostly sand or mangrove swamp, it's difficult to keep sufficient produce to feed the growing population. Still, there are substantial gardens, herds and grains.'

Holloway pointed to two large iron tanks.

'There's a galvanised tank to every house and building and there's a large well to receive surplus water. On the rising ground, higher than the buildings, there are two additional iron tanks. Obviously, the buildings and tanks require constant maintenance,' he said. 'Most of this work is carried out by the inmates themselves. In fact, besides one carpenter from Brisbane, the inmates have carried out all the building works and plumbing. As one would expect, there are local Aboriginal men and women employed for day-to-day tasks.'

'Is there any entertainment on the island for the inmates?' asked Hamish.

'Apart from the work required to keep the place running, there is very little distraction for the inmates,' Holloway paused for a moment, then went on, 'Inmates sometimes take the long walk through the bush to the other side of the Island,' Or they sit around the fires and stew tea. Admission to the asylum is technically voluntary and inmates are legally able to leave if they choose, however, circumstances are such for the majority, they have nowhere to go, and no means of supporting themselves if they do leave.'

Most of the men Hamish could see working in the gardens and patching the fences and tanks, appeared to be relatively healthy. It was obvious they had suffered difficult lives, old before their time, hardened by the sun, personal hygiene akin to that of the bush rather than the city, but still not too bad. These men seemed infinitely better off than the poor he read about in the workhouses in England, working at dangerous jobs in unhealthy factories and sitting filthy in overcrowded cells. They seemed well able to work and did so. Surely these men and women could have earned a living in Brisbane.

Hamish could see that apart from those busy working at sustaining the community, there were also individuals who were frail and disabled. These were the people of greatest interest to him. Hamish caught the eye of an old fellow sitting on the veranda of the male ward. Seeing the line of his gaze, Holloway announced the fellow was 95 years old.

'A testimony to our healthy environment here at Dunwich,' he said proudly.

Hamish strolled over to greet the old man. He had one arm and one eye. Hamish held out his hand to the man who used his good arm to shake it firmly. The man told Hamish his name was Tom, and he fought at Waterloo. His story, well-rehearsed by this time in his life, recounted a progression of government bungles through which he lost his pension and was left to destitution and transportation to Dunwich. Apart from his missing limbs, the fellow seemed in reasonable health, and as clearheaded as a man half his age.

'What does an active fellow such as yourself do all day?' Hamish asked.

'I fish,' he said, 'And watch the goings on here. And aren't there some goings on to watch?'

He grinned a toothless grin and winked. Hamish agreed with Holloway, the man's longevity must surely attest to a healthy lifestyle at Dunwich.

The group next made their way to the building referred to as the blind ward. Once inside Hamish noticed one inmate who had lost the sight of both his eyes. Hamish blinked. A yellow discharge dried at the rims of the man's eyes and there were deep pockets beneath them where the flesh was dark and swollen. His eyes themselves were colourless, swimming with a milky cream that covered the iris.

'Good day to you,' said Hamish, taking the man's hand in his own.

The elderly man held Hamish's hand as though it were something precious.

'Does your condition cause you intolerable pain,' Hamish asked quietly.

'A great deal of pain,' said the man, squeezing Hamish's hand. 'I would rather have these eyes surgically removed from my head than go on with the pain, Sir.'

Hamish squeezed his hand back.

'I wish there was something I could do to ease your burden,' he said.

But there was nothing. The pain caused by any disease of the eye was the most difficult to treat. Hamish squinted as his own eyes began to water.

In the corner of the ward Hamish noticed a collection of well used Bibles with raised letters for the blind.

'Can you still read?' he asked the man.

'No sir, but I never could, so that's no loss, as it happens.'

Hamish felt the red heat of shame creep up his neck.

'T' others as can read aloud, give us comfort,' the man said, as if eager to reassure the doctor, 'I get comfort from the words of the Lord.'

Hamish squeezed the man's hand once more before he released it to move on with the group. He wondered that in all his suffering, the man had been eager to absolve him of his shame.

Finally, they reached the hospital, a fine airy building facing the bay. It seemed to Hamish that Holloway became a little nervous as they entered this, the largest of the buildings, yet at first glance everything seemed orderly and clean. The inmates were tucked into neat beds, nurses were helping them to eat or drink, cleaning them up and generally maintaining order. The dispenser provided medicines for those who needed them. It was as satisfactory a scene as Hamish had witnessed in any rural hospital. Surveying the row upon row of beds, he noted one old boy who was feigning ignorance of the group's presence. Hamish walked directly to his bedside and as soon as he came near, the fellow sat up.

'This is Doctor Hart,' announced Holloway, following Hamish closely.

'Good day to you, Doctor,' the man said.

'Good day,' replied Hamish. 'How goes it with you, friend?'

'My only complaint, Sir, is my lack of appetite,' said the man. 'I've not eaten a morsel in days.'

'I'm sorry to hear it,' said Hamish, glancing toward the Matron as he spoke.

Brigid Holloway rolled her eyes.

'Ah Doctor, a little drop of spirits would make me eat,' winked the man.

Hamish smiled knowingly and directed a nurse to obtain a 'tonic' from the dispensary for the man. The nurse shot an enquiring glance at Brigid.

'The inebriates will have their doses measured at midday,' Brigid said curtly.

The nurse glanced from doctor to matron, unsure of what to do, then put her head down and scurried to the back of the ward. Hamish knew she would not be taking direction from him while her matron stood glaring at her.

'Sorry friend,' he said, and the man's face opened into a cheeky grin that suggested he had not expected success.

Men and women were separated into different sections of the hospital, just as the inmates were separated in the main living wards. Hamish asked if the nurses were trained and was not surprised when

Holloway informed him they were not. Formally trained nurses were scarce enough in the city hospitals, it would be unusual to find them in a rural out-post.

Unlike most of his colleagues, Hamish favoured the new concept of professionally trained nurses. Many of the doctors Hamish knew preferred to work with their own nurses, women who had been with them for years, had learned to anticipate their ways of working and to respond to their individual needs. But Hamish understood the value of process and standardisation. He wanted to believe that nurses could provide care within the scope of their discipline without constant supervision of a doctor. He looked forward to a day when he could walk into any hospital ward and find the nurses there providing the same consistent care and support to the patients as could be found anywhere in the civilised world. Holloway told him that most of the nurses at Dunwich were inmates themselves, or members of the Aboriginal community at Myora.

Nothing he had seen so far alarmed Hamish. He noted the rawness of disease at the asylum, but the place was relatively clean and there was sufficient staff to care for the inmates. Day to day hygiene was being attended. What more could be asked of unskilled and unqualified workers? Callahan seemed satisfied with the inspection. When they entered the dining room, the inmates were enjoying beef stew and haricot beans. There seemed to be plenty.

* * *

When the party returned to Holloway's cottage, they were joined by Vissen. Wallace delivered a delicious meal of soup followed by roast pork and vegetables. As Hamish sipped on a surprisingly tasty cabbage and pepper soup, he asked Holloway, 'Do you have a medical background, Sir?'

Holloway's embarrassment was instantly obvious.

'No. I do not,' he answered curtly.

'I'm surprised,' began Hamish, 'That there is no one with medical training here.'

Holloway was clearly self-conscious about his lack of formal qualification.

'Dunwich is an exceedingly healthy place,' he said. 'The inmates have an abundance of wholesome food, sufficient clothing and comfortable quarters. They're well cared for by my wife and they have industry, they're out of the way of temptation.'

'There are men and women with significant medical need nonetheless,' pointed out Hamish.

Holloway sat very straight in his chair. Brigid kept her eyes down, and Vissen seemed mildly amused.

'The inmates are in reach of medical aid. A three-hour notice by telegram to Lytton is sufficient to bring the health officers here,' said Holloway. 'It is however obvious,' he continued, 'that the great bulk of those who come down to end their days at the Benevolent Asylum are not likely to receive much permanent benefit from medicines.'

Hamish opened his mouth to speak, but Callahan cut him off.

Callahan took on a tone of polite condescension, as if he were explaining something complex to an irritating child.

'There are those in Brisbane who argue it is not right or Christian to banish old people who've been thrown upon the State for support, to a lonely, unapproachable spot where they cannot be visited easily by doctor or clergymen,' he said. 'I assure you Sir,' he directed himself to Hamish, 'the majority of the inmates have come upon this misfortune through improvidence in their early days. Our drinking propensities and facilities are largely to blame for the pauperism among us.' He finished his statement with a long sip of wine.

'Nonetheless,' cried Hamish, 'Surely we can't leave them to disease and death?'

'Certainly not,' replied Callahan. 'However, I do recall that when the asylum was in George Street, the majority of the inmates were utterly beyond control inside the building and an unmitigated nuisance outside. They were inveterate cadgers of 'threepence please, your Honour, for a drop of something to warm me up' from every likely passer-by they met in the street. This would inevitably be the case again should we bring them into the vicinity of a town.'

'I have heard,' said Hamish, 'there's been talk of moving the asylum to Ipswich.'

'Tosh,' said Holloway, turning his head away from the table. 'The fact is the inmates at Dunwich are persons sent here so society can be rid of them. It's very unlikely that a new site will return them to the midst of civilised society. They're not here for the improvement of their own health, Doctor, so much as to remove their offensive presence from infecting or otherwise disturbing the good citizens of Brisbane.'

Hamish agreed wholeheartedly this was the intent of the administration in Brisbane. He had the impression Holloway believed this intent showed sound judgement.

By the time the last of the plates had been removed and tea was being poured, even Hamish could sense the group had tired of the conversation. He didn't want to annoy Holloway any more by his visit than he already was. Changing the tempo, he said,

'I'm impressed with what I've seen of the asylum so far.'

Quickly, Callahan took advantage of the change to announce he'd be settling himself in the Superintendent's office for the afternoon to examine the books.

'You will find,' Holloway said, 'That monthly reports have been prepared with meticulous accuracy and sent to Brisbane in a timely manner.'

Hamish assumed that as long as the reports were coming in, neatly and according to guidelines, vague though they were likely to be, the Brisbane office would prefer as little as possible to do with the asylum out on Stradbroke Island.

* * *

Relaxed after a heavy meal and a mug of beer, Hamish set out to wander the grounds alone for the afternoon. He headed toward the outbuildings. Coming upon the kitchen first, he recognised Wesley Wallace outside. He was hunched over a bucket of cabbages, peeling away the outer leaves and rolling them over, checking for burrowing insects. There was a small, scruffy terrier snuffling away at his feet. The dog's coat was long and wiry and a startling red.

'Complements on the meal,' said Hamish cheerfully. Wallace looked up.

'Lunch,' said Hamish, 'Very enjoyable. The inmates here eat well.'

Wallace didn't respond. He turned his attention back to the cabbages, picking a fat, green caterpillar out of the heart of one with his finger.

Hamish's stomach lurched a little at the site of Wallace's thick, dirty fingernails. He imagined the cook differently. The image in his mind was of an especially clean man.

Hamish was struck by how compact Wallace seemed with his back curled over as it was. Short and stocky, he required less space than most men. There was something unobtrusive about his demeanour as well as his physical size. He glanced sideways at Hamish. He had a slightly yellowish complexion, and while his eyes were the palest crystal blue, the whites were a dirty cream. He had the look of a man with a liver disorder.

Undeterred by the man's silence, Hamish squatted beside him and continued his quest for communication.

'You have an enormous task here,' he said, 'Feeding four hundred people.'

Wallace continued with his work at the cabbage.

'Surely the asylum is not completely self-sufficient,' Hamish tried again, 'There can't be enough produce grown in these gardens to feed everyone.' Still no response.

Hamish could see an Aboriginal woman moving about in the kitchen. The kitchen itself was a model of cleanliness. There was a cooking range about seven feet long and four feet wide. At the back of the range were three enormous boilers, he assumed to be for soup and porridge. The Aboriginal woman's movements were steady, not rushed. Her fingers moved skilfully as she peeled some form of root vegetable. Hamish stood up and took the few paces between himself and the kitchen door. He stood on the step, unsure of whether he would be welcome inside.

'Thank-you for lunch,' he called out. 'They seem well fed - the inmates I mean.'

Without hesitating in her work, the Aboriginal woman called back, 'Not so well as the bosses.'

Hamish gave a nervous smile then returned to Wallace, determined to try his luck once more.

He reached down and placed his hand on the dog's head. It looked up at him and let out a low growl. It didn't strike Hamish as threatening, so much as an expression of irritation at being disturbed.

'What's his name?' asked Hamish.

Wallace took his eye off the cabbages long enough to glance sideways at the dog.

'Red,' he said.

'Ah, that would be because of his colour,' said Hamish.

'No. That's because he is a socialist.'

Hamish laughed.

'We will get along well,' he told the dog, still stroking its head.

The dog's brown eyes softened. He obviously appreciated a man who shared his political views.

'I am surprised by the absence of any medically trained personnel at the asylum,' Hamish said. 'I've been wondering about the Superintendent's background. What brings someone to such a place?'

Wallace was clearly ready to engage in this new topic.

'Holloway was a lime burner for the City Lime Company at New Farm before he came to Dunwich,' he began. 'He heard about the position from one of the sub-contractors who sold coral and shell from Moreton Bay to the firm he worked for. The Colonial Secretary's Office was desperate for a replacement. They'd already removed the old Superintendent.'

'Why was that?'

'The previous Super was a doctor in Warwick before coming to Dunwich. They charged him with drunken behaviour and accused him of being a dangerous lunatic.' Wallace chuckled.

'They dropped the charges later but they wanted him gone from the area. So, he was posted to the position of Medical Superintendent here.'

'Good Lord,' exclaimed Hamish.

'As luck would have it,' Wallace continued, 'the isolation and eccentrics here at Dunwich made his condition worse. They found him wandering in the bush in a delirium after he'd been missing for three days.

The authorities in Brisbane removed him from the post. Then there was some urgency in Brisbane, so when Holloway applied, they gave him the job. The truth is, there was no one else willing to come here. Holloway could read and write, and he'd managed a handful of men at the New Farm kiln. They reckoned he would do nicely.'

No wonder Holloway was defensive.

'Was he married when he came?' Hamish asked. 'Or was the Matron employed later?'

Wallace snorted.

'He was married when he came here all right, but not to her,' he said. 'When he moved to Dunwich, he brought with him his first wife Lily. She was frail, and she hated the Island, sickly from the moment she left the boat. She didn't want to work with the idlers and drunks at the asylum. More than that, she was terrified of the deranged inmates. She took to her bed within six months of arriving and didn't leave it again. She died from pneumonia during her first winter.'

'Good Lord,' cried Hamish a second time. 'Then where did the current Mrs Holloway come from?'

'Can't say from exactly where,' replied Wallace, his fingernails deep in the heart of a cabbage. 'Holloway petitioned the government for additional wages to meet the expense of a housekeeper after the death of his wife, but before they completed the paperwork, he met Brigid. He was over town for a few weeks and came back with her. I reckon he considered her a better prospect. She is a strong woman and can help him run this place. One thing I know, he's a lot more confident since Brigid joined him. He's always been anxious about those officials in Brisbane. He doesn't think they respect him as they ought.'

Hamish agreed they probably didn't.

'Nonetheless,' he said, 'Callahan seems satisfied with his inspection.'

Wallace snorted. 'Holloway shows him what he wants him to see.'

Red had sniffed out something interesting under the kitchen. He was burrowing furiously into a hole. All that could be seen of him was his red tail waving wildly.

Changing the subject, Hamish said, 'I hear one of the inmates committed suicide last night.'

At this, Wallace stopped picking at his cabbages and stared at his fingers.

Hamish continued. 'Who found her?'

'I did, Sir,' said Wallace.

He didn't look up, and he didn't move, however, his fingers curled tightly around the cabbage.

'She hanged herself on the track,' he said quietly, 'Halfway between Myora and One Mile.'

The depth of emotion suddenly apparent in the old cook surprised Hamish.

'I'm sorry,' he said.

'Naught to be sorry for,' Wallace's eyes were filling with tears. 'Just dangling there, she was. Her boots swingin'.'

Hamish inspected his own hands, his long, pale fingers splayed on his knees. He acknowledged the difference between his own hands and those of Wallace. He appreciated the differences in the life experiences represented in those hands.

'Where is she now?' Hamish asked the older man.

'With the good Lord, I expect,' answered Wallace, with a note of surprise.

'No. I mean the body. Where's the body?' said Hamish.

'She's in the back of the hospital. That's where we put 'em. Coolest place,' he responded.

Red emerged from his hole triumphant. He held a small, dull, grey mouse between his teeth. Hamish turned away quickly. The image of mice under the kitchen made him nervous. Still, he left with a growing admiration for the terrier.

Hamish made his way back to the hospital. He had seen no indication of a body there when he visited in the morning.

* * *

Hamish entered the hospital and looked around, wondering where '*in the back*' might be, exactly. He wasn't sure what he expected to find, examining the poor woman's body, but professional curiosity compelled him forward.

'What can I help you with, doctor?' The Matron asked when he caught her attention.

She used a tone that Hamish knew well. In his experience, nurses used it to exert authority over their territory.

'The woman who hanged herself,' Hamish answered politely. 'I wish to see the body.'

The Matron continued to glare at him. Hamish guessed she was as used to medical men who display a ghoulish interest in dead bodies as he was to territorial nurses. She must have seen no harm in it though, because she led him to the back of the building without further question.

'This is where we keep them,' she said, 'While they await burial. It gets very hot in the summer,' she added, 'even in here we can't keep them very long.'

Hamish looked down at the woman on the long wooden table.

'There's a crew coming to pick up the body in a minute.'

The idea occurred to Hamish that the dead woman must have been beautiful in her youth.

'These women who come here are deranged,' snapped Matron, as if she could hear his thoughts. 'It's a blessing for them when they find peace in death.'

Hamish could recognise the signs of asphyxia. He even noted a small trickle of saliva still present in the corner of her mouth. But something seemed wrong to him. There was a blueish, purple ligature mark around the neck.

'It's very clear,' he said quietly.

'I beg your pardon?' enquired Matron.

The only other hanged body Hamish had seen exhibited abrasions, a lot of redness around the ligature mark. The rope had left a mess. In this case, the line was clean, a fine blue line around what was otherwise clear, pearl skin.

'What did she hang herself with?' he asked.

Matron showed him a length of roughly hewn ship's rope.

'Must've taken it from the stores,' she said.

A rush of panic gripped Hamish.

'Don't let them take the body,' he said.

He ran to the Superintendent's office and hurtled through the door.

Holloway was sitting on the edge of his desk chatting to Callahan, who was resting comfortably in Holloway's leather chair. They both looked up, surprised to see Hamish crashing in.

'The hanged woman,' he began, gasping for breath, 'She didn't hang herself.'

'What?' snapped Holloway.

'What are you blathering about, Hart?' demanded Callahan.

'The woman who hanged herself last night. She didn't hang herself,' cried Hamish.

'What the devil are you saying, man?' groaned Callahan.

'I don't know how she died,' repeated Hamish, 'but she did *not* hang herself.'

Callahan and Holloway glanced at each other while they tried to grasp the implications of what the doctor was saying.

'Rubbish,' burst out Holloway.

'What makes you think so?' asked Callahan quietly.

'For one thing,', began Hamish, 'The marks on her neck are inconsistent with hanging. I think she was strangled.'

They both stared at him.

'The mark is thin and clean,' he said, 'From something like a wire, not from the rope that she was swinging from.'

They continued to stare at him.

'And she has skin under her fingernails. Like she scratched someone in a struggle.'

'Nonsense,' cried Holloway. He was standing now, ready to fend off any suggestion of trouble under his command.

'The woman was deranged. She was found hanging from a tree, dead. She hanged herself. She took the rope from the stores. Vissen has already checked. She's being buried now as we speak. That's the end of it.' He slammed his fist on the desk for effect.

'She's not being buried now,' replied Hamish, 'I've directed the Matron not to release the body.'

'You have no right,' declared Holloway, lurching toward the doctor.

Callahan stood up slowly.

'Actually, he does have the right,' he said calmly. 'If the doctor thinks something is amiss, he can keep the body from being removed from the hospital until he is satisfied.'

Holloway appeared anxious. Hamish could see that he was not used to being told what to do on the Island, though he assumed he was used to obeying orders from Brisbane.

'The body will not keep long,' said Holloway in another attempt to influence events.

'You can bury her tomorrow morning,' Hamish said.

'I'll be heading back to the mainland on the ferry this afternoon,' said Callahan, 'but as Dr Hart is staying anyway, I'll look forward to a report from him about the woman's death. I expect you to give him your full co-operation, Holloway.'

Hamish asked for a file with Emily's details and Holloway handed it to him with a sneer. Hamish then hurried back to the hospital to guard his body. It wouldn't have surprised him if they'd already carried her out and buried her despite his orders.

Hamish stood beside the body of Emily May Baker and took in all that was before him. She didn't look deranged as she lay in peace, all the trauma and disappointment of life behind her. Hamish read her file quickly so he could catch up on what little there was on record about her life.

Emily May Baker. 24 years old.

Admitted 30 May 1884.

Treated for wounds inflicted by her husband, Avery Baker. Husband in same hospital being treated for head wounds as a consequence of a violent altercation between husband and wife.

Husband claims wife is deranged and violent, refuses to have her back.

Brisbane Hospital despatched the wife to Benevolent Asylum at Dunwich, as she appears to have no family to support her.

Hamish took a deep breath. He wondered if the woman on the table before him had been deranged, or had she been caught in circumstances she couldn't control? Whatever led her to Dunwich, she met a violent end at the asylum.

He examined the ligature wounds around her neck closely, noticing two finger shaped marks on one side of her neck. Had Emily been trying to grasp at the material that was tightening around her throat? Hamish held her hand gently as he scraped skin from beneath her fingernails. He unpacked the microscope his mother gave him when he graduated from medical school and peered through it at the tiny scrapings. The edges were rough and torn, and there were tiny dots of blood. There were no scratch marks on Emily. The skin belonged to someone else. It convinced Hamish there was another party involved in Emily's death.

He carefully removed her tattered brown tunic, a uniform of sorts for the women at the asylum, then stepped back to take in her pale torso. There was a slight thickening at the waist. With brows furrowed, Hamish pressed against her lower abdomen with his hands. He carefully felt for the tell-tale signs with his fingers. Palpating down from the lower end of the sternum, he clearly identified the shape he was searching for. He stepped back again. There was no doubt in his mind. Emily was with child when she died. He smoothed her hair back from her forehead and carefully replaced her tunic.

'I'm so sorry,', he whispered, aware that 'sorry' was not the right word for the emotion brewing in his belly.

Someone had murdered this woman and strung her from a tree expecting that no one would question that she suicided. She was only an inmate, after all. She probably didn't have any value as a human being to any of the people in charge at Dunwich. An intensely felt shame flooded through his body. Emily had been silenced. He had to give her a voice. She deserved that much, at least.

Hamish returned to his tent to begin his report. But first, he scribbled a quick note to his friend, Rita, who was working in Brisbane.

My dearest Rita,

The most baffling event greeted me on my arrival in Dunwich. A female inmate, a woman of twenty-seven years, has been found hanged just beyond the confines of the asylum. I am certain she was murdered, though the Superintendent here disagrees. I also know she was with child when she died. I am hoping, my friend, you can find time to investigate a little about her background in Brisbane, as I aim to convince the Superintendent she did not die from her own hand. The Superintendent is the most insufferable man, full of misplaced arrogance, and I suspect also quite dim. Nonetheless, I find I must give this woman a voice. I must at least try to make the Superintendent see her as a whole person, not just an inmate, with her death an unfortunate inconvenience.

I do understand how busy you are. My appreciation of your attention to this request is heartfelt. The woman's name is Emily May Baker. She was discharged from the Brisbane Hospital to Dunwich Asylum in May of this year.

Your friend and greatest admirer, Hamish.

Hamish ran all the way to the ferry with the note. He presented it to Callahan just as the ferry was about to cast off from the jetty. It was Tuesday. There would be no more contact with Brisbane until Thursday. The rush of adrenaline from his morning's discoveries began to subside. Now that he had passed on the request for more information about Emily's past, Hamish felt he had met some ill-defined responsibility that he felt toward the murdered woman. He trudged back to his tent, reminding himself that his purpose on the Island was to collect information and write an article on the health of the inmates. It was not to investigate a murder.

Hamish was resting in a fold-away chair that Holloway lent him, when a voice startled him.

'Sorry sir. The Superintendent would like to know when we can bury the body, sir.'

Hamish opened his eyes. 'Who the devil, are you?' asked Hamish.

'They call me Chooky, sir.'

Hamish saw a man with a protruding stomach and stick thin legs that barely seemed able to support him.

'Why is that?' he asked.

'Don't rightly know for sure, sir. I think it's on account of me skinny legs.'

Hamish looked the man up and down and decided the name suited him.

'What is it you want, Chooky?' he said, trying to remember if the man had already told him why he was disturbing his rest.

'The Super wants to know when we can bury the woman who hung herself, sir. He said we might do it first thing in the morning, if you say so.'

'Tell the Superintendent you can bury her in the morning,' replied Hamish wearily.

'Also, sir, he said you could dine with him and Mrs Holloway this evening.'

'Thank him for me, will you? But I would rather be alone this evening to settle in,' said Hamish.

Chooky turned to leave.

'What time?' called out Hamish.

'Time?' he called back.

'The burial?' answered Hamish.

'Oh,' replied Chooky, 'About eight, I think the Boss said, sir.'

He scurried off toward the Superintendent's house. Hamish rested his eyes. The fact Holloway had asked his permission to bury the body amused him. It must have been painful, he thought.

Hamish slept fitfully that first night in his tent. There was light rain through the night, and though his tent kept him dry, he found the sound of the rain on the canvas troubling. In addition, the wail of the curlews was new to him. Given the events of that day, he found their calls eerie and unsettling, like babies screaming. The tent was hot and humid and the persistent hum of mosquitoes darting in and out of earshot kept him on edge. Vissen had provided him with a stretcher from the stores and Hamish was grateful to have it because it kept him up off the wet ground. But the stretcher was narrow, barely supporting his body, even if he lay on his side all night. Hamish watched the pool of water gathering at the opening of his tent, gradually swell and creep toward the trunk that held all his belongings. The night was long. He finally fell asleep as the air hung close and heavy on his body.

* * *

JULY 1869
EMILY

A tattered grey rat scuttled across the floor just within Emily's vision. She grabbed her pillow and launched it at the creature. Its tail disappeared in the dust under the wardrobe.

Night's silence had just been restored when she heard her mother's call. There was an urgency in the sound that led her to leap out of bed and run across the hall to her mother's room.

'What is it?' she cried, watching her mother lift her nightgown out of the pool of water swelling at her feet.

'It's my waters,' she cried. 'The baby is coming.'

Emily's heart was pounding.

'It's too soon,' she cried. 'Surely it's too soon!'

She helped her mother lift the nightgown over her head.

'Can you get me another?' her mother asked, reaching toward the tallboy. 'Not that one, an old one.'

Emily grabbed a worn linen tunic, wondering why her mother needed to wear anything at all during this process. She slipped it over her mother's arms and supported her swollen body as she climbed back onto the bed.

'I don't know what to do,' said Emily, the panic evident in her voice.

'Send your father for the midwife and the doctor. You're right, the baby's coming too soon. I fear we'll need the doctor.'

'Is he at home?' Emily glanced across at the space in the bed where her father would be if he were not out drinking.

'I think so,' her mother said. 'Tell him to hurry.'

Her face contorted with pain as her muscles contracted. Her swollen body pressed against the linen tunic.

Emily's mind was spinning. The house was small, a front entrance, two small bedrooms and a kitchen at the back. If her father were at home why had he not come already? She went to the kitchen and found him bent over the table, an empty whiskey bottle perched precariously in one hand. His greasy hair lay across his face, but there was no mistaking his condition. He had passed out drunk, too drunk to know his wife was in labour and his daughter was terrified.

Emily took him by the shoulders and shook him with all her strength.

'Wake-up!' she shouted.

His head lifted a little, then flopped back down. Emily grabbed the water jug from the washstand and tipped its contents over his head. He spluttered onto the table, then lifted his head properly.

'What the hell'd you do that for?' His eyes were bleary.

Emily was sure he didn't even know who she was at that moment.

'The baby's coming,' she shouted at him as if he were deaf. 'You need to get the doctor and the midwife.'

He looked as though he might nod off again. Emily grabbed his hair and held his head up.

'Go for the doctor,' she shouted into his face.

He grumbled, stood up and staggered to the door. Emily wasn't certain he had understood. She wondered if she should go for help herself, then she heard her mother cry out and knew she had to stay. She had to trust in this stupid man. This man she hated. She used the water left in the jug to moisten a cloth and wiped her mother's brow.

For eight hours she held her mother's hand while her body convulsed and rested at increasingly frequent intervals. She wiped the sweat from her mother's brow, she put water to her lips, and she prayed. She didn't know whether anyone heard her prayers, but she liked the idea that someone was there to help her mother if she failed. By the time the morning sun was heating the bed, her mother had tired. The contractions kept coming, but her ability to move with them, to push against her own body, was waning. Emily suspected something was seriously wrong. How long did it take for a baby to be born? She'd heard women talk about as many as twenty-four hours in labour. She couldn't see how her mother could sustain another ten hours of exertion. Where was the doctor? Where was her father? Her mother's cries sounded less like the effort of birth, and more like the agonising terror of encroaching death.

* * *

Eventually, the small blue bundle burst from her mother's womb, lifeless and covered in milky grease. Emily was there to catch it. She wrapped it in her mother's shawl and placed it in an empty fruit box. Her mother stopped screaming when she gave birth and a few moments later she went still. As still as the thing in the fruit box. Blood was everywhere. Emily fetched water and boiled it in the copper then gathered the sheets, dipped them in hot water and wiped her mother's translucent skin, her thighs, and between her legs where the blood had pooled.

She wiped her mother's face and hair. Her beautiful mother. Terror and tears marked the last twenty-four hours in equal measure. Now that it was over, it seemed pointless to be crying. As Emily bundled the wet sheets against her, she heard footsteps outside.

'Let us in,' a voice called. 'It's the Doctor. I have a midwife with me as well.'

'A lot of good that will do my mother now,' thought Emily. She opened the door silently.

The doctor walked past her and on to the bedroom where her mother lay.

About ten minutes later her father arrived, drunk and incoherent. Emily left them all together.

'Let them tell him.' She continued to the laundry with the wet, bloodied sheets.

CHAPTER THREE

There is a nicely laid out cemetery situated overlooking the sea, a mile distant from the dwellings. Some hundreds of people are buried there, 'where the wicked cease from troubling and the weary are at rest.' On enquiring who did clerical duty or officiated at the burials of the deceased persons, the answer was, 'Sometimes the cook, sometimes the man from the office.' None of the old residents at Dunwich remember having seen a minister of any denomination at the funeral of the inmates. - Queensland Times, Brisbane. Thursday 15 April 1886

---

24 SEPTEMBER 1884
HAMISH

When Hamish emerged from his tent in the morning, the community was already abuzz with activity. The inmates were out of the wards and at work. Someone told him that breakfast would be at seven. Hamish decided to wait until after breakfast to tell Holloway of his discovery. He was not hungry, and he was not ready to face Holloway so early. He walked instead, down to the mudflats that stretched from the jetty along the shoreline in front of the settlement and sat on a log that lay across the mud. Mangroves stretched about one hundred yards to his right before being subsumed by dense, matted foliage. The smell of the sea and the salt in the air was soothing as he gazed over the oyster beds marking the tidal line. Blackened timber spikes rose like crooked teeth from a sea of quicksilver. She oaks whispered and gossiped behind him, the sound of a thousand voices in succession, waves of sound reaching first one way and then the other.

On the shore's edge he could see a little girl he imagined to be about nine or ten, sitting with her legs stretched out to take in the cool of the lapping water. She had a full head of tangled black curls that tumbled down over her face. Her limbs were long and brown. Hamish assumed she was a local girl from Myora, probably belonging to one of the staff at the asylum. He smiled at the sight of her. She seemed an innocent vision in this community of misfits and inebriates. He noticed the dog Red was sitting beside her, staring out to sea.

To his left Hamish could see two long rows of crosses. There were twenty-six in all, wooden crosses spaced neatly along the grassy ledge before a drop to the sand. There were other cement markers, randomly set about the grass, and there was a hole freshly dug amongst them. This was obviously the asylum cemetery. There were two grand graves that stood like sentinels over the smaller mould ridden plaques. One larger than the other, but each with a cement sarcophagus and a wrought-iron fence.

'That's Dr Bellows there,' said a voice behind him. Wallace sat down on the log beside Hamish. 'Dunwich used to be a quarantine station,' he said. 'The ships came in here before going to Brisbane. Those crosses there mark where the passengers of the *Emigrant* were buried. Typhus, it was what killed them. An evil disease. I've had experience of it myself. When it takes over a vessel, it's like the jaws of hell have descended and swallowed those aboard. The innocent and sinful alike. There's no judging who'll die and who'll live. I was spared myself while others more worthy, children, great men and women, were devoured.' He collected himself. 'Those graves there, with the fences, that's the ship's doctor and the Surgeon-General of Queensland, David Bellows.'

At the sound of his master's voice, Red came racing up from the shore. His short legs couldn't carry him as quickly as his enthusiasm warranted. He stopped at Wallace's feet, his body trembling from the exertion and the excitement. Wallace gathered the mass of red fur into his lap.

'The cement markers with numbers on them, are they the inmate's graves?'

'Yes,' said Wallace. 'They don't even rate a name on their graves, poor folk. Society did away with them when they sent them here.'

Four men struggled down to the cemetery with a plain wooden coffin.

'There's Emily,' said Wallace, his voice barely a whisper.

They had prepared a hole in the ground overnight. Mounds of fresh dirt stood guard on three sides of the grave. Emily, tucked away in the simple coffin, was unceremoniously tipped into the ground by the men who had carried her there. Then each picked up a shovel and began filling in the hole. No words were spoken. Only Hamish, Wallace and Red sat by, watching. Hamish heard each plod of earth fall on the coffin and said his own silent prayer. It surprised him to see a tear roll down Wallace's cheek. They sat together in silence as the men completed their work. Such a simple process, the disposal of a body. It was all over in half an hour and the men wandered off; shovels slung over their shoulders. Was that all life was worth?

A few moments passed while Hamish reflected on the young woman who found herself here on this remote Island, and the circumstances that may have led to her life being taken from her.

'Can you show me where you found her?' He asked at last.

They walked back to the kitchen slowly, Red trotting happily behind. The kitchen hand, Mabel, was standing in the doorway watching them. Wallace and Mabel caught one another's eyes and Hamish had the impression that with that one look, an entire conversation took place between them.

Then Wallace directed his assistant to get on with the soup for lunch and motioned Hamish to follow him.

'Do you know anything about Emily?' asked Hamish as they headed for the bush track. Red darted in and out of the bush, leaping at insects.

'Too many of them to know any properly,' he said.

Neither man spoke for some time. Hamish glanced at the cook's arms. His skin was weathered and burnt from the sun, but there was no sign of scratch marks. Hamish quickly shifted his focus to the track. He hoped Wallace hadn't noticed him checking for Emily's dying scratches.

'She was a kind girl,' Wallace said.

'How so?' asked Hamish.

'She used to take treats to the kids at Myora. Cakes, pies from the bakery, whatever she could get her hands on. Used to walk out there and back every afternoon. Looked after the other women too. I watched her stand up to Brigid once. She gave her a mouthful when she tried to punish Old Margaret.'

Hamish nodded for him to go on.

'Old Margaret was at the privy this one time and that mongrel Jim Grimes followed her in there. He lifted her skirts and was about to get up to no good when Brigid came along. She clipped him across the ear and sent him packing. Old Margaret was screaming. Brigid dragged her back to the ward blubbering and left her there. Next day she refused to come out to work. Scared she was. She works in the laundry and she was afraid Grimy would get at her again.

Brigid transferred her to the hospital and put her on bread and water rations until she was prepared to get out and work. Old Margaret's not right at the best of times. Anyway, Emily gave Brigid a piece of her mind and escorted Old Margaret back to the female ward. She brought her meals to her there until one day, a week later, she just got up and went back to work in the laundry.'

'I thought they locked the wards during the day, to stop the inmates from staying in bed.'

Wallace laughed out loud.

'The locks are no good, the inmates can get in and out whenever they want. No one wants to sit in those hot boxes all day, not unless they are sick or scared.'

'Didn't Matron try to discipline Emily?' asked Hamish.

'Nah. No point. The Holloways make a show of discipline, but when it comes down to it, they leave well enough alone. Unless there's something in it for them. When they know Judge Callahan is coming, they put the inmates to work cleaning up. No one likes an outsider, so none of them talk.'

'I have to say the wards were clean when I saw them,' said Hamish.

'Yeah. That's because you saw what Holloway wanted you to see,' scoffed Wallace. 'He takes the Judge around the same circuit every time he comes. You didn't see Ward 10 or the Asiatics, did you?'

'Asiatics?'

'The Chings.'

Hamish jolted at the use of the term, and they both stopped.

'Here it is, the hanging tree,' announced Wallace.

Hamish still had the reference to Ward 10 and the Asiatics swirling around in his mind. He would have asked about them, but the arrival at the scene of Emily's death was too compelling.

He inspected the ground beneath the tree, looked up into its branches and explored the track closely for fifty yards on either side. Red also investigated every inch of the area, scratching at the sand below the tree, sniffing around the trunk. The evening's rain had cleaned away any sign of footprints. There were no signs of a struggle, or indeed, that someone had been hauled up on a rope tied from the lowest branch. If there had been anything left lying about, Red would have sniffed it out. Hamish stood still and tried to listen for a sign, a message that he should look this way or that, uncover this stone or lift the trailing branches of that bush. There was nothing but the sound of birds. Weighing up his options, Hamish decided there was nothing more he could do. With a sigh, he said to Wallace, 'Might as well get back then.'

'If it's not an impolite question,' began Wallace, 'what are you looking for?'

'I don't know. I don't know what to look for. I can only tell you that Emily did not commit self-murder.'

Wallace coughed. 'What are you saying?'

Hamish looked the smaller man in the eye. 'Emily was murdered,' he said.

Wallace's pale face grew paler, the red tinge from the sun fading to Ivory in patches, sweat dripping from his brow.

'Are you sure?' he mumbled.

Hamish nodded. 'And she was pregnant,' he added, watching Wallace closely.

'Yes,' he said. 'I know.'

'How did you know?' Hamish was almost too afraid to ask. 'Did she tell you?'

'Not in so many words. But I knew.'

Hamish and Wallace walked back along the track in silence. Red trotted beside Wallace. After a while, Hamish struggled to keep up. Beneath the hard leather of his boots, sand irritated his skin. The sand was invasive on the Island, it was everywhere. Now it had infiltrated his thick woollen socks.

He went over the story he had to present to Holloway. Emily May Barker was murdered. Pregnant, and murdered. These were the two things he knew for certain. He was aware that Holloway wouldn't want to believe either of them. That something like this should happen to a woman under Holloway's care indicated serious neglect of his duties. That a woman had hanged herself was unfortunate, but murder showed another level of incompetence. Hamish doubted he could convince the Superintendent to announce the death as a murder and in so doing, initiate an investigation by the authorities. Still, it really wasn't his job to convince the Superintendent of anything. He was obliged to present the facts to him, as clearly as he could. It was also his responsibility to convey the facts, as he saw them, to the Colonial Secretary.

Hamish reminded himself his purpose for visiting the Island was to examine the conditions and illnesses at the asylum and write an article for the Courier. By the time he made it back to the asylum, he had decided to return to his primary goal.

'Don't become involved in matters that are not your concern,' he told himself.

He would go directly to Holloway and relay his findings, then write to the Colonial Secretary and that would be the end of it, in terms of his involvement. If the authorities decided not to take the matter further, it was of no account to him. He was almost convinced by the time Wallace was disappearing into his galley. Then Hamish heard himself call out to him.

'Is there anyone from Myora I could talk to about Emily?'

Wallace looked back at him.

'You can talk to Mabel,' he said. 'My offsider.'

He nodded into the kitchen where Mabel was moving about efficiently as always.

'She's not afraid of strangers.'

Hamish and Mabel sat out the back of the kitchen and boiled water for tea over a fire. Red curled up at the woman's feet, peering at Hamish with his brown eyes peeking out under wiry red hair. He was watchful, as suspicious of this newcomer as anyone else on the Island.

'Worked here most of me life,' said Mabel. 'Seen the place grow from about sixty people to what it is now. They send all the people they don't want messin' up their towns. White people just throw away anything they can't use. This is where they dump their rubbish.'

'Is that what Emily was?' asked Hamish. 'white rubbish?'

Mabel's eyes flashed. For a moment Hamish was afraid he had angered her. Then she settled, and her eyes grew soft again.

'Nah,' said Mabel. 'Emily was kind. She was good to us. She used to steal food. She preferred our company to those of her own kind. Used to come out to Myora a lot.'

'Did the Matron mind her coming to Myora?' asked Hamish.

'Ha!' cried Mabel. 'Emily paid no mind to that bitch. Emily did her own thing. That bitch and her husband don't control nothin'. They just pretend they do for the bosses on the mainland.'

Mabel smiled a toothless grin.

'She had a mouth on her, Emily did. She could swear better than most men.'

'Do you know why she was here?' asked Hamish.

'They said she was crazy. But Emily wasn't fuckin' crazy. Not like the other women in 'ere...all mutterin' to 'emselves and that. Nothin' wrong with Emily. Pretty, too. Some of our women, you know the black ones, didn't like that at first. Thought she was after our men. But Emily wasn't like that. She just...' Mabel stopped. She didn't want to finish that sentence.

'Do you know anyone who would want to harm her?' asked Hamish.

While he was framing the question, he was mulling over in his mind whether to mention the pregnancy. He decided he would not.

Mabel said nothing.

'Mabel?' prompted Hamish.

'I gotta get back to me work,' she said.

Mabel tipped the rest of her tea onto the dirt and returned into the kitchen. Red followed as far as the steps and stood there, defying Hamish to follow.

Curious, Hamish thought as he watched her go. He shook himself and braced for his next task.

He couldn't avoid Holloway any longer. He had to speak to him. Hamish headed to the Superintendent's office where he found Holloway bent over his desk.

'Pregnant?' cried Holloway when Hamish told him. 'Those bloody Blacks!' he said loudly. 'I told Brigid it would do no good letting her run around with the savages the way she did. Not doin' no harm, she said. Well, there is bloody harm now, isn't there? No wonder she killed herself.'

'She did *not* kill herself,' declared Hamish.

'That's merely your opinion,' responded Holloway quietly.

'No. It's a fact,' said Hamish.

At that moment, Holloway's wife joined them.

'Matron', nodded Hamish.

'He says she was bloody pregnant,' burst out Holloway. 'The Baker woman was pregnant!'

Both men stared at her.

Brigid Holloway fidgeted uncomfortably, unable to find somewhere satisfactory to put her hands.

'What?' demanded her husband. Gradually, something that would never have occurred to him before this moment began to take shape in his mind. His face reddened.

'You knew?' he seethed.

'Of course, I knew,' said his wife. 'The women can't hide something like that in a place like this.'

'Why the devil wasn't I informed?' Holloway's voice had become low and steady.

He looked like an animal ready to pounce.

His wife responded with a gush.

'I was going to tell you, she would have had to go to the mainland soon anyway, to wait for the baby to be born. There was no point telling you sooner than necessary. What could you have done?'

Holloway's eyes narrowed. 'There is nothing I despise more than deceit,' he warned her. 'Particularly from my own wife.'

'It's not deceit,' cried Brigid. 'I ...didn't want to bother you.' She fidgeted, squeezing her hands together.

'Who is the damn father?' Holloway said.

'No one knows,' answered his wife. 'The girl has taken that secret to her grave.'

She showed neither triumph nor resignation. She stated it as a simple fact.

At that moment Wallace poked his face through the door.

'Will the doctor be joining you for lunch?' he asked.

APRIL 1873
EMILY

Emily heard a faint tapping that sounded like it was happening in another world. She turned over and pulled the sheet over her head, but the sound didn't go away. It became present, something real in the here and now. She threw back the sheet and lifted her head from the pillow, squinting, her swollen eyes making it impossible to see. She wiped the tears from her face and the moisture from her nose.

'Oh God. Mrs Chambers,' she said out loud. 'It must be rent day.'

She burrowed her face into the pillow again.

Tap...tap...tap.

Emily tried to decide whether she would rather die of starvation or explain to Mrs Chambers that she had been abandoned with no money to pay the rent.

Sluggishly, she hauled herself out of bed and made it to the door. She unlatched the lock, the door flew open and Mrs. Chambers burst through, thrusting a sugary cake into her hands.

'It's my special tea cake,' she said, 'Loaded with extra sugar and cinnamon. I know how you enjoy your sweeties, luv.'

Mrs Chambers stood before Emily with her hands clasped tightly in front of her ample body.

'I assumed you would be lonely and depressed,' she said. Then quietly she added, 'He's not going to be back, is he pet?'

Emily immediately collapsed into a sobbing ball on the floor.

Mrs Chambers managed to grab the cake just before Emily dropped it. Great, heavy sobs contorted her entire body. She heard Mrs Chambers whisper, 'You can be no older than thirteen or fourteen.'

Emily sobbed for some time, then looked up to see Mrs Chambers with a perfectly respectable morning tea laid out, waiting patiently for her to stop crying.

She pulled herself to her feet and flopped down in the chair opposite Mrs Chambers. The older woman poured her a cup of hot tea and passed her a slice of teacake.

Emily took a deep breath and drank the tea then she hungrily ate the cake.

'No,' she said. 'He won't be back.'

During the morning tea Mrs Chambers extracted from the girl a detailed account of her young life so far, beginning with her escape from her father's house with the salesman who was renting the tiny flat from Mrs Chambers, and ending with the part where the salesman, her 'husband' who was not her husband, tired of her, blamed her for making him feel ashamed of the fact, and then left her.

Mrs Chambers and Emily agreed to an arrangement whereby Emily would move into a single room on the first floor and work daily as a cleaner. There was no more crying, and she made the move within the same day.

CHAPTER FOUR

To take poverty in a spirit of submission and a religious point of view is, of course, the proper course; but when one is deprived of all the happiness of life, men do not feel religious. As [Charles] Kingsley says, it is easy to feel religious and grateful to God for daily blessings when you have everything you want, because naturally, the heart feels uplifted and thankful when the body is well and nourished and the blessing of riches is about us, but it is very difficult to realise our lot as a happy one when one has nothing, even toil as he may.' - Geelong Advertiser, Vic. Saturday 18 July 1885.

25 SEPTEMBER 1884
HAMISH

Hamish was even more restless on his second night. The wind batted against his tent, and the curlews wailed. He heard voices outside, sometimes one or two whispered voices and sometimes hundreds of voices singing, in a language he didn't understand. The sounds swirled around in his head. Chanting songs grew louder and louder until he tried to block his ears with his blanket. On several occasions he was certain someone was pulling his toes, but when he opened his eyes, no one was there. Willing himself to get some sleep, he pretended the voices in his head were not real. He told himself they were part of a nightmare. But even while he was telling himself that, he knew he was awake, and the singing was still going on, relentless, ancient sounding, like something deep within himself.

Finally, he convinced himself it was the sound of the wind in the she oaks, and he drifted off.

Hamish didn't wake until Chooky poked his head through the flap in his tent.

'The boat is in, sir,' he said. 'There's something for you.'

He handed Hamish a thick envelope.

'The boat leaves in an hour sir, if you want to send a reply.'

Chooky looked uncertain about whether to stay or go. Then he stumbled on his skinny legs before slipping quietly away.

Hamish opened the envelope with his name written on it in Rita's elegant hand and removed the paper folded within. He felt a warm glow as he recalled meeting Rita Cartwright for the first time. It was during his first months as a junior doctor at the Melbourne Hospital. One of an endless string of experiences in his life that left him feeling like an outsider looking in. The other doctors came from wealthy families and had all known one another most of their lives. Hamish's father had money, new money from the goldfields, and he continued to increase his wealth as a bookmaker. But this was not wealth that had validity, family depth, class and entitlement attached to it. Rita was two years his senior and had completed her medical training in London. She attended the London School of Medicine for Women. She graduated with Honours, but women were not allowed on the medical register, so she practised as a chemist when she returned to Australia. Hamish knew her to be one of the brightest stars to graduate in medicine. To be that brilliant and competent and not be able to practise was a tragedy in his mind, for Rita personally but also for the patients she could have treated. Her diagnostic skills were second to none. He often referred to her quietly when a case stumped him. Rita was exceptional.

Hamish was stirred from his memories by a sharp pain in his legs. He'd been sitting in the same position for too long. He put down Rita's letter so he could read it later, savour every word. He rose to half his height and dipped his head further to get through the flap of his tent. It was good to stretch his legs. The pain melted away as the blood rushed through his veins once more. He shook out one leg and then the other.

Hamish brushed the hair back from his face and noticed the build-up of activity as a result of the incoming ferry. It was low tide. A succession of Aboriginal men carried large quantities of supplies on their backs, trudging from the *Kate* to the rocky causeway, through a hundred yards of soft, grey mud. Inmates took over carriage of the supplies once they reached the shore.

Among the lines of men carting wooden crates on their shoulders, Hamish noticed a thin little girl with wild hair. He recognised the girl as the one he had seen sitting at the shoreline on the day he arrived. An Aboriginal man held her hand and was pulling her along. The girl was resisting vigorously. Hamish was too far away to hear the words, but he could see that she was shouting at the man tugging at her hand. Hamish considered intervening. None of the inmates were taking any notice of them, men simply stepped sideways to avoid them if they came into their path.

She was dark, like the man who was now dragging her in his wake. He took stride after stride that was far too long for her little legs to keep up. Now and then she ran a few paces. She had given up the struggle and was allowing herself to be swept along, her feet hardly touching the ground at times. Hamish decided it was not his place to interfere. It was clear the man and the girl belonged to the Aboriginal community at Myora.

Hamish returned to his tent, still contemplating the little girl when he was surprised to see Wallace appear out of nowhere. Red scurried in and out between his legs as he walked.

'I came to see if you want to have breakfast in the Mess,' he said.

'Thank-you,' said Hamish, 'I was just going to boil up some tea and drink it here.'

He took up his pannikin.

'I would love you to join me, but I only have one mug.'

'Always have one with me,' cackled Wallace as he drew a metal mug from his coat pocket.

Hamish laughed. 'Sit down, will you?'

'Do you have a bowl for the dog?'

'The dog drinks tea?'

'Of course.'

Hamish brought an enamelled bowl that he used for shaving from his tent. He was reluctant to provide Red with tea in his shaving bowl, but he decided that as he didn't have to drink out of it, he could live with the arrangement.

Wallace perched himself on the log set up outside the tent while Hamish started the fire and put the billy on to boil. He piled tea leaves from a rusty tin into both mugs and placed a scoop into the shaving bowl.

'I received correspondence from a friend of mine,' Hamish said. 'She trained as a medical doctor.'

'A lady doctor?' queried Wallace.

'Yes,' said Hamish. 'Well, she works as a chemist, actually. She has a degree in medicine, but women can't register to practice medicine in Australia.'

'How is it that a lady would want to be a doctor then?' asked Wallace.

'Rita is a woman with no boundaries,' Hamish said.

Wallace smiled. 'How'd that lead to her studying medicine?'

'Rita's father sent her to England to study. She made it clear to him she would not marry any of the young men in his circle, so he shipped her off. I suppose his plan was to provide her with a career to fall back on. Or maybe he thought she would find a young man to marry in England. Rita told me she had always wanted to study medicine, so that's what she chose to study.'

'Did she find a man to suit her?'

'No,' said Hamish. 'She returned from London with a medical degree and a firm resolve to pursue a career. Her family told their friends that Rita was married to her work and destined to be an old maid.'

Hamish and Wallace laughed together, but the laughter was a little hollow. Hamish had no qualms about sharing Rita's story with Wallace. He knew that Rita would do so herself, with the same light touch, if she were present. He felt comfortable with this man, for all his rough exterior. He imagined he could trust him.

'I didn't know Rita at that stage,' explained Hamish. 'She told me her story as soon as I met her. She's alarmingly open. We became close friends. I think she believed I needed protecting.'

'Protecting from what?'

'From the sharks. Rita calls the established doctors, sharks. They prey on the young graduates. They love to humiliate them in front of others. That's how they indoctrinate them into the hierarchy. Always carry the mantle of superiority, humiliate everyone beneath you and maintain the status quo of power in the institution. Obviously, they are worse to women who work in medicine in any capacity than they are to us.'

'You don't see yourself as one of them?' asked Wallace.

Hamish was passionate in his response.

'My interest is in science. My commitment is to serve through medicine. I have no inclination for elitism or false superiority. I see too many mistakes made, costly mistakes, to believe in any kind of superiority for the medical profession. I use all the information I can lay my hands on and then pray to the Good Lord that I make the right decisions.'

'I can see why you need protecting,' Wallace said. 'Your attitude would make you a threat to the sharks.'

Hamish knew Wallace was right. There'd been many times when the older doctors had taken exception to his constant questioning of their authority. His medical training had taught him as much about what the medical profession didn't know, as what it did.

'I worry about how little we understand of how disease pathways progress, of how a person's social circumstances impact on their propensity for disease, or their prognosis when they become ill,' he said, becoming more animated the longer he spoke. 'The people here at the asylum, for example, how much does poverty have to do with their diseases? Do they become poor because they are ill – or do they become ill because they are poor?'

Red bared his tiny white teeth and growled. He mistook Hamish's animation for aggression toward his master.

'It's all right Red. You would agree with me, Mate, given your political persuasion.'

Wallace examined the back of his hands. 'I think we all know that disease afflicts the poor more readily than the wealthy,' he said.

Hamish continued. 'In a place like this, with fresh air and good food, we should be rehabilitating people, returning their strength to them. Many could return to society and contribute, live useful lives.'

'Ah,' said Wallace. 'This lot may be set in their ways, I think.' He glanced around the asylum grounds.

'Most of them wouldn't want to return to society, as you call it. Not permanently, anyway. They wouldn't mind a visit to the town with all its entertainments, but they wouldn't want the responsibility of making their own way. Not most of them.'

Red ran around in circles in an attempt to include himself in the discussion.

'You think being here is easier than making one's own way in town?' asked Hamish.

'For those who are relatively fit it is. No responsibility. For those who are ill, that's another matter. I wouldn't want to be ill in this place. They don't last too long once they are confined to those stinking hot wards. No access to medical care. No one cares much at all about the sick. More of a burden to the Superintendent than anything else.'

'What about those with mental ailments?'

'Ha! I'd say that is just about everyone here, wouldn't you?'

Wallace had finished his tea.

'Well, back to work,' he said as he stood to leave. Red stopped circling to see what would happen next. He skipped alongside his master back toward the kitchen.

Hamish reflected on the connection growing between himself and the old cook. Hamish trusted him. More than that, he liked him. He hoped his intuition was accurate and the cook was not involved in whatever sinister events had led to the death of Emily.

Hamish went back into his tent to retrieve the letter from Rita.

He opened the envelope, flattened out the sheets of paper and admired his friend's handwriting. He wished his own could be as elegant.

Hamish read the summary of circumstances surrounding Emily May Baker's life that Rita sent him.

Hamish Dear,

Emily May Baker, born Mountford, in Brisbane in 1860.

Mother passed during childbirth when Emily was nine. Infant was stillborn.

Emily lived with her father until she was thirteen.

From then on she lived and worked in a boarding house in Spring Hill owned by a Mrs Frieda Chambers. Emily and Mrs Chambers were close by all accounts. I visited the address to ask her about Emily, however I was informed that Frieda Chambers had passed.

Emily married Avery Baker in October 1882. They moved into a flat in South Brisbane in January 1883. Neighbours report that the marriage was not a happy one. More than once they were disturbed by loud outbursts from both Avery and Emily. A final, apparently violent, argument in May 1884 led to both husband and wife being hospitalised. They discharged Emily from the hospital to Dunwich Asylum when her husband had her declared insane and dangerous. Neighbours of the couple say that Emily didn't appear to be insane in her interactions with them and were shocked at the decision.

I am sorry I couldn't find out more. By all accounts Emily kept to herself and her only close friend was Frieda Chambers, who is now, as I said, deceased.

I am glad you are looking into the death of this poor girl, Hamish. It is so like you to care.

Your dearest friend, Rita

Hamish stood outside his tent, looking across the scattering of buildings before him. What did Emily think about this strange place?

Hamish remembered the male and female wards they had shown him on his first day on the Island. He recalled the caution made by Wallace, that he had not seen the worst of the asylum. Tucked behind the main buildings were several others in various stages of repair. He made his way to one of the less well-maintained buildings and entered. The door was closed but not locked. Once inside, Hamish took a few minutes to adjust his eyes to the darkness. Already in September, the ward was hot and close. There were windows on each side of the building, but they were too dirty to let light in and they were closed. The odour in the ward was nauseating. Hamish regained his focus and noticed there were several men in their beds. Each was of Chinese appearance.

'Obviously the Asiatic Ward,' he thought.

Some men, their eyes barely open, were watching him. They appeared to have neither the energy nor the inclination to lift their heads or to speak. These men hadn't been cleaned in days. The smell of urine and faeces was overwhelming. He stood by the bed of the man closest to him, looking down at a small, frail, Chinese man with his eyes closed and his face pinched. Hamish lifted the hessian covering him and let free a wave of putrid decay that caused him to step away in horror. The man's body was visibly decaying at several points where his bones, barely covered in flesh, rested on the hard surface of the bed. There were gaping holes of flesh, oozing a creamy excrement.

Just as Hamish was trying to comprehend the shock to his senses, the door opened and light flooded the room. A nurse came in and stood defiantly before him. It was the same nurse he had directed to bring a tonic to an inmate on his first day. Aware she had not responded to his directives then; Hamish was determined she would do his bidding now.

'I want this man cleaned up immediately,' he said sternly.

The woman, who was more used to taking orders than Hamish was of giving them, scurried away to retrieve a bucket and some rags. Without the Matron present, Hamish was accepted as the point of authority.

Hamish removed the tattered shreds of clothing from the man as gently as he could. When the nurse returned, he showed her how to turn the frail body without causing further damage.

'Here, like this, at the elbow,' he said. 'Then there will support without causing more pain.'

The two of them held the collection of bones together, the muscles and tendons having long since diminished to a point they could no longer do the job. The disturbance must have caused the man some discomfort, but he didn't call out. Either he was so relieved to be rid of the filth, or he didn't have the energy to object. When Hamish and the nurse had sufficiently cleaned his frail body, Hamish ordered the nurse to find him a dish and some tweezers. He sat patiently picking maggots from the man's wounds and dropping them into the dish.

'I want all the inmates in here washed,' he said. 'And I want fresh bedding for them all.'

'The Asiatics do not get clean bedding routinely,' she said with determination.

The icy look on Hamish's face nonetheless sent her from the ward to track down the bedding.

When he finished plucking maggots from the Chinese man's body, Hamish wrapped his wounds in clean bandages. He tucked bunched up rags under his hips to prevent the pressure points from resting against the hard surface of the bed. He then moved to the next inmate to repeat the process. None of the other men suffered wounds as significant as the first, however they were all thin, pale and close to death.

As he was leaving the ward, Hamish noted a sign on the wall. It was grubby, but clear. It said, '*Every man admitted is to maintain the utmost cleanliness inside the ward and on the veranda. The ward is to be properly swept by the inmates. The blankets must be aired thoroughly every Tuesday and Friday, and the pillowcases are to be washed every fortnight by the inmates.*'

Hamish shook his head. How on Earth could these men carry out these duties for themselves? The idea was ludicrous. It was clear to Hamish that Holloway had no capacity to enforce any of the rules he made. The rules served as a scapegoat for lack of care. Hamish assumed that once the sign was in place, in Holloway's mind, it became the inmate's responsibility to keep the ward and his own bedding clean although they had no capacity to do so. How could Brigid Holloway allow this neglect?

Upon leaving the Asiatic Ward, Hamish strode across the grounds toward Holloway's office. He found Holloway expecting him, already tipped off by the nurse.

'You have to understand,' began Holloway before Hamish could speak, 'We have insufficient funds, no support at all from Brisbane, and we make do with what we have.'

Hamish stood mute. He could not find words to describe the neglect he had witnessed.

'The Asiatics have to be our last priority,' declared Holloway, 'You must agree. They cannot live with the other men; they carry diseases against which we have no defences.'

Hamish caught his breath.

'The Chinese carry no disease other than those which inflict all of humanity', he said. 'I have instructed your nurse to clean all the men in the ward and to provide clean bedding for them. I will now instruct you to be sure they are cleaned daily, their wounds attended, and their bedding changed twice weekly.'

Holloway looked defiant.

'Surely, you cannot think that these men have been neglected.' He puffed up with indignation and glared at Hamish as if he expected him to apologise for impertinence.

Hamish glared back from beneath his unruly fringe.

Finally, Holloway let out his breath and said,

'Nonetheless, I cannot meet your demands. I have neither the resources nor the inclination. This is a finely balanced community of misfits, shirkers and criminals. There are men who would cut your throat without the slightest hesitation. Among the inmates, the Chinese are the worst. Who knows how many of our own have been seduced by opium? They are worse than the Aboriginals. You have no idea how I have worked to manage this place without serious incident to trouble the Colonial Office. Tend to the sick while you are here by all means, for all the good it will do them, but do not interfere in my administration of this asylum.'

'The inmates here deserve humane treatment,' cried Hamish. 'All of the inmates. It's not for you to decide who deserves care and who does not.'

While Hamish was admonishing him, he was looking for any sign of scratches on his face or arms. The skin on his face was clear, but he couldn't see his arms. He was wearing his usual thick woollen jacket, even though the day was hot.

'Surely a medical doctor has been called in to attend those men in the Asiatic ward?' he said.

'What is the point? Those men are close to death. It's beyond me how they hang on so long. What can a doctor do to improve their lot?'

'It's certainly too late now to improve their prospects for life. But what about nursing care? They need clean bedding, they need to be protected against bed sores, medications for their pain...'

'The staff here do what they can. As I have already informed you, we have insufficient funds, insufficient qualified staff and my poor wife is intolerably over extended. You can put that in your report to the Colonial Office.'

'Don't concern yourself,' said Hamish, 'There will be a great deal in my report to the Colonial Office. His parting quip was the one that cut to the bone for Holloway. As he turned on his heel to leave, Hamish said, 'I will be making the strongest recommendation to the Colonial Office that a medical officer be placed in the Superintendent role.'

* * *

Hamish sat in his tent adding to his report of the morning's events. He wrote with righteous indignation and knew he would have to rewrite it later when he calmed down, but he kept going anyway. At some point he became aware of snuffling sounds outside his tent. He stopped writing to listen. Footsteps back and forth, snuffling and grunting. He was thinking it must be Red, but then a hairy pink nostril lifted the canvas at ground level. A pig was chewing at the bottom of his tent. A man's voice called the pig away and Hamish waited a few moments for the spectacle to pass, but it went on. The man appeared to push the pig because it made a massive bulge in the canvas. Hamish burst out of his tent into the light.

'What the devil is going on?', he cried. The pig had circled around behind the man.

'The pig's out,' he replied.

'I can bloody well see that,' said Hamish. 'Get him away from here.'

'Yes sir,' said the man.

He hollered at the pig as an indication of his goodwill toward Hamish and the pig sauntered off on its short, little legs.

'What's your name?' asked Hamish.

'People call me Grimy, Sir.'

'Yes, I can see why.'

The man called Grimy shifted from one foot to the other but showed no sign of leaving with his pig. He appeared to be a white man under all the dirt. Hamish recalled Holloway saying the man who looked after the piggery was Aboriginal. Grimy had long, thin, greasy hair and a similarly lightweight beard that covered most of his face, albeit sketchily. Sharp cheekbones were his only visible feature, aside from small, pale eyes. Hamish checked his bare arms for scratches, but there were none. It was hard to tell through the dirt whether there were scratches to his face.

'People say you're asking about the dead girl,' Grimy ventured.

'That's right,' said Hamish. The man had his full attention.

'That bun she was carryin' was Black,' Grimy said. 'If that ain't a good enough reason to hang y'self, I dunno what is. Course, he might've done it too. Them Blacks can't be trusted.'

Grimy hurried off after the pig, which was now digging in a garden in front of the top tents.

Hamish watched him go. If Emily's baby had an Aboriginal father, what would that mean in relation to her murder? Was she murdered by her lover, as Grimy suggested? Or was she murdered by someone else living at Myora? How did the white community feel about an inmate having an Aboriginal child? Hamish shook himself. Best thing to do was to complete his report about the asylum and get to work on his article.

Diabetes. He would begin with an account of the diabetics at the asylum. A great deal of great work was being done in that space in Europe. He might even have an opportunity to do some good. Get an intervention in place for the poor sods with the disease on the Island.

He walked to the Telegraph Office to ask Holloway for the medical records. No one was in the office, so he found them himself. There were several journals, neatly arranged, with the names, dates and diagnoses of each inmate. Hamish skimmed down the list and copied the names of each resident with diabetes into his journal. He suspected there were many more that had not been diagnosed or had not had their diagnosis recorded on entry to the asylum. It occurred to him he should have asked Rita to send reagent papers. He could have tested everyone.

'What are you doing in here?' cried Holloway.

Hamish answered without lifting his eyes.

'Research,' he said.

'Downright rude of you to help yourself to my office, and my journals.'

'My apologies,' said Hamish. 'Do you object to my reviewing the patients' files?'

'That's not the point, Hart. You can't come in here without my knowledge, that's all.'

'There are a number of people here with diabetes,' Hamish said, switching to a topic he hoped would be less disagreeable.

'What of it?'

'I'm not accusing you of anything. I wondered what treatment plans are in place for these people?'

'What are you talking about? Treatment plans? There is no treatment for diabetes.'

'But there is, Superintendent. The diabetics ought to be on a restricted diet, no breads or sugar. Plenty of greens. And you should be monitoring the levels of sugar in the urine. I suppose they get plenty of exercise here, working at the asylum?'

Holloway stared at him as though he were mad.

'Research from Europe is very clear,' said Hamish. 'There is much to be gained in improvement for diabetics from a well-managed diet and exercise. The reagents now for testing are very convenient. I mean to ask for test papers to be sent over.'

'This is not a health spa,' cried Holloway. 'For pity's sake the inmates are not here 'to take the waters!'

'You misunderstand me. It's a simple matter and entirely within your capacity to provide an appropriate diet for those with diabetes, Holloway. It would cost nothing and require no additional labour. The urine testing is a simple process. I can train your nurses to do it. They provide paper strips now, embedded with a chemical that will turn black if there is too much glucose in the urine. It's most convenient.'

'These people are not here on holiday, Hart. They're paupers, deranged, they're not fit to receive the benefits of the health cures available to the wealthy in Europe.'

'Those who are ill deserve the treatment that science has available.'

'Treatments are wasted on them doctor. They're here to receive the basest of requirements until they die. For the most part, they die sooner rather than later, and that is for the best. For them and for society.'

'Nonetheless, Superintendent, I will be testing all these people for diabetes, and creating treatment plans for them, which I expect you to follow. I will contact Callahan and have him check that you're doing so at each of his visits.'

Holloway was pale. Hamish saw his eyes darken, then Holloway turned away from him and marched from his own office. Hamish continued to copy down the names of inmates with diabetes.

When he completed his list, he made his way to the kitchen where Wallace was cleaning mullet; he braved the smell to sit with him.

'I've had a troubling conversation with Holloway,' said Hamish.

Wallace chuckled. 'That's hardly surprising,' he said.

'I'm concerned about the diabetics here. Holloway doesn't seem to understand that the longevity of diabetics can be positively influenced by a restricted diet.'

'Can it now?'

'Certainly.'

'What's involved in these dietary restrictions, then?'

'Simply avoid giving them breads, grains and sugars.'

'They might object to being excluded when the bread and puddings are put out,' said Wallace. 'But it's no difference to me.'

'If I leave you with a list, will you provide these people with more greens and less bread and sugar?' asked Hamish, surprised that the old cook seemed inclined to support him in this.

'Like I said, no difference to me. The inmates might object, though. And what are you going to do about their drinking? Plenty of sugar in alcohol, I would've thought.'

'True,' said Hamish. 'Small steps.'

Encouraged by this small success, Hamish broached a new subject. He described the man with the pig.

'Yeah, that would be Grimy,' said Wallace. 'He's an inmate. One of the drunks. Frank runs the piggery; he's a good man. But Grimy helps out. In fact, he has a finger in almost every pie at the asylum.'

Hamish noted a tone of intense dislike in the cook's voice, but he decided not to enquire about it.

'He told me that Emily's baby could've been black,' he said instead.

'He's lazy and a liar,' added Wallace.

'So, you don't think the baby had an Aboriginal father?' asked Hamish.

'Dunno,' he said, 'but it ain't so just because Grimy says it.'

Hamish wondered if he was telling him the whole truth. He had the feeling that Wallace knew more than he was prepared to say.

'Grimy gets drunk and aggressive himself.' Wallace went on, 'Remember I told you he chased old Margaret into the privy and had her skirt up over her neck. Brigid heard Margaret screaming and came running like a bat outa' hell. She chased him across the paddock with his trousers around his ankles.' Wallace shook his head. 'You couldn't put it past that bastard to kill a woman himself.'

Hamish considered the inference.

'He didn't look to me like he was physically capable of killing a healthy woman like Emily,' he said at last.

'The drink gives 'em strength,' said Wallace. 'But as you like.'

Was Wallace trying to shift him away from his original question about the baby's father?

'Of course, Grimy may have raped her,' said Hamish. But why kill her?'

'Maybe he expected to keep visiting,' suggested Wallace. 'But she wouldn't have it.'

'Then why draw attention to himself at all? Where does Grimy sleep?' asked Hamish.

'In the inebriates' ward,' said Wallace, pointing to one of the back buildings.

Hamish made his way to the inebriates' ward, thinking he would talk to this Grimy fellow and ask him exactly what he knew about Emily's pregnancy and death. He found an assembly of men lined up before the dispenser who was handing out measures of alcohol.

'Their medicine,' he said to Hamish by way of explanation. 'The Superintendent believes that a controlled approach to alcohol is superior to with-holding it. These men are alcoholics.'

Hamish knew well enough the consequences of cutting off a supply of alcohol to those who were addicted to it.

'Where is the alcohol kept?' he asked.

'In the dispensary,' responded the man, 'I measure it out and dispense it daily.'

'What are your qualifications?' asked Hamish, smelling alcohol on the man's breath.

'I am a man of science,' he declared defiantly. 'I studied apothecary.'

'Never mind that,' cried a voice from the back of the line. 'He's a bloody inmate.'

The fellow was pushing his way to the front. Hamish recognised him as Jim Grimes.

'No better than the rest of us,' he said.

'An inmate?' asked Hamish.

'That's right,' said the dispenser. 'Doesn't mean I ain't qualified.'

The inmates took their measure of alcohol in their turn. Hamish indicated to Grimy that he wished to speak to him, while the others returned to their various tasks doing whatever was required to sustain the asylum community.

Grimy waited while Hamish studied him closely. He leered back at him. Broken, yellow teeth, liquid dribbling down his chin. Hamish could see him committing murder, but he was not convinced he could lift a healthy woman up to hang her from a tree.

Still, if he had help.

'I wanted to ask you about the woman who was hanged,' Hamish began. 'You said the father of the baby was an Aboriginal man.'

Grimy looked wary. 'That I did,' he said.

'How do you know?'

'I seen 'em together with me own eyes, didn't I?'

'Do you know the name of this man?'

Grimy grinned. It was a sly grin and made Hamish uncomfortable.

'Well now, that would be telling wouldn't it?

'Good Lord, man. You've already volunteered the information that you saw the woman with a black man. What more does it cost to say the man's name?'

'Maybe I don't know his name,' said Grimy. 'Maybe I just know he's from Myora, where they all come from 'round here.'

Hamish glared at him. He tried to sum him up. There were not that many Aboriginal people who frequented the asylum grounds that Grimy wouldn't know all their names. Holloway had made clear that only the Aboriginals who worked at the asylum were allowed in Dunwich.

'You don't know the name of the man? Or are you being obtuse and don't want to tell me his name?'

'I don't know what you mean, sir.'

Frustrated, Hamish shrugged his shoulders and dismissed him with a flick of his hand.

* * *

Hamish returned to the kitchen and caught up with Mabel as she was leaving. Lunch was over, her shift was finished, and she was heading home to Myora. Hamish quickened his pace to keep up with her. Mabel didn't acknowledge him when he drew alongside. He kept pace with her, anyway.

'Did Wallace tell you?' he asked.

'Tell me what?' snapped Mabel.

'What Grimy said,' replied Hamish.

'That scum,' scoffed Mabel. 'You don't want to waste ya time listenin' to him.'

'Did he tell you what he said though?'

Mabel stopped and turned to Hamish. 'So, tell me then. What did the scum say?'

'He said,' began Hamish, 'that Emily's baby had an Aboriginal father.'

Mabel's face went red.

'Anything happens around here and it's gonna be the blacks to blame,' she spat on the sand and strode away quickly, her anger apparent with every step.

Hamish decided, wisely, it was not the right time to accompany her to Myora.

10 MARCH 1881
EMILY

Emily spent the day of her twenty-first birthday preparing for the dinner party Mrs Chambers had arranged in her honour.

'Is everyone joining us for dinner?' she asked Mrs Chambers.

'I believe so. The tenants have all confirmed they'll be present. The new fellow is particularly keen. It'll be the first opportunity he has to meet everyone in the house,' said Mrs Chambers.

'I've not met him myself.'

'Exactly the right time then. Who would've thought you would be turning twenty-one so soon?'

At precisely six o'clock Emily made her entrance into the dining room. The male guests all stood as she entered. She greeted them all warmly, however one gentleman stood out. He wasn't handsome, but pleasant looking with fine features and fair eyelashes. His hair was already showing signs of thinning, even though Emily guessed his age to be in the early thirties.

'Emily,' said Mrs Chambers, 'I would like to introduce you to Mr Avery Baker. Avery has moved into Number Four upstairs.'

Emily held out a small, gloved hand to Avery, who gently kissed it.

'A pleasure to meet you,' said Emily. She detected a glint in Mr Baker's eye.

Mrs Chambers motioned for Emily to take her seat alongside him, and she did so happily. He smelled of soap. His small white hands rested on the table on each side of his plate, and Emily noticed that his fingernails were clean and pink. He had the cleanest hands she had ever seen on a man.

'What work do you do, Mr Baker?' she asked.

'I am a clerk,' he said, 'at the bank.'

Emily smiled and settled comfortably by his side at the table.

She was careful to share her attention among all the guests, but she could not ignore Avery's attempts to dominate the conversation.

'The meal is superb,' he said to Mrs Chambers, 'I don't believe I've ever eaten better. Of course, my mother was a great cook, but your skills are a match for hers.'

The guests all agreed wholeheartedly.

'Thank-you,' said Mrs Chambers graciously, 'Emily assisted me. She has been cooking all afternoon.' Mrs Chambers smiled warmly at Emily across the table.

'Do you have the same culinary skills as our host?' asked Avery. 'If so, you will be a great catch for a lucky gentleman.'

His voice was quiet when he said it, so that only Emily could hear. Emily's eyes were caught and held by his own.

Finally, she looked down at her hands.

'I fear not,' she said. 'I am not skilled in the kitchen. For all the energy Mrs Chambers has invested in teaching me.'

'Modest as well,' said Avery smiling.

Emily smiled sweetly in acknowledgement, but in her heart, she knew that modesty had nothing to do with it.

That evening, as Emily lay in bed, she felt a confusing set of emotions. She was not sure how she felt about the attention Avery had paid her.

He had a good job; he seemed well-mannered, and she enjoyed the attention of a man after so many years tucked safely away in Mrs Chamber's house. She wondered, for the first time, if she ought to seek a life of her own, independent of her friend and employer. Avery didn't set her heart alight as the salesman had done when she was sixteen, but then he had proven to be a poor choice. Perhaps what she needed was stability. A match not of passion, but rather the pursuit of a sensible life.

Avery gathered the courage to ask her to walk out with him by the following Friday.

'Would you be willing to accompany me on a stroll in Queen's Park?' he asked as though it were a business arrangement. 'With Mrs Chambers as chaperone, of course,' he added.

'I think I would like that very much,' replied Emily.

'Fine,' he said. 'I will invite Mrs Chambers to join us.' He hesitated as if he might say more, then he turned toward the kitchen.

Emily sensed this was the beginning of a monumental change in her life. Change was exciting, but there was also a hint of foreboding.

Mrs Chambers couldn't contain her excitement when she told Emily, Avery had asked her to chaperone them on a trip to Queen's Park.

'What will you wear?' she cried.

Emily hadn't thought about it.

'The cream poplin?' she asked.

'With the long neckline set off the shoulders, yes, perfect,' declared Mrs Chambers.

'That's fortunate, for it is the only good dress I have,' laughed Emily.

Mrs Chambers spent the morning before the outing, curling and twisting Emily's hair into the modern style. She ran her hands from Emily's trim waist to the wide skirt, fluffing the fabric. She tried to fix a bustle cushion to the back, but Emily backed away laughing.

'No,' she cried, 'I'm not wearing that. How will I sit if sitting is required?'

Mrs Chambers reminded her that ladies do not sit in parks.

'What do they do when their legs become tired? Emily asked.

Mrs Chambers gave in and threw the bustle aside. She didn't wear one herself, so she could hardly force the thing on Emily. She insisted on pulling her corset extra tight and left it at that.

When the group met in the entrance hall, they were all looking their finest. Avery appeared to have taken as much care of his appearance as the women. They caught a carriage to the entrance to Queen's Park, where they arrived to the sounds of laughter and merry chatter. There were people everywhere enjoying the afternoon sunshine. They promenaded along an avenue lined with Hook Pine, nodding at the other couples doing the same. Emily breathed in the sensation of suitability, of belonging to society, for the first time in her life. She had not known that so many ordinary folk, like herself, were out enjoying themselves on a Saturday afternoon. They reached the grand fountain at the centre of the formal gardens and Emily stopped to gaze at it. Its ornate beauty stunned her, and she wondered if it would seem more at home in the gardens of the great European houses than in this backwater of Brisbane.

Emily was admiring the startling red blooms of the Poinciana against the sky when Avery said, 'What impressive exotics the curator has introduced.'

She agreed. Having been born in Brisbane, she knew nothing other than the dazzling light of Queensland.

'Colours pulse in this light,' she said.

'I prefer the muted tones of England,' said Avery, who had come to Australia as an adult. 'However, there is no denying the great talent of Mr Hill in designing this Park. He is a client of the bank, you know. I am acquainted with him, at a professional level.'

Emily nodded in approval and they walked on, Mrs. Chambers remaining a few steps behind them.

Emily saw that a game of cricket was being played on the lawn at the other side of the park. A crowd had gathered to watch.

'Shall we watch the game?' cried Emily, as she moved to join the crowd. Avery took her elbow in his hand and held her firmly.

'We will walk around the lawn this way,' he said, guiding her, 'to the river.'

Emily followed him, stretching her neck to look back over her shoulder at the crowd of applauding spectators.

They reached the river in time to see a steamer make its way slowly toward Petrie Bight. A group of fashionably dressed women stretched across the railing to wave at them. Emily waved back enthusiastically. Emily, Avery and Mrs Chambers followed the river around the curve, ending up at the other end of Alice Street, where they had first started. They'd walked almost a complete circle, skirting Queens Park and the Botanical Gardens. They carried on to Queen Street, stopping for sodas before they caught a carriage and rattled back up the hill to Leichardt Street.

Emily thought about how she would have liked to join the laughing crowd watching the cricket. She wondered if Avery ever laughed. He seemed so serious all the time. Still, it had been a pleasant afternoon and she liked the sense of propriety that accompanied stepping out with a man like Avery.

CHAPTER FIVE

On Mr Henry George's work, 'Progress and Poverty': In concluding his address, he said that avoiding the large question of land nationalisation, with its hope of social reform, he believed in 100 years to come – or say two hundred years – the theological idea of the universe would be altogether discredited. Then the humanitarian ideal would take its place, and half the money spent in war, if not more, would go to humanity; more than half of the money spent in missions would go to humanity; and the new ideal would not lead a man when he has prosperity to give 30,000 pounds to build a church, but his worship of God would take the form of a gift to humanity. - South Australian Register, Adelaide. Saturday 5 December 1885.

---

26 SEPTEMBER 1884
HAMISH

Friday dawned with Hamish faintly aware of the thud of footsteps outside his tent. It took him a few moments to place himself on the Island and to remember the events of the past three days. As he lay half-awake trying to focus, he became aware of Aboriginal voices reverberating across the grounds. The words were foreign to him, but the urgency was clear. He quickly dressed and stood outside his tent. There was candlelight in the Superintendent's house, and in his office. The main wards remained dark.

Hamish set his eye to the light in the Superintendent's office window and made his way toward it. Once inside, he was shocked to find Mabel alone and in tears. She was sitting on the floor holding her knees and rocking. Hamish sat down beside her.

'What's happened?' he asked.

She looked at him with swollen eyes.

'Dead,' she said. She continued rocking and sang a quiet song in a language she shared with her ancestors.

'Who is dead?' he asked.

'Simon,' she sobbed. 'The hanging tree.'

Hamish tried to piece together what he could. The tree where Emily was found had become known in the community as the hanging tree. Simon was clearly someone close to Mabel. He waited for more information.

Mabel began talking to him in a low voice. Some seconds passed before he understood that she was no longer singing, she was telling a story.

'Emily and Simon met because I took her to Myora with me,' Mabel was barely whispering. 'She wanted to know about our ways, and I let her know too much.'

'What do you mean, too much?' asked Hamish.

But Mabel continued as if he hadn't spoken.

'Emily and Simon went swimming together at the Springs. Our girls were jealous because Simon belongs to them. But Emily and Simon loved one another. I tried to make Emily leave him alone because those girls might fight her. Or your mob might kill Simon. We had a blue, but nothing in this world would keep them two apart. Emily wanted to live at Myora, with Simon. She wanted to bring up that baby our way. We have plenty of babies from white fathers, so I hoped our mob might get used to it.'

As Hamish came to understand that Simon, who was hanging from the hanging tree, was the father of Emily's child, he wondered if Simon had in fact killed himself, or if he was also murdered. He knew he had to get to Holloway before anything was done with the body.

He considered for a moment going to the hanging tree himself. But no, the body would be down by the time he got there. Would the Aboriginal community allow him to examine the body?

When Mabel finished her story, she resumed a melodic chanting. The curlews began wailing just outside the office, long mournful cries woven in and out of every note. A strange energy was building with the song. The hair on Hamish's arms and the back of his neck stood upright and, for a moment, he was frozen. When he finally moved, he couldn't shake the sensation that something was moving with him.

Holloway returned to his office just as Hamish was about to go out and look for him. He slumped down into his chair and held his head in his hands. His elbows on the desk.

'I need to examine the body', declared Hamish.

'Of course you do,' sighed Holloway wearily, 'Although I doubt his family will allow you to do that,' he said, lifting his head.

Mabel chipped in immediately. 'We want the doctor to examine him.'

The chanting had stopped.

Holloway looked genuinely surprised, both that she was still there, and at her assertion.

'Well,' he said with a level of resignation. 'The body is in the hospital. You know where to find it.'

Hamish looked toward Mabel, but she was quiet, staring into space.

'I believe Simon worked for you,' he said to Holloway.

'Yes,' replied Holloway. 'He was a good worker.'

Holloway put his head down again.

'I have no idea what this is about,' he said.

Hamish strode across the grounds to the hospital. As he did so, he had the feeling there were others walking with him. He was determined to examine the body for a sign the death was anything other than suicide. Two deaths, two people hanging from the same tree, two people intimately linked, all in one week. It was disturbing.

* * *

On the table before Hamish was the strong, muscular body of a man who would have been no more than thirty years old.

His neck was broken. There was blackening of the skin around his neck consistent with the rope that was found around his throat. Otherwise, the man was unmarked. There was no indication that he died by any other means than his own hand. There was no obvious evidence to suggest murder.

Hamish examined the body again. He ran his hands over every part of the corpse on the table, trying to keep an objective eye, a scientific eye. He was as thorough as possible. Still, his mind couldn't stop wandering on paths that were less than scientific. Perhaps Simon killed himself out of grief, or perhaps he murdered Emily and then killed himself. Guilt was a powerful emotion. He searched for evidence that would confirm a cause of death other than suicide. But there was none. Whatever the reason for Simon's death, Hamish had to conclude it was most likely suicide.

Hamish returned to the Telegraph Office to find Holloway still resting his head in his hands.

'I can see no evidence for a cause of death other than suicide,' he said.

Holloway sighed. 'Well, at least that's something.'

'Perhaps he killed Emily and then himself,' suggested Hamish.

'The Dunwich community has already decided on that theory. The rumours about Simon being the father of Emily's baby have spread across this community like a fire in the westerly winds. Apparently, they see Simon's death as something of a confession that he killed her,' said Holloway.

'We have no evidence of that,' cautioned Hamish. 'What do the people of Myora say?'

'What do you think they say? They say Simon didn't do it.'

'Despite what people think,' Hamish said carefully, 'there is no evidence that Simon killed Emily.'

'Evidence? Evidence plays no part in a place like this. What people think is all there is. If you hadn't started blathering about murder, we could have put the whole thing down to a double suicide. We wouldn't need to charge anyone with murder.'

'Emily was murdered,' said Hamish. 'Someone killed her, and someone needs to be held accountable. But there is no need to rush into an accusation against Simon.'

Holloway had returned to his prior position with his head in his hands. He didn't look up or offer a response, so Hamish left him.

* * *

Hamish knew that Myora was the key to some of his questions about Emily's death. He needed to visit the place. He set off toward the kitchen, determined not to be put off this time. He waited around for Mabel to finish work.

'Can I walk to Myora with you?' he asked.

She nodded, '*Moongalba*,' she said.

'Sorry?' asked Hamish.

'We call the place *Moongalba*,' said Mabel.

They head off across the gardens to join the sandy track. They walked silently for the first part of the journey and both missed a step in their stride as they passed the hanging tree.

Mabel was eventually the first to speak.

'Simon was a good man,' she said.

Hamish didn't want to risk saying the wrong thing, so he said nothing.

'There was a cotton plantation out that way,' she said pointing ahead, 'In my grandfather's time. He worked there as a young man. Didn't last long. Then the missionaries came. They didn't last long either. 'Passionists'.' she said quietly.

As the track widened into a clearing Hamish was surprised to see a jumble of European style dwellings, makeshift and constructed from second-hand materials, but without mistake, European in style. Some had fences and gardens. Already tangled among the native trees and grasses were guava trees, lemon and orange trees, mango trees and banana stands. In the gardens grew cabbages and sweet potatoes.

'Europeans been living with us mob for generations now,' said Mabel. 'First white men came when my grandfather's father's father was a boy. Fishermen, government people running that depot down at Dunwich, some that came for the oysters. They tried farmin', even got cattle in the scrub on the other side. I been working for the asylum since I was twelve, cleaning mostly, a bit in the laundry, then some years back I went into the kitchen. I was taught by the white fellas to speak English. No good to them for work if we can't speak English. We were beaten if we spoke our own language. Even my father wouldn't let us kids speak language. Future is in speakin' English, he said. We all been given European names, alongside our true names, our Aboriginal names.'

'Do you have an Aboriginal name?' asked Hamish.

Mabel threw him a sidelong glance. She didn't respond.

'This is it,' she said.

Hamish stood back. Under a salmon sky, roughly hewn huts sat within a glade of trees, on a hill gently sloping to the beach. Cockatoos called out a racket and a swarm of white and yellow feathers made its way across the pink sky. Flying foxes called out too, waking from their day of sleep, ready to feast on the sweet juices of over-ripe mangoes.

'Fresh water comes up from the spring,' explained Mabel. 'We get government rations. Most of our people who work at the asylum are paid in rations; meat, rice, sago, tapioca. There is always some cash work around. And we mostly eat fish.' Mabel hesitated beside him for a moment, then said, 'I'll leave you to it then.'

She disappeared into a tangle of corrugated iron forming a doorway into the lower section of one of the houses.

Hamish was overcome by contradictory sensations. Firstly, he could see the poverty, the disorganised, half-finished ramshackle appearance of the buildings. Trees and vines were growing up through some structures, as if nature was slowly reclaiming the space. Still, there was serenity, intense beauty. And despite the impression of poverty, there was abundance everywhere, from the heavily fruited trees to the carelessly built garden beds bulging with their mixture of vegetables and weeds. Hamish walked around the gardens drinking in the pungent smell of herbs. There was no one around.

Gradually he became aware of a low wailing moan. Following the sound, weaving his way between buildings, he came upon a group of women. Mabel was one of them. The women sat cross-legged before a fire, heads bowed and crying. Their cheeks were wet with tears, their skin shining in the yellow glow of the evening sun. The sound of their cries twisted Hamish's stomach in knots. As the sun faded, they became shadows against the glow of the fire. Somewhere in the distance was the untroubled call of children.

Hamish sat a short distance from the women and waited. He didn't know what else to do. An older man, tall and thin, came and sat beside him on the ground. His bearing was proud.

'You find out who killed Emily,' the man said. His voice sounded like water falling over rocks.

'There are some who say Simon killed her,' replied Hamish.

The man stared at him with milky blue eyes. It startled Hamish. He had never seen an Aboriginal man with pale eyes.

'The ancestors will not let this rest,' he said.

'Why do your ancestors care about the death of a white woman?' asked Hamish.

'Simon's child was murdered.'

Hamish felt the familiar flush of shame travel up his neck and across his face. He had been so incensed at the way Emily was being dismissed; he had not thought to consider the murder of her child, Simon's child. When he turned to look at the man, there was no one there. He had left silently, melting into the dark.

Realising the women would not be finished with their ritual any time soon, Hamish got up and wandered between the houses looking for someone to talk to about Emily and Simon. At the back of a cluster of houses, on a hill overlooking the sea, Hamish stumbled on a group of men. They were silently working rope into fishing nets. Hamish called out a cheery 'hello.' But the sound of his voice fell into the sea. He walked closer to the men, and as he did, one man raised a sinewy arm and waved Hamish away.

'Fuck off,' he growled.

The whites of the man's eyes shone in the emerging moonlight. Hamish did as he was told. Why had he come to Myora? What made him think these people would want to talk to him? Well-meaning indignation hung like a heavy cloak. He was as foreign in this place as he was anywhere.

Down on the shoreline, more men were hauling a dugong carcass over the edge of a small wooden boat. Hamish watched from above as they lay the carcass on the sand and used fishermen's knives to begin carving it.

'They'll share out portions among the families,' said someone behind him.

Hamish had not seen anyone approach. What was it about these people? They seemed to be able to appear in one place or another without travelling the distance. It was disconcerting.

'I'm Ned,' The man said as Hamish turned toward him. 'Simon's brother.'

'I'm honoured to meet you,' said Hamish, holding out his hand. Ned didn't move. Hamish quickly dropped his arm and wiped his hand nervously on his thigh.

'What is it you want to know?' asked Ned.

Now he had the opportunity; Hamish was not sure what question to ask first.

'I want to know what happened to Emily,' he said. 'I don't think Simon killed her.'

'Emily was killed by one of her own. That place, the Asylum, it's full of evil. Simon was killed by the evil there. He told me he would make someone pay for the death of Emily and his child. Then he hanged. Simon didn't kill himself. Someone stopped him from taking his revenge.'

'Did Simon say who he thought had killed Emily?'

'No.'

'Did you ask him?'

'He would've told me if he wanted me to know.'

'When you say Dunwich is full of evil, what exactly do you mean?'

'You'll find out. The answers are at the asylum, not here with us.' With that he returned to the group of men tying rope into fishing nets.

Hamish made his way back through the tracks between the houses, sometimes seeing shadows moving about inside, sometimes seeing a child duck behind a door when he came into view. His scientific mind, his expensive education and the cultural norms he wore against his chest like a vest that was too tight, seemed to do nothing but disconnect him from life, and from death. He concluded that no one else at Myora would talk to him, let alone answer his questions about Emily and Simon. Why should they? There was no reason for them to trust him, and they were in mourning.

Hamish found Mabel still with the women and told her he was heading back to Dunwich. She didn't look surprised.

'Will you be safe?' she asked.

'Yes, yes, of course,' he said. 'There's only one track.'

* * *

Hamish set off quickly, aware he had to walk back in the dark. Ned told him there was something evil about the asylum and he was becoming more convinced that was true. There was a façade that seemed reasonable at first, but beneath that there was neglect, disinterest and incompetence. All these things were regrettable, but evil implies something deeper. Hamish was prepared to believe that evil lurked in the dim buildings, in the isolation, in the overriding sense of hopelessness. But what specifically was it that constituted the evil? He needed more than feelings, he needed something tangible. He needed evidence. Ned said that Simon was killed because he planned to have revenge for Emily's death. That made sense, but there was no sign on the body that Simon was murdered.

With each step away from Myora, Hamish began to lose his confidence. What was he doing pursuing this investigation? He was certain Emily had not killed herself, but what business was it of his to be digging about in people's lives? He could appreciate the sensation of there being dark secrets at the asylum but uncovering them would be a job greater than him. It was his responsibility to report his findings about the two deaths, objectively, to the Colonial Secretary. That's all. The Superintendent had every right to put forth an alternative explanation. Let others follow-up if they found an investigation warranted. With each step along the track, Hamish managed to distance himself further from Emily Baker and her murder.

It was then he heard voices in the distance. The sound was not coming from Myora behind him, strangely it came from all directions. The more carefully he listened, the less he was able to pinpoint the source of the chattering voices. It sounded like a large group of people all talking at once. Hamish looked about anxiously. The silver moon glowed in the sky and cast an eerie light across the trees. But there was nothing to see apart from branches, leaves, and clusters of ferns clinging low to the ground. Hamish picked up his pace. As he strode on, a shadow caught his eye to the left of the track. It was fleeting, as though moving quickly behind the trees. Hamish tried to focus on the shadow but when he looked in its direction, it was no longer there.

He walked on; long purposeful steps designed to propel him forward regardless of fear. Again, he caught the fleeting image alongside him. The sound of the chattering voices became louder. He stopped and peered through the trees, expecting to see people gathered around a fire, but there was nothing but the sound. He stood there concentrating for some time. Finally, a shadowy figure came into view, shorter than a man, but taller than a child, and it was staring back at him. As the clouds cleared from across the moon, a silver beam of light illuminated the figure. It was stocky and had long brown hair. A tingling sensation travelled up the back of Hamish's neck and he was frozen to the spot. His mind couldn't work out what he was seeing. This was something outside his experience, yet he tried to convince himself it could be explained.

The moonlight caught the figure's eyes and at that exact instant it turned and loped away through the bush. Hamish ran also, his heart thudding in his chest. Even though the figure was running away from him, not toward him, his only aim was to get back to the asylum as quickly as possible. In his haste he tripped over an exposed tree root and fell, hitting the ground heavily. The sound of hundreds of voices crowded around him. He couldn't move his legs or lift his chest. He put his hand to his lip and touched a sticky pool of his own blood. He must have split his lip in the fall. That was the last thought he had that night. He slipped into unconsciousness and remained where he was until dawn.

The first warm rays of sunlight on his aching back woke him. He struggled to his feet and looked about, confused. There was a large Moreton Bay Fig to one side of the track and twisted roots spread across the sand. There was a dull ache in his head and his face was crusty with dried blood.

Apart from that, he seemed fine. He diagnosed no broken bones. Looking around, he recognised the curve in the track ahead and acknowledged that he was only about fifty yards away from the hanging tree on the Myora side.

A glint of sunlight dancing on the sea through the trees caught his eye, and he heard men yelling to one another. Working his way through the scrub to have a better look, he tripped and almost fell again. A group of old fence posts twisted in fencing wire broke his fall. It struck him that the wire looked exactly the right gauge to match the wound on Emily's neck.

Before he had time to fully process the idea, the sound of men's voices distracted him. He came into the clearing above the beach and saw the men from last night who were walking waist deep into the water with fishing spears. Ned was among them. A pod of porpoises was herding a swarm of fish into an ambush. The men circled the fish and speared them easily while the porpoises swam back and forth, ensuring they couldn't escape. Hamish watched fascinated for some time as the men and the animals worked together to facilitate the catch. When the young men filled their spears with fish, they threw some back to the porpoises, happily springing from the water to catch them. Some of the porpoises were bold enough to take the fish directly from the men's spears.

Hamish returned to the track, marvelling at the way the men and the animals worked together. Heading on toward Dunwich, he soon reached the hanging tree, and he stared up at the branch where Emily and Simon ended their lives. Nothing sinister was evident in the light of day. It was just a tree. Hamish kicked around the bank at the side of the track aimlessly, then caught a glimpse of sunlight in the bracken. He moved closer. It was a pair of glasses. He picked them up and tucked them into the waist of his trousers.

Walking on toward Dunwich, a shadow fell across the path. An enormous bird circled above, dipping and diving in ever-widening circles. Hamish had never seen a more magnificent bird. It appeared to be travelling with him. But that was surely his fancy. It was travelling toward the Bay, just as he was. Then, it suddenly dropped directly downward, swooping so low the breeze from its wings ruffled his hair. He caught its eye, black and shining. It seemed to look right through him, then it swooped back up and away, tipping the tops of the trees with its wings as it went. His pulse quickened.

Hamish had never been so relieved as when he caught the first glimpse of his tent from the ridge. He was tired and sore and desperately wanted to lie down. He knew he looked a mess, and his lip was bleeding again, but he didn't even want to wash. He pushed open the tent flap and was ready to fall onto his bunk. He stopped himself just in time. Curled up in his camp cot was the largest python he could have imagined. It was at least nine feet long and as thick as a tree branch. Its skin had a black and beige pattern that reminded Hamish of an expensive carpet. There it was, sleeping comfortably on his bed.

Hamish let the tent flap fall and walked backwards a few steps. He didn't hear Grimy coming up behind him, he simply stumbled into him. Hamish let out a squawk.

'Is there some trouble, Sir?' asked Grimy.

Hamish pointed toward his tent.

Grimy opened the flap and looked in, letting out a chuckle.

'Oh, that ain't nothin',' he laughed. 'I'll put you right.'

He entered the tent and placed one hand against the snake's jaw and slipped his other arm through its coils. He lifted the snake slowly. The snake gradually uncoiled and wound itself around Grimy's left arm, while he held its head in his right hand. Fully draped in the snake, Grimy walked past Hamish.

'I'll let him go down by the creek,' he said, smiling his greasy smile.

Hamish fell into his bed exhausted and slept the rest of the day.

In his dreams, a giant python appeared over the hill behind the asylum and slithered its way down into the settlement. The python crushed buildings in its wake until it reached the beach. There, the python curled up and gave birth to three eggs, each as big as a building. The python lifted its great body to reveal a man trapped beneath it. At first it seemed that the man was him then the face became clear. It was Vissen. Hamish woke up immediately.

'Good Lord,' he thought. 'Now Vissen of all people appears in my nightmares.'

He remembered the python Grimy removed from his bed and shivered.

29 MARCH 1881
EMILY

For their second outing together, Mrs Chambers suggested Emily and Avery attend the Music Hall. 'There's to be a wizard, I believe,' she said.

'A wizard?' cried Emily.

'I don't think the Music Hall is quite the place for young ladies...' began Avery.

Emily's eyes flashed. 'But I've never seen a wizard!'

From the moment they entered the Music Hall, it enthralled Emily. It was her first experience of any kind of public entertainment. The stage sparkled.

'Professor Anderson, all the way from the theatres of New York, to entertain and delight!' shouted the Host.

The Professor wore evening attire, and over that a glistening blue cape that fell from his shoulders. A conical cap of the same deep blue with silver stars was perched on his head. In his first few minutes on stage Professor Anderson produced an enormous quantity of fresh flowers, toys and sweetmeats from an ordinary top hat. Next, he extracted a rabbit, two geese and a live boy out of a portfolio about two inches thick. The audience cheered, and so did Emily.

The Professor's next trick was called the 'inexhaustible bottle.' He asked the audience if anyone would enjoy a glass of gin? The crowd called out at once. Professor Anderson chose a gentleman two rows in front of Emily and poured him a glass of gin from the tall blue bottle. Then he asked if any of the ladies had a desire for lemonade. There were several shouts from the audience. The Wizard filled a large glass with lemonade from the exact bottle he had poured the gin. This continued with the bottle producing copious amounts of rum, whiskey and soda for members of the audience. Everyone applauded.

Then a man in the audience called out,

'You have a quick hand and a clever way about you, stranger. But there is one trick I would like to see you do. As clever as you are, I'll wager you cannot do this trick.'

The Wizard laughed.

'What is it you would have the Professor do?' he asked.

'I say stranger, you can't turn a black nigger white! You can't do that!' The man spat on the floor and put his hands deep in his pockets.

The audience cheered.

'Settle down now,' said the Professor.

He pointed to a sturdy black man who happened to be sitting in the front row.

'Will you come up on stage?' said the Professor.

'Who me, Sir?' asked the man.

Emily recognised the accent. Her mother had a friend with the same accent when Emily was a child, he was American. The Professor motioned to him and he climbed up onto the stage. A large table was brought forward, together with an enormous basket, tall and narrow like a giant extinguisher formed out of wicker work and covered in cloth.

Everyone was on their toes as the black man mounted the table. He stood still while they placed the wicker extinguisher over him. The Professor fired a pistol at him, and a hush went through the crowd. On removal of the extinguisher, there stood a perfectly white-skinned American with white curly hair.

'It's flour! It's flour!' cried the audience.

Professor Anderson invited audience members to examine him. They found his skin was indeed white. Avery remarked that in changing colour the man appeared to have become taller. Still, round after round of applause greeted the Professor. Emily clapped the loudest.

'Let me change him back again,' said the Professor. He replaced the extinguisher - the pistol fired, and there a minute later stood a black man. The Professor bowed several times as the audience stood and applauded for ten minutes.

Emily and Avery left the theatre arm in arm. Emily was animated and talkative, full of the joy of the evening's entertainment. As they emerged from the crowd in front of the entrance, they saw a group of men arguing on the roadside. A small child stood helpless just beyond the tussling men. Emily was about to walk toward the child and speak to her, ask her if she was alone, when a well-dressed gentleman appeared out of the gathering onlookers and took her hand. The man said a few words to the child, and the child followed him. Emily watched for a moment, unsure. There seemed something unnatural about the interaction. The child kept looking back over her shoulder at the fighting men.

'Come now,' said Avery, leading her in the opposite direction. They walked around the block before turning toward home to avoid the crowd that had gathered to cheer on the fight.

The following morning Mrs Chambers read a piece from the Brisbane Courier aloud.

'A child is missing,' she said.

'Apparently, the father was involved in a quarrel in Roma Street, and the Police were called. He was taken to the Police Station, but no one could find the child.'

A cold shiver travelled up Emily's spine. Had she seen the child led away? Was that the missing child? Emily reflected on it only briefly and decided she was reading too much into a simple image of a man leading a child away from a street fight. It was surely a relative, and quite right that the child should be removed from such a scene.

CHAPTER SIX

Ah! What pleasant visions haunt me,
As I gaze upon the sea,
All the romantic legends,
All my dreams come back to me.
Longfellow.
The Queenslander, Brisbane. Saturday 14 April 1883

---

27 SEPTEMBER 1884
HAMISH

It was mid-afternoon when Hamish woke up. He wandered down to the beach in front of the asylum and entered the calm bay waters. The saltwater stung his wounds and cleared his foggy mind. As he left the water to dress, his skin prickling from the salt, he felt refreshed. He ran his hand down the side of his face and his fingers touched the scarred flesh there. At least his scar had not been torn in the fall. He strode toward the Superintendent's office where he found Holloway, his wife, and Vissen in conference.

'We can't bury him at the cemetery,' Holloway was saying, 'And at the same time declare him a murderer.'

'It was a tragic love story,' cried Brigid. 'Star-crossed lovers. He killed her and the baby, then killed himself. People will accept that.'

'I think the Colonial Secretary will accept that,', said Vissen. 'But I don't think we should bury him at the asylum. Let him lie with his people at Myora.'

Holloway wrung his hands anxiously. 'Yes. Yes,' he said. 'The tragic story of lovers that could neither belong in one world or the other, and that will be the end of it.'

Hamish was standing in the open doorway to the office, but no one had yet noticed him.

He coughed.

The other three turned in astonishment to see him standing there.

'There is a problem with your solution,' said Hamish. 'There is no evidence it's true.'

Holloway stood up. 'There is no evidence it's not true,' he barked.

'Damn it, Hart, if it were not for your blathering about murder all over the Island, there would be no problem. Double suicide would be the most convenient explanation by far. In fact, we only have your say that this was not the case.'

'You can't claim double suicide,' said Hamish. 'There is clear evidence that Emily did not self-murder.'

But Holloway had talked himself around to a position and become dedicated to it.

'Actually,' he said, 'I believe we should take that position. It avoids any further interference from Brisbane. We'll go ahead with the funeral tomorrow afternoon. We'll bury Simon at Dunwich in the Aboriginal quarter and talk about two ill-fated lovers who ended their own lives rather than be parted. The report will be clear and succinct.'

Vissen was anxious to have the matter closed satisfactorily.

'Hear, hear,' he said.

Brigid looked nervously at Hamish, while the two men avoided his eye.

'My own report will say otherwise,' said Hamish calmly.

'So be it,' declared Holloway, straightening the papers on his desk and rising to go.

'You have no evidence to prove any alternative. The mark on the woman's neck means nothing. Not when the whole story can be packaged so neatly, and further trouble in Dunwich avoided. Double suicide.'

Hamish knew that on one level Holloway was probably right. If an accusation of murder against Simon could be avoided, the people from Myora would accept the story. The Colonial Secretary would also find it far more convenient to accept that one of the asylum inmates committed suicide, rather than have to investigate a murder case. Even though the inmates at Dunwich were society's lowest misfits, if a native murdered one of them there would be consequences. The fact the man was dead had some advantages to it. No one would have to be tried; however, the murder couldn't go uncommented upon in official circles. There would need to be some warning to those living at Myora that the murder of a white woman is intolerable. Also, murder implies poor management, and something would have to be done about the lack of discipline at the asylum.

By the same token, the odd suicide in such a group of people is hardly surprising. That a woman declared deranged, chose to end her life rather than live out her days in an asylum, a woman pregnant with a black bastard no less, was understandable. And one more dead native would mean nothing to the Colonial Office. Hamish could feel his frustration rising. He tucked his fingers inside his collar and ran them around his neck to allow some air to reach his skin. He struggled to find the words he needed to convince Holloway that Emily had not killed herself, whatever the truth about Simon's death might be. The events of the evening before, and his own frustration, exhausted him.

Holloway and his wife pushed past Hamish to leave the Telegraph Office. Vissen waited.

'What happened to your lip?' he asked.

'I fell,' said Hamish.

'Will you be needing access to the office this evening?' asked Vissen.

'No,' said Hamish.

He left Vissen locking up behind him. After a few steps Hamish turned back.

'Do you believe that Simon killed Emily?' asked Hamish.

Vissen's face darkened. He didn't look directly at Hamish or answer as he strode away.

Hamish made his way to the kitchen to see if there was anything left of the evening meal. Wallace was sitting outside with a billy on the boil and a bowl of cabbage soup. He ladled another bowl from an enormous pot and handed it to Hamish.

'I haven't seen you eat for days,' he said.

Hamish took the soup and drank it hungrily. He hadn't noticed, but it was true. He hadn't eaten much since his first day at Dunwich. Wallace tore a large mound of damper apart and handed Hamish half.

With his mouth full of damper soaked in cabbage soup, Hamish said, 'I am no closer to the truth.'

Wallace stared into the fire.

'They're holding a funeral tomorrow and they will say both Simon and Emily committed suicide,' said Hamish quietly.

Wallace took in a deep breath and poked at the fire with a stick.

'The truth is, Emily was murdered,' went on Hamish. 'There's no doubt about that.'

Wallace didn't look away from the fire.

'Not always important in a place like this,' he said, 'the truth.'

'I can see that. The thing is, I have my article to get on with. I've been here five days and I haven't even started yet. I've been completely distracted by these deaths. I'm not qualified to investigate one murder, let alone consider the potential that two have been committed.'

Wallace poked about in the ashes with a stick.

'Still,' he said, 'Emily was a good woman.'

'I found these glasses near the hanging tree,' Hamish said holding them up to look through them. Wallace looked nervously at the glasses, but he didn't comment.

'Simon didn't kill Emily,' said Wallace.

'I know!' cried Hamish. 'Everyone who knew him says that. But someone killed her.'

Wallace suddenly seemed to remember something.

'Grimy used to follow her about. Sneaky little cunt. Saw him follow her onto the track one night not long before she died. I wanted to go after her, but I had the supper to do. Mabel had already gone home.'

'Why didn't you tell me this before?' asked Hamish.

'I don't trust the filthy little fucker, but I seen nothin' but him following her onto the track. And she was well and fit the next day.'

They were both silent for a while.

Red came out from under the building, his hairy face caked with dirt.

'Been hunting mice again, Mate?' said Hamish.

The dog ignored him and put his front paws on Wallace's knee. Wallace pulled him onto his lap.

Hamish needed to calm himself, and Wallace seemed to have a calming influence on him. The need for a friend on this Island was overwhelming.

'How did you come to be in this place?' he asked.

'Came up from Melbourne looking for work,' said Wallace. 'I cook, they needed a cook.'

'Were you always a cook?'

'I was a ship's cook,' he said. 'Since I was a boy of fourteen, I worked in ship's galleys. Never knew any other life as an adult, than on a ship.'

'How did you find yourself in a ship's galley at fourteen?'

'Father died when I was twelve. By the time I was fourteen, we were likely to starve during the winter if something wasn't done. My mother remarried, and her new husband didn't want me around. He had connections on a vessel, so he sent me on board to work in the galley.'

'That must have been rough for you,' said Hamish.

Wallace laughed.

'Quite the opposite,' he said. 'The Captain took a shine to me. I spent most of my time in the Captain's quarters. He taught me to read literature, introduced me to poetry.'

Hamish looked surprised.

'Isn't that unusual?' he asked.

Wallace laughed.

'Not really,' he said, 'Many of the Captains took a liking to a lad. Voyages are long.'

The look of surprise turned to one of shock as Hamish watched him continue.

'It's not so bad,' said Wallace. 'He was good to me. I spent four years with him. Two voyages around the world and back. I experienced more in those years than most people could imagine in a lifetime.'

Hamish was confused. 'Was the relationship...?'

Wallace spoke before he could finish.

'There was... he was... like an Uncle. I was under his protection, so I didn't suffer like the other apprentices. The Head Cook was too afraid of him to chastise me.' Wallace laughed again. 'Oh, for sure there were sly looks from the others and plenty of jokes behind my back.'

'What happened to your Captain then? How did it end?'

'His wife decided to keep him at home. Ha ha, she retired him. She decided she had spent long enough raising their four daughters alone. I wasn't upset about it. By then I wanted to spread my wings a little. The next two years were a wild ride, I can tell you.'

'What made you take to the land?'

'It was that last voyage. The last one I ever sailed,' he said quietly.

'I lost my will for the sea,' he added. 'Besides I was getting too old. Too much drink had taken its toll.'

'What happened?'

Wallace seemed to turn the answer over in his mind. He chewed on the end of his pipe.

'We were coming down the Southern Ocean,' he began, 'We were aboard one of the Great Clippers. Beautiful ship she was. Making our way from Plymouth to Port Phillip with a cargo of immigrants and a Captain hell bent on making it in less than seventy-five days. We were overcrowded, too right. The Captain knew it.'

Wallace paused to stroke the dog's ears before going on.

'Just as we reached the Southern Ocean, the storms hit. One after another, each lasting for days at a time. The wind hissed and screeched night and day, belting the sea into a fury. Waves of sixty feet lifted the vessel into the sky, held her, then dumped her back into the sea. Each time there was an almighty crash as the bow hit the bottom of the trough. With every wave, the ship would lurch to one side, dive deep until the decks were underwater, then pitch back again and right herself. This went on and on for near three weeks.

On one of the last nights of the greatest hurricane yet, passengers screamed in terror. It swept some from their bunks as they slept. Drowned in the belly of the ship. The galley was chaos. Pots and pans crashed from one side of the ship to the other. It smashed anyone who tried to move around against the ship's sides. It crushed skulls and broke limbs. My best mate was swept off a ladder going from the galley up to the lower deck. To this day, I have no idea why he was climbing the damn ladder. He was torn from the ladder by a mighty torrent of water that washed him across the deck and out to sea. I caught his eye in the split second before he lost his grip. He looked sorry. His eyes were saying, I'm sorry. What the hell do you think that is about?' pleaded Wallace, his own eyes red.

Hamish couldn't speak. He wanted to say something comforting, but no words came.

Wallace continued, 'The storm kept raging for three days and there was no time to grieve. We were busy struggling to survive, every one of us.' He paused again.

'Then came the typhus.'

'Good Lord!' Hamish cried, recalling Wallace had mentioned this earlier.

'The weather settled and then the passengers began coming down with fever. It was just two or three at first, and they were ill for four or five days before death came. Then the number of cases grew, but the small hospital on the ship was full. People were dying in their bunks. Soon the fever would grip a person and they'd be dead within hours. They dispensed with more than ten in one go. Wrapped 'em up in bedding and mattresses, tied up tight, and tipped the lot overboard. When we finally made it to Port Phillip we weren't allowed to come ashore. That voyage was my last.'

Wallace's story overwhelmed Hamish. He had always loved the *idea* of an adventurous life at sea. He had even entertained becoming a ship's surgeon at one point.

'Do you ever miss it?' he asked.

Wallace smiled dolefully.

'I have the stories,' he said. 'I enjoy telling the stories. But I guess I miss something,' he stared out across the bay. 'I miss conversation the most. No one here can bloody read,' he laughed.

Hamish nodded slowly.

Wallace continued telling stories of the sea. He told Hamish about a crossing at Bass Straight during which the waves were higher than the main sail. There was a sea monster, a fish as large as a house with a gaping mouth you could drive a carriage into, teeth like shattered glass. A series of stories melted into one as Wallace talked. Every now and then Hamish made a sound in respect for the enormity of the tale.

Walking back to his tent later, Hamish felt relaxed. The urgency of his need to find out what happened to Emily had dulled. He liked Wallace, he believed him to be an honest man. But he couldn't help acknowledging to himself that Wallace had yet again shifted his focus from the deaths of Emily and Simon.

In his dreams that night Hamish was floating in a vast sea. He was in a boat only large enough for him to remain within its confines if he bunched up his legs, his knees under his chin. A sea eagle floated across the sky above him. He had no paddles for his boat. Sharks were circling. The tips of their fins were just visible above the water line. He looked about the boat anxiously for something he could use to push the sharks away should they come close to the boat. But there was nothing. More and more sharks were joining those already circling his boat. Then the sea eagle dipped its wings and swooped down to the sea level right beside the sharks closest to him. Those sharks turned outward and the sea eagle took another dive, aiming directly for the next round of sharks.

The sea became choppy as sharks tried to turn tail, and the sea eagle dipped its great wings in and out of the water. The waves were making the boat unstable and Hamish was clinging with all his strength to the sides. Just as the boat was about to tip, Hamish tried to balance himself by standing. He fell into the sea, and then all at once he was awake. He was on his bed, his sheet was tangled around his body, his forehead wet with sweat.

Hamish settled himself. The tent walls were flapping wildly. He could hear that a strong wind had blown up outside. There was the light patter of rain on the canvas and he felt a chill in his chest, despite the sweat. He straightened out the sheet and lay back down, listening to his breathing become calm. The wind was threatening to upend the tent; the canvas pulling at the pegs. It occurred to him he should check they were sound, but he didn't have the strength. He drifted back to sleep, barely aware of the wind ripping at the canvas and the rain that came in squalls. He slept feverishly throughout the night and the following day. The wind formed a constant backdrop to his sleep. The sound fell somewhere between consciousness and unconsciousness. He wondered that no one came to check on him, but then it was Sunday and Holloway and his wife would be busy with the Bible. Who knew where Wallace might be? In between the preparation of meals, he was likely as not drinking with his mates.

Hamish passed the day waking, attempting to get up, then feebly falling back onto his bed. At one point he briefly considered the possibility of concussion, however his mind was not sharp enough to form the thought.

When he woke up the next morning, Hamish felt slightly more like himself, however the continued wind and rain that came in fits and bursts discouraged him from leaving his tent. He heard some movement at the jetty, and the horse and dray passing with the night soil pans, but little else. It seemed the whole settlement was standing firm, waiting for the wind to drop.

7 OCTOBER, 1882
EMILY

Emily woke up with a start on her wedding day, clammy and nauseated. Pulling the sheets up under her chin and closing her eyes, she tried desperately to calm herself.

Mrs Chambers knocked twice and then entered without waiting for a reply.

'You look enchanting, Pet,' she said. 'Like a porcelain doll.'

'I feel sick,' said Emily.

'Of course you do, dear. It's your wedding day. We are, all of us, nervous on the morning of our wedding.'

Emily forced herself to smile.

'What would you like me to bring you for breakfast?'

'I couldn't possibly eat.'

'I'll bring us both a fresh pot of tea then.' Mrs Chambers turned back. 'Don't worry, married life will suit you,' she said.

Emily lifted her dress from the hook behind her bedroom door and held it against her skin. It was a subtle colour. When Mrs Chambers made it, it was white, but Emily had her stain it with cold tea. She did not want to wear white. The tea colour suited her, it was barely a shade darker than her skin.

When Mrs Chambers returned, Emily was still clutching the dress to her chest.

'Look at you,' Mrs Chambers began, 'You have survived your early mistakes, worked hard and now you have found a steady man to wed.'

Emily told herself she was making a mature choice. Avery didn't make her heart pound faster, but he was steady, as Mrs Chambers said. She braced herself and concentrated on what she had to do to get ready. The following three hours collapsed into moments and Emily emerged from the bedroom draped in silk and lace, her hair rolled and tucked and adorned with matching silk flowers. She was clutching a posy of angel's breath and white roses.

At precisely 11:00am Emily stood beside Avery in the small white Presbyterian Church in Ann Street. Mrs Chambers stood beside her as her only guest. Avery was adamant that they only needed one another. If they had not required a witness, he might not have let even Mrs Chambers attend. The church was eerily quiet. Emily focussed on the beams of coloured light streaming through the stained-glass windows on the back wall. The colours passed over her to dance on the pulpit. Tiny flecks of dust blinked on and off in the light as the Minister began his sermon. Keeping her eyes focussed on the coloured lights helped to still the nausea.

'Words are just words,' she thought, as the Minister rattled on, saying words that had no meaning for her. It was like being in a dream, watching on from a distance, as unrelated moments passed.

'Emily May Mountford, wilt thou have this man to be thy husband, and wilt thou pledge thy faith to him in all love and honour, in all duty and service, in all faith and tenderness, to live with him, and cherish him, according to the ordinance of God, in the holy bond of marriage?'

Suddenly Emily was aware Avery, Mrs. Chambers and the Minister were staring at her.

'Sorry...I do,' she stuttered.

'Repeat after me,' the Minister said.

Her throat closed over. How would she ever say the words? She panicked.

'I, Emily May Mountford,' chanted the Minister. Emily swallowed heavily. She mouthed the words, but no sound would come.

'A little louder please,' the Minister leaned forward. 'Take you, Avery Baker,' he went on.

Emily repeated the words as clearly as she could.

'They are only words,' she kept telling herself.

God would know her doubts. But she just had to say the words, and it would be over.

'As long as we both shall live,' she said.

'Husband and wife,' said the Minister.

'Wife,' thought Emily. She belonged to someone. She mattered.

CHAPTER SEVEN

M. Bucy has devoted years of patient experiment to the subject of metallotherapy, or the alleviation of disease by the application of pieces of metal – gold, iron, copper, silver, zinc etc. to the skin, or administered internally. He has certainly from time to time produced startling results, in the presence too, of the sceptical. Thus, his assertion deserves serious consideration, that he has attended fifteen patients and prescribed 'metals' along with the waters, and has completely cured them of fatty diabetes, a malady up to the present accepted as mortal. - The Age, Melbourne. Monday 8 March 1880

---

29 SEPTEMBER 1884
HAMISH

It was Monday morning and Hamish woke to the sound of light drizzle on his tent. The wind had finally dropped. He pulled the cotton sheet up under his chin. He was hungry, but he didn't want to join the Holloways for breakfast. He particularly didn't want to explain why he had been closeted in his tent since Saturday evening. The alternative was porridge with the inmates in the mess tent. If he wanted to take that option, he would have to get up immediately. He wondered at the soreness in his back and legs, given that he had spent the last thirty-six hours on his bed, apart from the occasional step out to relieve himself. Reluctantly, he rose and pulled on his trousers, shirt and coat. He put his hand to his face and felt the rough texture of the stubble accumulated there. He realised he would have to shave. There was sufficient water left in the jug, so he lathered his jaw and cleared the stubble with a quick razor. He tucked the collar up under his ears and made his way out into the rain.

Hamish noted that the men around him fell silent as he sat down at the long wooden table. It was a familiar pattern at the asylum. Most of the inmates were suspicious of him since word got around he was interested in the two recent deaths. The men were all thin and some had terrible disfigurements. The man to the left of Hamish was missing a foot. His trouser leg was rolled up to reveal an inflamed stub at the bottom of his leg.

'What happened?' asked Hamish.

The man was willing to answer.

'Sugar,' he said.

'Diabetes?' corrected Hamish.

'That's right,' the man said. 'Took one foot already, and the other will go the same.'

Hamish glanced across the man at his other leg. A foot peeped out from the ragged hem of his trousers. It was black.

'Necrotic.' The man was right, the other foot could not be saved.

Hamish noticed the man was eating a large slab of bread.

'You know the diabetes can be managed if you cut out bread and sugar. Might give you a little longer before you lose that foot.'

The man looked at his blackened toes.

'Too late for me, doctor, I reckon.'

'Do you think the people here would accept a restricted diet that would do them some good?' asked Hamish.

'Dunno,' said the man. 'Doubt it.'

Hamish wished there was another physician to talk to about this terrifyingly backward, yet interesting place.

At that moment Chooky came into the Mess and caught his attention.

'You are needed in Holloway's office immediately,' he said, with sufficient dramatic effect, every man in the room looked up intrigued.

Hamish had no idea why he was being summoned. He hoped no one else had turned up dead.

When Hamish entered the office, Holloway sat behind the desk looking stern. Vissen stood to his left, red faced and huffing. It was only then that Hamish noticed the third person in the room. He let out a cry of delight.

'What...?' he began and lost his voice thereafter.

Standing before him, calm and steadfast was his friend Rita.

'Good morning, Doctor,' she said. 'I have come at the request of the Colonial Secretary. I am to gather data on the health of the inmates.'

'What?' repeated Hamish. Then, at risk of sounding like an imbecile, he gathered his wits. 'My apologies,' he began. 'It's just a shock to see you here. Welcome. Welcome,' he added.

'You know one another?' the Superintendent asked dryly.

'Of course,' explained Rita, the medical community in Brisbane is very small.'

What's she up to? thought Hamish. But out loud he said, 'I was only just thinking how important such a task would be. What a lucky coincidence!'

'Lucky coincidence indeed,' said Holloway.

Vissen objected.

'I really must protest,' he said. 'There's been no word of this visit. No notice. It's not acceptable that people turn up here unannounced in this way. First Hart, and then you,'

He shot Rita a look of contempt that could've turned a lesser woman to tears.

She smiled at him, unmoved by his contempt.

'Nonetheless,' she began, 'Here we are. And with orders from the Colonial Secretary, no less. Will I sleep in the nurses' quarters?' she asked.

'There are no nurses' quarters,' replied Vissen.

'You can sleep in a tent,' said Holloway, 'As Hart does.'

He drew his brows together in what he hoped to be a menacing frown and added,

'I expect you both to be on the next barge to the mainland on Thursday. Hamish has already been here for the week that was approved. I would have expected your departure on the barge today,' said Holloway, 'not the arrival of another visitor to examine us as though we were insects.'

Hamish and Rita left the office together. Rita had been given permission to set up a tent alongside Hamish.

'I believe he let us stay together because no one wanted me anywhere else,' Rita laughed.

'He probably thinks he can manage us better if we're close together.'

Rita assumed a reasonable impersonation of the Superintendent. 'To hell with morality, any woman who takes on a man's profession is beyond saving, anyway.'

They both laughed like children.

A trio of inmates, Grimy among them, helped pitch the tent and set Rita up with everything she would need. Hamish and Rita sat brewing tea outside Hamish's tent.

'Why have you come, really?' asked Hamish.

'I want to find out who killed Emily,' Rita replied. 'While I was investigating her past, I became quite fond of her, besides did you think I was going to let you have all the fun?' she added with a cheeky laugh. 'Now you have to bring me up to date.'

Hamish recounted the events at the asylum since his arrival, ending with Simon's death.

Rita listened intently.

'So,' she began, 'the potential killers are Grimy, who resented Emily's affection for Simon; Simon, who had no reason to kill Emily at all that I can see; Mabel....'

Hamish stopped her. 'Mabel?' he cried. 'Mabel can't have had anything to do with it. Why would she?'

'Well,' said Rita, 'she may have wanted to protect her nephew. She may well have feared they would punish him when news of the baby came out.... Anyway, then there is Holloway...'

'What? Why?' cried Hamish.

'To prevent a scandal.'

'I don't think he even knew about Simon and the affair.'

'And Wallace,' finished Rita.

'Now wait a minute,' objected Hamish. 'Why would Wallace kill Emily?'

'I don't know,' said Rita. 'Do you?'

Hamish had to admit he didn't know either way.

'There are plenty of people here,' he said. 'Almost anyone could have done it, either from Myora or from Dunwich.'

'Yes, but has anyone else's name come up?' she asked.

Hamish tried not to admit to himself that he didn't want to think of Wallace as a murderer.

'Then again, he did seem nervous when I showed him the glasses...'

Hamish and Rita drank their tea while Rita tried to come up with a methodical way to proceed. Rita decided that Hamish would continue to talk and listen, while she concentrated on the inmate records, in case there was anything there that would link someone else to Emily.

'I don't know if I want to investigate Emily's death,' said Hamish. 'I would rather focus on writing the article if it comes down to it.'

'Tosh,' said Rita. 'You can't remain silent while they pass off this woman's murder as suicide. It reduces her life to nothing. Anyway, it seems to me you've done nothing but think about the murder since you arrived.'

'How would you know what I think about?' asked Hamish.

Rita tilted her head to the side. Her brown eyes said she always knew what he was thinking.

He shifted uncomfortably at the thought.

'How did you convince the Colonial Secretary to authorise your project here?' he said.

'Easy,' said Rita. 'He owes my father a favour.'

* * *

While Hamish spent the morning catching Rita up on the details of both Emily's and Simon's deaths, the rest of the community was preparing for Simon's funeral. The wind and rain had derailed the ceremony with the Myora community refusing to agree to the funeral until the weather cleared. Simon's body had been taken by his people and held at Myora. Hamish hoped the rain would stop within a day or two, or the body would become a significant problem. The people of Myora had assured him they had ways to delay decomposition, but Hamish wondered exactly what that involved. He decided they must be keeping the body under the cool water of the springs. Then he caught himself wondering if that was the same spring they drank from, and he became anxious again. On the morning of the funeral, Simon's body was picked up by horse and cart to be placed in a coffin and delivered to the cemetery.

Hamish and Rita were sipping tea by the fire when they saw Mabel coming from the kitchen.

'I'm sorry for your loss,' said Hamish, unable to think of anything that would more genuinely reflect his feelings.

Mabel didn't respond.

'May I ask you a question?' asked Hamish.

Mabel glared at him. 'You and your bloody questions,' she said.

Hamish lowered his head.

'Go on then, ask your question.'

'Why are you allowing Holloway to have Simon buried here,' he said. 'Why wouldn't you bury him at Myora?'

'Simon was proud of his people,' Mabel began, 'But he was also proud of his job here. Holloway said they will remember him for his work at the asylum. We want people to know that Simon was a good man. We want people to remember him. White people as well as our own. Simon didn't kill Emily. Holloway will say that, publicly. Then it will be over.'

Hamish accepted her answer and kept his misgivings to himself. It wouldn't be over. He was sure of it.

Soon after midday, Hamish and Rita set off toward the cemetery. Hamish was keen to know what the Superintendent would say about the deaths.

As they approached, they could see people from Myora gathering. There were six Aboriginal men, naked and decorated with white clay, sitting around the open grave clicking clap sticks. The sound was hypnotic. It had been humid that morning after the rain and the afternoon was building toward a storm with dark clouds gathering over the bay and a strange green glow cast across the cemetery. Hamish and Rita were sweating uncomfortably by the time they reached the grave site. Again, Hamish was curious about how and where Simon's body had been kept since its removal from the hospital, but he didn't dare broach the subject with Mabel. He wondered if he ever could.

The Aboriginal mourners kept coming, a slow procession down the sandy track to the beachfront and into the cemetery. They were mostly silent, apart from a group of children who were skipping about the graves squealing. When the trickle of mourners came to an end, there must have been more than one hundred people gathered. There was an uneasy tension in the air. When everyone was present, and the stifling humidity had reached its peak beneath the heavy sky, Hamish noticed Holloway, his wife and Vissen striding across the fields to join them. The sound of the clap sticks provided the rhythm for Hamish's heart, and he knew that the whole congregation was tuned into the same rhythm. The sky above continued to darken, and the taste of the sea grew salty in their throats.

When Holloway stood before the crowd and spoke, the clapping ceased. Hamish imagined the congregation taking in a single breath. There were several inmates and workers from the asylum present. They stood apart, away from the grave, giving the people from Myora room to be close to their loved one. Hamish caught the eye of Wallace for an instant. Wallace quickly looked down at his feet, not wanting to reveal anything. Hamish noticed the difference in the two funerals. Emily's funeral was lonely and stark. Simon's was full and colourful.

The Aboriginal people were comforting one another, hugging, supportive and reassuring. It tugged at Hamish's sense of fairness that Emily had no one to mourn her passing at her burial. Both the populations of Myora and of Dunwich had turned out for Simon. Hamish acknowledged the importance of what Mabel had said to him. This was acceptance of Simon as a 'good man'. It was a show of solidarity from the people of Dunwich; and for the people of *Moongalba*. It was a symbol of closure. They had endured the two deaths, the reasons for them explained to everyone's satisfaction, and this was the end of it. Rita took Hamish's hand and squeezed it. He felt reassured, she always knew when he needed reassurance.

When Hamish returned his attention to the speaker, Holloway was describing Simon as a solid worker and a fine man respected by all. He spoke of heartbreak, and a murmur swept through the crowd. He said the word suicide and there was a palpable spike in the tension. A whirring sound descended from above, and a shadow fell across the open grave as an enormous sea eagle swooped from the sky. The white belly and outstretched wings came low over the crowd. Some could see the bird's yellow eye as it dove into the grave, turned abruptly and swooped up again directly into the sky.

As they lowered Simon's body into the ground, the sky darkened even further and there was a deafening crash of thunder. Jagged knives of lightening shot across the bay, while the sea and sky merged in a deep grey-green haze. Large, heavy drops of water fell as individual community members stepped forward to drop plods of sand into the grave. There was an echo as the sods hit the wooden coffin. The drops of rain gathered in frequency and the asylum staff and inmates scurried across the fields to find shelter. The Aboriginal community remained by the gravesite, paying their last respects.

As Hamish and Rita rushed forward with the others, Hamish brushed past Vissen. He was muttering something to Holloway, and he and Rita heard the words, 'filthy Blacks', as they passed. Brigid shot Hamish a glance. It could have been fear, or it could have been shame. Could it be that Brigid had doubts about her husband's decision to disregard the possibility of murder? Or was she shamed by Vissen's overt distaste for the original inhabitants of the Island? The moment passed quickly, and Hamish wondered if it had happened at all.

Hamish was furious that Holloway publicly referred to both Emily's and Simon's deaths as suicide. Emily's death was being reduced to a convenient story, as though her life had no value and the circumstances of her death mattered little. Holloway's only concern was his reputation and keeping enquiring eyes away from the asylum. Hamish said as much to Rita and she nodded.

'I can't let this go,' said Hamish.

'And you shouldn't,' said Rita. 'You have support now. I'll help you. Together we'll find out what happened to Emily... or we'll at least make the authorities in Brisbane listen.'

'Did you notice the look on Brigid's face?' asked Hamish.

Rita nodded. 'I'm not sure she agrees with her husband's approach. And I get the sense she doesn't like Vissen at all.'

* * *

Sub-tropical rainfall was too substantial to ignore, so Hamish and Rita decided to spend the afternoon indoors examining medical records. The record books and registers for the asylum were neatly kept and well organised. There were ledgers which carefully listed supplies and costs, and ledgers which detailed assets and buildings. Livestock kept by the asylum and produce from the gardens were neatly recorded. The asylum was expected to be self-sufficient, and to the extent that this was possible, it seemed to be true.

Records confirmed that there was a tannery, inmates worked at making candles, there was a butchery and a bakery. Inmates also turned milk into butter and cheese. It appeared that often food was short, with supply of many staples depending upon seasonal changes and the availability of water. Hamish noted that the skill set of the individuals responsible for the production of the community's daily needs was largely dependent upon that of the particular inmates residing at the asylum at any given time. When there were people with specific skills; they were put to good use. Still, it appeared that inmates with little experience in a task would sometimes find themselves working twelve-hour days at that very task. Necessity and survival would soon translate into experience and expertise, Hamish supposed.

'The asylum is loosely modelled on the theory that inmates will be rehabilitated through meaningful activity', Hamish said aloud.

'There is merit in that theory,' said Rita. 'Tanning leather to produce shoes for the community is certainly meaningful activity.'

'There's no training for people who've never worked in these trades before. It doesn't make sense, to simply expect that the community will be sustained through sheer hard work.'

'Consequently, people who have never had so much as a vegetable patch are responsible for growing crops sufficient to feed a whole community in sandy soil, with limited rainfall,' said Rita.

'Exactly,' agreed Hamish.

When they began reading the medical notes of the inmates, Hamish and Rita were interested to find that while there was a large number with a diagnosis of diabetes, and many cases of tuberculosis, the greatest number of inmates were listed as inebriates. There was the inebriate ward, which Hamish had visited, but there were also individuals scattered throughout the asylum listed as 'inebriate' or 'alcoholic'. In terms of mental health status specifically, there were a few inmates registered as 'deranged', however the majority had no mention of their psychological status.

After three hours of data collection, Hamish sat back and brushed his hair from his face. 'These people are not sent here because of their mental health at all,' he said. 'They're sent here for social reasons.'

Rita looked up at him. 'Absolutely,' she said. 'It surprises me that you're only now coming to that realisation.'

Hamish stared at her in silence.

'Really Hamish,' she said, 'You know as well as I do that the majority of people believe that the poor live as they do, because of their own inferiority. The middle-classes believe God blesses them with wealth because He favours them.'

'Wasn't it Herbert Spencer who said that the defective nature of citizens will show up in whatever social structure they are arranged into?'

'Yes, it was. And when Spencer promised competition would lead through social evolution to unparalleled prosperity, he was talking about prosperity for the middle-classes. Sending the frail and dysfunctional souls here to isolation is probably more than many of the well-to-do in Brisbane would think necessary. It would seem to many that such State based support encourages laziness and dependency,' said Rita, still shuffling through documents.

'Progress in this country has nothing to do with social evolution to a new 'fit' society,' said Hamish. 'It's about the exploitation of labour to exert power and control over resources.'

'Yes, well, thank-you Karl Marx,' said Rita. She seemed distracted by something.

'What are you reading?' asked Hamish, looking over her shoulder.

'I started looking through this journal that documents complaints,' she responded. 'Look.'

Hamish forced his eyes to focus on the page she was showing him.

It was a written account, entered by Holloway, of a complaint made by Emily May Baker in relation to abuse at the hand of Cornelius Vissen. According to the account, Emily reported to Holloway on 6 August, that Vissen, Storeman at Dunwich, had physically assaulted her, attempting to force himself upon her in an explicitly sexual manner. Emily stated that she fought back and pushed him away from her, at which point he called her a 'filthy slut' and restored his trousers. Holloway notes that he spoke to Vissen regarding the incident, and he gave a wholly different account. As there was no witness to the incident, Holloway concluded that the events could not be proved either way. Rita looked intently at Hamish. 'And so, we have another name to include on the list,' she said.

Just at that moment Holloway appeared at the door.

'It's getting late,' he said. 'I thought you might be ready to finish for the evening.'

Hamish and Rita did feel weary. They had been peering at ledgers under candlelight.

'Yes,' replied Hamish. 'We're finished for now.'

He closed the ledger Rita had been reading, unsure of whether Holloway could see which one it was.

2 JANUARY, 1883
EMILY

Emily appreciated the routine of married life. She woke early to make sure Avery's business clothes were laid out for him, she prepared his morning meal and kissed him on the cheek before he left for work each day. Then she cleaned her own flat and the rest of the building for Mrs Chambers. After lunch she boiled the laundry for herself, Mrs Chambers and the lodgers who paid for the service. At four she prepared a meal for herself and Avery in the large kitchen downstairs and took it up to Avery so he could eat in private, as was his preference.

One of her greatest challenges was the management of meals. Avery assigned a different meal to each day of the week. If she served corned beef on lamb stew night, Avery would push his plate aside and announce he was bitterly disappointed. He would retire to the lounge with his pipe without eating a morsel. One night when Emily prepared roast beef, he took two tentative bites, wiped his lips carefully with a napkin and said, 'I regret my mother cannot be here to teach you how to prepare a proper English roast.'

Emily was disappointed in herself for not being a better cook, but she was determined to improve.

When Avery suggested they enjoy a picnic at Queen's Park one Saturday, Emily was overjoyed. They hadn't left the house together for months. She ran downstairs to ask Mrs Chambers if she would like to join them.

'You know, I believe I will,' she said. 'The fresh air will do me good.'

Mrs Chambers filled a basket with leftovers for the picnic. Emily skipped upstairs with the basket and called out to Avery as she entered their flat, 'Mrs Chambers is joining us.'

Avery stepped into the room. 'I beg your pardon?' he asked.

Emily stared at him unsure what to say.

Avery moved very close to her and said, 'I'm afraid you should not have invited her without checking with me first. I prefer we go alone.'

'I'm sorry,' Emily said. 'I didn't imagine you would object.'

'I do object.' Avery's eyes were cold.

In little more than a whisper, Emily said, 'I can't go back on the invitation now.'

Just as she spoke Mrs Chambers called up the stair well, 'Ready?'

Avery's jaw was set in an unattractive scowl, but he took the basket from Emily and followed her down the stairs. He took her arm as they walked out onto the street and held it firmly. Emily continued chatting to Mrs Chambers as though his fingers were not digging into her skin. No one would know he was hurting her.

She tried not to mind that he wouldn't allow her to have friends visit the flat, or that he was angry if she spent too long at the market. She was careful not to do anything to provoke him. She wore the clothes he approved, and she maintained his schedules as carefully as she could. Her life revolved around the flat, her work for Mrs Chambers and her husband. It was a small life, but it had an element of security. As long as she didn't anger him.

One morning, about thirteen months into the marriage, Emily felt desperately unwell. She woke up dizzy and nauseated. Each time she tried to step out of bed, she fell back onto the sheets while the room spun around her. She lay on the bed for an hour staring at a single point on the ceiling, trying to coax the room to stop spinning. She heard a knock at the door and knew it would be Mrs Chambers looking for her. She managed to make her way to the door but had to hold back the compulsion to vomit.

'Are you well?' asked Mrs. Chambers. 'You look like death.'

'I feel sick,' Emily said. 'I think I am going to....'

At that point, she made a dive for the chamber pot.

'What is it that is ailing you?' asked Mrs Chambers.

'I don't know,' she said as she vomited. 'Nothing eases the nausea. I have never been this unwell.'

'I think you may be with child,' suggested Mrs Chambers.

Emily's eyes widened. The notion was terrifying.

'What makes you think so?'

Mrs Chambers smiled at her.

'All your symptoms would suggest so, Pet,' she replied gently.

Tears welled in Emily's eyes.

'This is a normal progression of married life,' she said. 'A fine thing.'

'When did you last need to use your rags?' asked Mrs Chambers.

Emily conceded that it had been a good three months.

She remembered a book her mother had given her, *The Book of Nature: A philosophy of Procreation and Sexual Intercourse* by James Ashton M.D. At the time Emily's mother told her to keep the book a secret. She said she hoped it would save her from a life of servitude. Emily didn't know what that meant when she was nine. But she kept the book close to her always. For one thing, it was the only item she owned that her mother had given her, and for another she found the book fascinating. When she was sixteen, she used it to direct her in a simple method of contraception that involved a small sea sponge and embroidery thread.

She opened the book now and read the contents page carefully. There was the chapter on how to prevent conception and to avoid childbearing. Why had she not observed those practices since her marriage? She grimaced at the idea that Avery should find out she knew of such practices. Later in the book there was a chapter on the rules for management during labour and childbirth. The bile rose in her stomach as she flicked through the pages of that chapter. She quickly hid the book away again.

That evening Emily told Avery about the possibility of a baby. At first, he was silent.

When at last he found his voice, he said,

'We'll have to move then. This flat is too small.'

He told her he would see to it in the morning and went to sleep.

Emily was shattered. Fear was gripping her like a vice. She was desperate for reassurance, but none came. And how would she go through this without Mrs Chambers? Why the need to move? It would be months before they needed more room. How much space did babies need anyway?

Avery organised a new flat for them within a week. Emily struggled to pack their meagre belongings and clean the flat thoroughly while she nursed her constant nausea. She cried when Avery told her the new flat was on the southern side of the Brisbane River and she would have to give up her job with Mrs Chambers.

'It is unseemly for a married woman to work,' he said. 'And it is deplorable for a pregnant woman. What kind of man will people think me?'

Emily wondered what people he had in mind. He did not allow them to have any acquaintances. But she was too sick to argue. She dragged herself through her last week with Mrs Chambers, weeping the whole time.

'I will miss you,' she said between sobs on the last morning they shared.

'I will miss you too,' said her friend, 'But your husband is right. You must stop working now. Be happy pet. We'll catch up from time to time.'

CHAPTER EIGHT

The steamer Crown of Aragon with bounty immigrants, arrived in Moreton Bay today. Twenty-four cases of virulent Scarlet Fever occurred during the voyage. Six proved fatal and there are five cases now on board. The vessel has been quarantined. - Morning Bulletin Rockhampton, Queensland. Thursday 26 June 1884.

---

30 SEPTEMBER 1884
HAMISH

The following morning, Hamish stood at the beach staring out onto the Bay. It was barely dawn, and he had come to the water's edge to splash away the remnants of a night tossing in his cot, unable to reconcile himself to the fact that both Simon's and Emily's deaths had been publicly declared suicide. He had spent a good proportion of the dark hours, penning his account of events to the Colonial Secretary by candlelight. As he stared toward Cleveland, Hamish was startled to find that overnight, a great vessel with tall rigging had appeared nestled into the cove of Peel Island. It was a shock to his senses to see it there, where for days there had been nothing, apart from the choppy waters of the Bay and a sky dotted with gulls. Peel Island shrunk in size beside the ship, a large immigration vessel.

Hamish noticed a small fishing craft inching its way diagonally across the water, bobbing precariously as it reduced the distance between itself and the ship. The person rowing the fishing boat had only just managed to overtake the strong current that runs a half a mile from Peel

Island, when there was a sudden gust of wind that sent him back again. The man struggled with the oars through the strong tide until he was back where he had been. Finally, he made it to the vessel and settled against the great ship's hull. Hamish felt a hand on his shoulder.

'*The Crown of Aragon* came in on the tide in the early hours of this morning,' said Wallace. Red sniffed around Hamish's legs and he bent down to greet the dog. 'Vissen has been sent out with provisions,' he said.

It was then that Hamish noticed the yellow flag flying from the ship's mast.

'What is it? Do we know?' asked Hamish.

'Don't know as yet. Vissen will bring back word.'

Hamish tried to suppress the fear in his voice, 'But if there is infection on the ship, what is to stop Vissen from bringing the contagion back?'

'Not much, I suppose. But the infected will be quarantined on the ship. They'll take them onto Peel Island later today. They'll be needing provisions; it might be days before they gain permission to enter the Brisbane River.'

Red was dancing about demonstrating his excitement as Rita joined them.

'Yellow flag,' she murmured.

'Yes, Vissen is boarding now. See.' Hamish pointed to the small figure being hauled up from the tiny fishing boat.

Hamish and Rita continued to watch the ship for some time. Wallace left them to prepare breakfast for the inmates.

Hamish and Rita reached the Telegraph Office as Holloway was preparing his communication for the Colonial Secretary.

'Scarlatina,' he said as Hamish and Rita walked in. 'It could have been worse.'

'Scarlet Fever is bad enough,' said Hamish. 'If it were to spread among the inmates here, with their depressed physical health, it would certainly be lethal.'

'There are only a handful of cases,' said Holloway. 'They remain quarantined on the ship for now. There is a surgeon on board. I'm sure the situation is in hand.'

At that point, Vissen entered the office.

'There are three additional cases this morning,' he said. 'A female of fifteen years of age and her mother, and an infant of twenty-four months.' Vissen turned to Hamish. 'The ship's surgeon asked me to pass on the message that he would appreciate your assistance Doctor. He asked if you could attend him on the ship. He would be grateful if the Matron could join them as well.'

'Who is in charge of the quarantine station?' demanded Hamish.

'I am,' said Holloway. 'I'm temporarily Superintendent of both the asylum and the quarantine station.'

'You must be joking,' said Rita.

'Indeed, I am not,' said Holloway. 'I'll tell my wife to join you at the jetty, Hart. Chooky can you row them out to the ship. I need Vissen here.

'I'm coming,' said Rita.

'No,' said Hamish and Holloway at the same time.

'Stay here and oversee the supplies for the Quarantine Station,' said Hamish. 'I have treated patients with Scarlet Fever before and not picked up infection.'

'My wife has also nursed the illness,' said Holloway.

'Vissen should be isolated,' said Hamish.

'If he develops symptoms, I'll consider it,' Holloway said.

'By the time he develops symptoms, it will be too late.'

'Doctor, you have been summoned to the ship, I suggest you make haste to the jetty and wait there. I'll despatch a telegraph to Brisbane communicating news of the new cases.'

Hamish turned directly to Vissen.

'Do not involve yourself in the preparation of supplies for the quarantine station. Show Rita where to find everything they need and then leave her to organise it. You should go to your quarters and remain there.'

Hamish and Rita left the office and walked toward the jetty. As they walked, a horse and dray passed them carrying carcasses of mutton to the kitchen.

'Is that the same cart that carried Simon's coffin to the cemetery yesterday?' said Hamish.

Rita had a closer look. She rolled her eyes.

'Yes,' she said. She hooked her arm through that of Hamish. 'Come on,' she said. 'Before you have a complete breakdown.'

Hamish kept pace alongside her, glad of her arm in his. Then a thought occurred to him.

'Where does the water supply come from?'

Rita stopped.

'I don't know,' she said, scanning the buildings.

At that moment, Vissen joined them with Chooky.

'Follow me,' he said to Rita.

Hamish watched as they strode toward the Stores, then he saw Brigid pacing along the jetty. Hamish, Brigid and Chooky climbed into the boat and Chooky began rowing, his sinewy arms proving to be surprisingly strong as they reduced the distance between themselves and the *Crown of Aragon*. Hamish thought he would have preferred Rita's assistance to that of Brigid, but he also couldn't help feeling relieved that Rita was safe on shore away from exposure to the disease.

The ship's doctor greeted them as they climbed from their boat onto the deck of the ship. He looked no older than Hamish and he appeared dishevelled and tired with grey circles under his eyes.

'We have corpses on board,' he began without greeting them, 'Sick bay is full and the well passengers are in a state of panic. I need to get the sick onto Peel and I need someone here to identify new cases and care for them.'

Hamish noted the chaos on deck. Passengers were gathered talking over one another in shrill voices, some already coughing and croaking with symptoms of scarlatina. The crew were dashing about trying to separate the ill from the well and convince those with symptoms to climb onto the rowboat waiting to convey them to the quarantine station.

'An infant has taken ill overnight,' said the ship's doctor, 'The mother is hysterical. Indeed, I fear for the child's safety myself. He was not a healthy baby to begin with, he has suffered dysentery throughout the journey and he's significantly underweight. I hoped you might look at him while I try to establish some order and get the other cases into quarantine.'

While they had been talking, Brigid had already become 'Matron-in-charge'. She barked orders at passengers and crew alike. In no time the atmosphere of chaos slipped into a procession of people hastily but calmly carrying out the tasks assigned to them. The first rowboat bursting with passengers in various stages of illness was soon bobbing toward the white beach of Peel Island. Hamish was impressed by how Brigid incited confident reassurance and engage people, replacing panic with positive action.

Hamish followed the ship's surgeon down an unstable ladder to a dark cabin beneath the deck. The infant he came to see lay on the bed naked, while his mother wept beside him. Hamish examined the small body. His skin felt hot with fever and was covered in a spray of red blotches that joined in places to create the impression the child was sun burned. His cheeks were flushed scarlet and there was a white patch around his mouth. His chest heaved and it was clear that he was struggling to breathe. Hamish felt the tears sting his own eyes. It did not seem probable that the child would survive.

'We have to get him to the quarantine station,' said Hamish gently. 'You will need to accompany him. You have been exposed so we'll observe you for symptoms.'

The mother nodded, her red eyes and swollen face giving away her belief that nothing could help her beloved child now. Hamish wrapped the child in a sheet, then cradled the baby under one arm while he helped the woman up the ladder with the other.

When they were all on deck Hamish handed the tiny bundle to Brigid. She took the child gently and looked at Hamish. Their eyes met and confirmed what they both knew. Brigid spoke kindly to the woman and helped her onto the next rowboat waiting to transport passengers to shore. Hamish watched as Brigid climbed in behind the woman and steadied her. They both sat down, and Brigid lay the poor little bundle in his mother's lap.

Hamish returned to the cabins below deck to look for more ill passengers. He couldn't believe the passengers with symptoms had not been quarantined earlier. At this point it was likely that everyone on the ship had been exposed to the disease.

At first light, Brigid returned to the ship with news from the quarantine station.

'The baby passed during the night,' she said to Hamish quietly.

'How is the mother?' asked Hamish. 'Does she show signs of fever?'

'The mother is overcome with grief and exhaustion. But there is no fever. She says she has no sore throat. I sat with her through the night and held her while she held her boy as he passed.'

'Thank-you,' said Hamish.

Brigid did not look up. She moved away quickly to attend to her next task.

For the following two days and nights Hamish cared for those who fell ill on the ship and helped to get them into the row boats for transfer to the Island. He hauled fresh fruit and vegetables onto the boats to provide nutrients to those who remained well and for the ill to build their strength. He washed his hands scrupulously. Brigid came back and forth from Peel, checking on patients at different stages of disease, feeding the weak and hydrating the feverish with fresh water from Stradbroke Island. Hamish grew to appreciate her stamina and even saw a compassionate side to her that he would not have imagined a week earlier.

30 MAY 1883
EMILY

When Avery finally delivered her to the new flat, Emily was shocked. The building itself was newer than Mrs Chambers place, but their own flat was no larger than the one they left behind. If the point of the move was to ensure more space for a child, this flat sorely missed the target. Her old home at Spring Hill was now more than one and a half hours walk away. She could not see how she and Mrs Chambers would be able to meet up very often. She missed the sense of purpose her job gave her, and she missed the company. She was now isolated, alone and ill most of the time.

One morning Emily was churning sheets in the enormous copper in the shared laundry at the back of the house when her neighbour Sheila came in carrying a basket of sheets of her own. All the tenants used the laundry, so Emily and Sheila ran into one another there every so often. Until this day, Emily and Sheila had only spoken of general topics, the weather, the price of soap. Emily shared news of her pregnancy with Sheila when she first became aware of it and Sheila congratulated her. She had seemed genuinely happy for her at the time.

This morning it was obvious to Emily that Sheila had been crying. Her usually pale features were red and blotchy, and her eyes were swollen. Emily pretended not to notice.

'I will have my wash out directly,' Emily said smiling.

Sheila tried to smile back. Emily let her eyes rest on the woman's face for a moment, then turned her attention back to the wash. She began wringing the heavy sheets and plopping them into a separate tub. Emily had strong arms and wrists. She had noticed many times that Sheila was thinner and frail.

'Let me take your basket,' said Emily as she removed it from Sheila's hands.

Emily replaced her own sheets with Sheila's and threw in a handful of soap flakes. She swirled the sheets around in the boiling water with a long dowel. Sheila stood watching.

'Is everything all right?' asked Emily when she could hold the question in no longer.

Tears rolled down the woman's cheeks.

'Oh dear,' cried Emily. She stopped churning laundry and took Sheila's hand in hers.

'What on earth is wrong?'

Sheila lent on the tub with one hand.

'It is nothing really,' she said. 'I don't know why I'm like this at all.'

'It must be something,' said Emily.

'It's just that... I thought I was with child, like you,' she said, sobbing now.

'You thought? But you are not with child?' asked Emily.

'That's right,' she continued to sob. 'I'm bleeding like never before. It's been ten weeks since my last time. I was so sure!'

Emily was still a little confused. She was so thoroughly terrified of her pregnancy, a revelation like this, that it was all a mistake and she was never pregnant at all – would have been wonderful news.

'I take it you are not relieved?' asked Emily.

'Of course, I'm not relieved,' blurted out Sheila. 'I'm shattered. There's nothing my husband wants more than a son. We've been trying for an age!'

Emily happened to know, because Sheila told her herself, that Sheila and her husband had only been married twelve months. Still, Emily accepted that it may seem like an age if you were desperately waiting for something to happen.

'It will come,' said Emily soothingly.

'I envy you so much,' said Sheila.

'I can only tell you,' began Emily, 'That it is I who envy you. I am terrified. At my wit's end. The birth itself frightens me nearly to death, but worse than that is my fear of being a mother. I can barely take care of myself.'

Sheila squeezed Emily's hand.

'You'll be a wonderful mother,' she said.

'I don't know if Avery even wants the baby,' Emily told her.

'Of course, he wants his own baby,' cried Sheila.

'He won't talk about it at all.'

'Never?'

'Never.'

Sheila looked shocked.

Emily had wrung out Sheila's washing while they were talking, she moved her things into a tub of clear water for rinsing, and then twisted the sheets again. Together they hung all the laundry from the line that went from the outbuilding to the fence.

'Would you like to join me for a cup of tea?' asked Emily.

They made their way upstairs to Emily and Avery's rooms and enjoyed an hour together chatting like old friends. It turned out to be opportune that Sheila's elder sister was an acquaintance of Mrs Chambers. This gave them common ground for sharing gossip, but also allowed Emily to relay a message to Mrs Chambers to let her know she was well, although fearful of giving birth. When Sheila returned to her flat, Emily had a nap.

That afternoon Emily was aware of Avery's footsteps in the kitchen, but she was struggling to wake up properly from an afternoon's rest. She was in that haze between wakefulness and sleep and the latter kept drawing her in. She hauled herself out of bed to find Avery aggressively wiping clean cups and saucers from afternoon tea.

'I'm sorry I didn't clear the table,' she said. 'I fell asleep.'

'Who was it that you had here?' asked Avery. His tone flat.

'Sheila came over,' she said.

'Sheila?'

'From downstairs,' said Emily. 'We've been talking while we do the laundry. I invited her to morning tea.'

'You haven't mentioned this woman before.'

'I know. We have only lately become friends.'

'Friends?' said Avery. 'I wonder that you could've become so close to someone I've never met or heard of, for that matter.'

'Would you like to meet her?' asked Emily. 'We could have her over with her husband. I've never met him myself, but I'm sure he's pleasant. You know, of all things, her sister is an acquaintance of Mrs Chambers?'

Avery groaned. 'I would prefer you don't have people in the house that I haven't met,' he said.

'Will we invite them over then?' asked Emily. 'So, you can meet them? Perhaps Friday evening, for dinner?'

'I think not,' said Avery. 'I'll be late home Friday night.'

'Saturday then?'

Avery sighed.

Emily gave up on having her friend to dinner. She retired to their small bedroom and curled herself into a tight ball. She worried that Avery had become increasingly cold toward her since she became pregnant. She understood he might be nervous; she was nervous herself. And he had always seemed disappointed in her. This was just one more disappointment. But even her swollen body seemed to offend him. He no longer looked at her with desire. His touch was formal and distant. When Avery joined her in the bed, she summoned the courage to ask him why he was indifferent toward her. He turned his back to her, but she persisted.

'A mother is a sacred thing,' he said finally.

'I am still your wife,' she said touching him gently on the shoulder.

He stiffened at her touch and flicked his shoulder to remove her hand.

'You are the mother of my child,' he said.

'What does that mean?'

'It means something different to wife. I fear you don't have the maturity for motherhood. You are barely sufficient as a wife.'

Tears streamed down Emily's cheeks, but she didn't make a sound.

Finally, Avery rolled over so that his face was inches away from that of his wife.

'I didn't want the baby,' he said.

Emily stopped crying immediately. The tears still stained her cheeks.

She looked directly into his eyes.

'Indeed, I am well aware of it. Unfortunately, for all of us, the child included, God has had the sense of humour to foist this upon us and see what happens,' she said.

In a flash, Avery's eyes turned dark and his face reddened. He sat up and slapped her with all his strength across the side of her face. Emily's head lurched to one side and her body followed causing her to fall off the edge of the bed and her shoulder to meet with the wall. Pain shot through her shoulder. She lay slumped against the floor for a few minutes while Avery regained his composure. When he did, he gathered her into his arms and lifted her back onto the bed. He held her to him throughout the night and whispered, 'I'm sorry,' several times. The next morning, he sent for a doctor to come to the flat and left for work.

A few days later Emily woke from her afternoon nap with an excruciating cramp in her abdomen and felt stickiness between her legs. She tried to get up, and found she was lying in a pool of blood. Emily struggled to the washstand and made an attempt to clean herself. Her instincts told her she was losing the baby and the consequent wave of relief caused her to hate herself.

Emily had been terrified of both the pregnancy and becoming a mother. But now she'd lost the baby she felt an emptiness so profound she could no longer function. She couldn't remember the daily schedules that had sustained her since the wedding. She was barely able to drag herself out of bed, and when she did, she moved without purpose. She didn't understand why the relief she felt initially had transformed into this dark cloak of despair. She could not find respite from the constant numbness. There was no joy, there was no longer hope.

Emily knew she had never loved Avery. She wondered whether that was what had ultimately caused the suffocation of any feelings he once had for her. If so, her current circumstance was as much her fault as his. Even so, where there had been a well-intentioned desire to please him, there was now hate. She was isolated and lost. Avery had separated her from her closest friend and shut down the possibility of friends entirely. He had lost her the one glimmer of hope, the spark she had not even dared to acknowledge, of bringing into the world a soul who would love her.

The sound of Avery's voice became like a red-hot poker on her skin. It was the only thing that penetrated the numbness. For this reason, she was almost grateful for the hatred she felt for her husband. She began to cultivate it. At least it was something she could feel.

One evening Emily could smell smoke and the tang of something burning, but she didn't have the will to move.

Smoke filled the house.

'Good God,' Avery screamed. 'Could you not smell the smoke woman?'

'He's home from work then,' thought Emily.

She felt him clutch at her hair and pull her into the kitchen. He pushed her head forward forcing her to look at the blackened pot. It all happened quickly and afterward Emily couldn't remember it. She was told by the police constable she had lifted a cast iron pot high into the air and cracked it down with some force onto Avery's skull. She supposed that must be what happened.

She was informed Avery insisted she was deranged and needed to be locked up. Emily was despatched by the hospital to the Dunwich Asylum.

CHAPTER NINE

It disgusts me to hear men say that poverty is but the effect of vice, is due to thriftlessness and want of self-respect. Nothing can be falser. And yet this ought to be so. Only the vicious and idle should be poor. All wealth is the production of human toil; therefore, the industrious man ought to be rich. If wealth were the result of work, our palaces would not be inhabited by those who do not toil for a living. Grasping what another has already produced is not work. Henry George. - Kapunda Herald, SA. Tuesday 16 June 1885.

4 OCTOBER 1884
HAMISH

'It occurred to me that you may enjoy a diversion tomorrow,' Holloway said. 'It's quiet here on Saturdays. My wife and I think it would be a shame for you to miss the beauty of the other side of the Island while you're here.'

Both Hamish and Rita silently acknowledged that he was trying to get rid of them for a day, nonetheless their curiosity was peaked.

'The other side of the Island faces the open sea,' went on Holloway. 'There's a gorge that'll take your breath away. Wallace can pack you a picnic. I'll get the horses ready. There's a single track from here to the other side, you can't get lost. You could diverge onto the track to Amity as well, if you wish.'

Rita summed him up carefully and then announced,

'Why not?' she said.

'What about our work?' Hamish whispered.

'There're only so many ledgers and so much data,' she whispered back. 'And we have covered them all.' She paused for a moment. 'Some clear air away from here will do us both good. It'll give us a chance to talk without the whole settlement listening in.'

As always, Hamish went along. Energy spent arguing with Rita was energy wasted. Still, he had an uncomfortable sense of foreboding. He was convinced that Holloway's version of events would be upheld and his evidence, based entirely on his observations of ligature marks on Emily's body would be dismissed. He and Rita had not found a single piece of evidence to suggest that Emily was murdered. She wasn't a woman who mattered to anybody in the grand scheme of life in the Colony, and her murder, if it was declared that, could bring unwanted attention to the governance of the asylum. This wouldn't only be a problem for the Superintendent, it would also be a problem for the Colonial Secretary. As for Simon's demise, there was no indication at all that he died from anything other than his own hand. Still, Hamish had a deeply held belief that Simon was also murdered. He didn't know what to do about it and he wasn't convinced it was his responsibility to do anything.

When Hamish woke at dawn to meet Rita outside Holloway's cottage, he was feeling quite hopeless about the inquiry into Emily's death. Perhaps the day's ride would be a welcome distraction after all. There was nothing more he could do. Holloway wouldn't tell him any more than was written in the complaint entry, should he ask. Gaining real trust with the Aboriginal community would take months of rapport building, not days, and he knew that he would never reach a point of honest communication with the Asylum inmates. By their existence at Dunwich they were defined as a group of individuals with little reason to trust authority or to abide by the conventions of civility. Secrecy and deceit were survival skills that many of them had sharpened to perfection.

Rita was already waiting for him outside the cottage. Holloway advised them to leave early before the heat of the mid-day sun made the ride uncomfortable. Rita was wearing men's trousers and shirt, tucked in and secured with a leather belt. She looked tiny, but the clothes fit snugly to her frame. Hamish thought they were made for a boy rather than a man.

She wore a broad brimmed felt hat of the style worn by bushmen. The hat cast a shadow across her small perfect nose. Her brown hair was cut short and tucked behind her ears. She was a handsome woman. Hamish was proud to have her at his side, even if he regretted that she could never be more than a friend. He joined her and they waited while Holloway led two sturdy horses from the stable. Leather saddle bags were packed with fruit, bread and cheese and flasks of water.

'Lunch,' said Holloway as he slapped one of the horses on the back side. 'The track is easy to follow,' he said. 'You keep going past Myora, then along the coast until the track veers right. There's a smaller track to the left that goes to Amity. You keep to the right and head across the Island. When you reach the sea, you'll see a lesser track heading uphill to a bluff that reaches out into the sea. This is where you'll find the gorge. Plenty of scenic spots for a picnic.'

Hamish and Rita both mounted, they had only been half-listening to the instructions. Hamish noticed Brigid Holloway standing in the doorway of the cottage staring at them. There was something odd about her expression. Rita raised her hand to wave, but Brigid didn't move. Why did she look so anxious? Hamish realised Brigid never seemed to be quite in sync with her husband and his friend. Vissen had an arrogance that was devoid of self-awareness, while Holloway exhibited a combination of bluster and bluff that was contrived. But Brigid had so far given away very little of herself in front of Hamish. She appeared stern, and she parroted many of her husband's views, but he sensed something deeper, something that set her apart from the others.

Hamish and Rita squeezed their horses into action and the animals trotted contentedly across the grounds of the settlement. They moved easily between the trees as they progressed along the sandy track, and they passed Myora without noticing it. The community was tucked away behind the trees, almost invisible from the track. Now and then they captured glimpses of sea through the trees to their left. Soon, they relaxed into the ride, the feeling of the soft breeze on their faces and the rhythmic rocking of the horses beneath them. They noted the range of bird calls, some shrill, others chattering. Each sound was different, but together the music they made was invigorating. Layers of sound cascaded away from them, deep into the bush.

Eventually the track to Amity appeared to their left. They were aware of the fishermen who camped there because they came into Dunwich for supplies. They had been told there was also a man who managed the oyster lease and a fellow who had been caretaker of the old Pilot Station until it closed down. Wallace had described Amity as a shamble of huts perched on the edge of the Island along the channel between Stradbroke and Moreton Islands. He had said it was a treacherous spot with widely varying tides and shifting sand banks, the main channel used by ships entering Moreton Bay to reach the Brisbane River. Hamish had no desire to see it.

Hamish and Rita led their horses to the right heading across the Island to the seaward side. Almost as soon as they changed course, the vegetation changed. The scrub became low and the land flat. They could see hills in the distance, but the track skirted them and the air seemed heavier. An eerie stillness descended on them as they moved inland. Mangrove and tidal swamp gave way to grey creeping grasses, flowering acacias, and low heathland. To each side of the track, as far as the eye could see, surprising bursts of grass trees dotted the land. Long brown spikes stretched upward, charcoal black stems emerging from under great skirts of green foliage.

There were small bushes with showy yellow flowers, and others that looked like balls made up of thousands of tiny white snowflakes suspended in mid-air. As they travelled further, the stocky banksias dominated the landscape. Strange flowers, large and boxlike, stood upright. This seemed to Hamish to be a vision from the ancient past. The Australian landscape, both when he was growing up in Victoria and here on the Island in the northern colony of Moreton Bay, always brought to him a sense of prehistoric time. When he visited England briefly, she spoke to him of age in terms of civilisation, but Australia spoke of an age that was infinitely older than man-made structures.

The ride was long, and they were becoming warm when the first glimmer of the ocean crept into view ahead of them. Hamish felt a flush of excitement at the sight of the sea. He was mesmerised by the turquoise horizon when his horse noticed something closer and came to a rapid stop.

Rita's horse careered to a halt alongside him, the head of her horse only missing his own horse's grey flank by a whisker. Startled into awareness, Hamish saw that five cows had wandered onto the track.

Hamish and Rita shouted at the cows and waited on horseback for them to move on. They indicated through their disinterest that they had no intention of doing so. The animals' ribs could be seen beneath patchy coats spotted with raw skin and covered in burrs. Their eyes were dull. Rita lost patience, climbed down from her horse and began chasing the animals, leaping, waving her hands about and shouting at them. The cows slowly began to move away, looking back at her every few paces wondering if she was likely to maintain this lunacy, or if she would disappear and they could meander back onto the track where they were. Hamish laughed at the display Rita put on.

As she mounted, he asked, 'How can anyone maintain cattle in this dry, sandy scrub?'

'It's cruel,' Rita said. 'They're a mess.'

As they rode on, sand dunes covered with bright daisy shaped flowers and spinifex opened out onto a white sand beach. The surf rumbled and spluttered onto the sand with a timelessness that made Hamish and Rita feel small. They rode quickly along the beach, enjoying the salty sea air in their faces. Even the horses seemed to be enjoying the break from the oppressiveness of the track.

There was a rocky headland ahead of them. At that point they turned back into the bush to make their way to the top. There was a track of sorts to follow but it was difficult, overgrown, not much used. The horses tripped on tree roots and stumbled through patches of native grass. It was a significant climb to the top of the headland, but the deep turquoise of the sea was worth the ride. Hamish could not remember seeing an ocean that particular shade of blue-green. They forgot about Dunwich, the asylum and the murder and drank in the beauty of the view before them.

Finding a shaded clearing, they set out the food. Simple as it was, it was delicious and welcome. The sun was warm on their backs, the sound of surf filled their ears, and their eyes were sore from the beauty of the scene. They joked and laughed all through their lunch and lay side by side exhausted after they had eaten. They stared at the sky through the irregular spiky leaves of the pandanus.

'What a strange place this is,' whispered Hamish as he dozed. He was content knowing that Rita lay beside him. He was glad she came to Dunwich to join him.

When they had rested long enough, Rita jumped to her feet and poked a fern frond up Hamish's right nostril. The move sent him leaping to his feet snorting.

'I think we should tie the horses up here,' she laughed, 'And walk the rest of the way to the gorge.'

Hamish did as he was told and secured the horses. They had to struggle through low scrub and loose rocks, but eventually they scrambled onto a rocky ledge that stretched out over the gorge. Rita went straight to the edge and called out to him.

'Come and look,' she cried. 'It's delightful down there.'

Sheer joy was evident in her voice.

In contrast, Hamish was sick to the pit of his stomach. He wasn't afraid of heights exactly. He was afraid of falling. Even from his position further back on the ledge he could see that the water below was deep though crystal clear. He could see the sand at the bottom of the gorge. Before his eyes a shadow in the water gradually took the shape of a green sea turtle. Rita cried out in delight again, causing Hamish to nearly lose his footing. He closed his eyes and swallowed down the panic. Together they inched further towards the edge and gazed at the turtle while it slowly made its way along the gorge towards the sea.

It was at this point, when the moment couldn't have seemed more perfect, that Rita said,

'Did you hear anything?' Her eyes were scanning the bush.

Hamish followed her gaze.

'I did hear a crunch in the scrub,' he said. 'Probably a kangaroo.'

Even while he said it, he couldn't help thinking about the strange creature that seemed to follow him in the bush.

'There was a Grey nibbling away at the grass when we ate lunch,' he said.

Rita looked uncertain, but they continued on anyway.

They made their way along the edge of the gorge, climbing over boulders and clinging to pandanus. They were heading in the opposite direction to the sea turtle. They scrambled towards the junction where the two great rock faces of the gorge met. From just around the corner, on the other side of the gorge, they could hear the blow hole. Occasionally enormous spouts of white water flickered through the trees. When they finally arrived above the blow hole, they caught sight of a platform of rock directly below. Rita didn't hesitate. She clambered down and out onto the platform. Hamish followed. They stared with awe into the crashing, boiling water below. The noise of the churning sea rang in their ears.

Hamish caught a movement in the corner of his eye, then froze with shock as he saw Rita's body hurtle over the edge of the gorge. She screamed as she fell forward over the rocks. A split second later, before he had time to react, Hamish felt a push from behind and was propelled forward... Then everything went black.

Hamish landed with a shot of pain that went straight through him. It was some time before he regained consciousness sufficiently to realise that he was on a rocky ledge not too great a distance from the water. The back of his head was bleeding and the whole left side of his torso and leg was raw. He had fallen down the gorge face, scraping his body against the rubble all the way. He looked up, but he couldn't see the top of the gorge. The ledge was hidden from view by a rough outcrop with a massive pandanus growing out of it. That had broken his fall and saved his life. The person who had pushed them couldn't see his body from the top of the gorge. Had the person already left, thinking the job was complete?

For the second time in his life Hamish understood the closeness of death, hovering like a shadow, a whisper away from him. Childhood memories flooded back of himself as a small child falling into a mine shaft. Shattered rock fragments ripped and tore at his skin then. He remembered his father saying of miners who were lost in their own tunnels,

'The more time that passes, the less likely it is they'll be found.'

Hamish lay on the rock ledge now, swamped by the emotions of a seven-year-old boy at the bottom of a mine shaft.

Gradually his senses returned to his present situation. He was no longer seven years old. He felt the cold hard surface of the rock beneath him and registered the ache in his back. Then he remembered Rita falling before he did. What about Rita? The thought that she may have been killed in the fall stung him like a knife wound. Struggling against the pain, he propped himself up on one elbow so he could look down into the gorge. Rita was on the ledge below. She was still.

'Rita!' he called as loudly as he could, but there was no change. For a terrifying moment he thought she must be dead. The cold spray blurred her face each time a wave crashed against the ledge. Studying her intently for any sign of life, he finally detected a slight rise and fall of her chest. While he was desperately trying to think of a way to get to her, he saw her start to struggle to lift her upper body. She was trying to sit up. She pulled herself up on one side so far, then her body crumpled. She fell back onto the ledge. It thrilled Hamish to see her body making even that small effort. At least she was alive and there was hope.

'Rita!' he called again. There was no sign she heard him.

Hamish examined the white foam that rose into the air beside her face as it grew higher. More of the sea crashed onto her rock with every wave. The tide was coming in and Hamish tried to calculate how long it would take for the waves to wash over her and for her to slip silently into the sea. He scanned the rock face between his ledge and hers below. It was a sheer drop. There was no way he could get down to her without ropes. And if he were to get down there, how would he bring her back up? It was no good. The only thing he could do was get help. It was Rita's only chance. If only God would still that tide before the waves took her.

'I'm going for help,' he yelled. 'I need help to bring you up.'

He hoped she'd heard him. It would give her hope to know he was alive and coming for her.

Hamish bundled all the determination and strength he could muster to lift his own body upright. He went through a quick process of self-diagnosis. No bones appeared to be broken. He began searching for a way up the rock face to the edge of the gorge. By clinging to a narrow ledge just above head height, he hauled himself up toward the pandanus outcrop. His knuckles grew white as he clung to tree roots, easing himself up a few inches at a time. His feet dislodged rubble clawing their way up to join his body. The left side of his torso burned, and his head was pounding. More than once he almost blacked out, but the need to get help for Rita kept him determined to make it to the top. If it had been only his life at stake, he was sure he would have given in to the pain and the extraordinary demand for effort.

Once he was sitting on the pandanus outcrop, clutching the knobbly trunk, he knew he would make the top. From there, he could see opportunities for hand and footholds. He rested for some time to gather the strength in both mind and body, then he heaved himself from narrow ledge to even narrower ledge up the face of the gorge. When he finally reached the top, he collapsed in the grass. The taste of his own blood woke him. He sat up and spat out the blood that had seeped from his head, down his face and into his mouth. He looked down, but he could no longer see Rita on the ledge below. He was relieved because that meant that no one else could see her either.

Hamish scrambled back to where he had tied up the horses earlier that day. The horses were no longer there. Had the same person who pushed them over the cliff set the horses free? Hamish braced himself for a long walk back to Dunwich. The sun had faded to a dull glow. He had no idea how he would stay on track once the night descended. It would take him hours to make his way back to the asylum.

Hamish reached the spot where the cows were on the track earlier in the day and noticed lights bobbing in and out of sight between the trees ahead. As the lights moved closer, he made out men on horseback. He first recognised Holloway and then Vissen behind him. Further behind them he could make out a man on a third horse, but he couldn't see who it was. He called out loudly when they were near enough to hear him.

'Here!'

Hamish didn't know who had tried to kill him, but he needed help to save Rita. Holloway was carrying a rifle. Holloway might either shoot him or help him. It didn't matter much to Hamish at this point, except that if he shot him, there was no chance for Rita. Holloway stopped alongside Hamish and dismounted.

'What happened to you?' he cried. 'Where is Rita?' He looked around as if he expected her to appear from the bushes.

'There has been an accident,' cried Hamish, keeping his cards close. Vissen dismounted behind Holloway, and now Hamish recognised the third rider as Wallace. He remained on his horse. Holloway looked incredulous. Hamish was acutely aware that blood soaked his shirt and matted his hair.

'Where is Rita?' he repeated.

'She is on a ledge above the waterline at the gorge. She was alive when I left her.' His voice trailed away, 'Though I am not sure she will still be alive now.'

The three men continued to stare at him.

'I climbed up the side of the gorge,' Hamish went on, 'But Rita is too badly injured. We will have to winch her up somehow.'

Holloway turned to Vissen,

'Go back and fetch the block and tackle,' he ordered. 'We'll need a canvas stretcher and another horse as well.'

Vissen stood stony faced.

'Go on, man,' said Holloway. 'Hurry!'

Vissen mounted his horse, turned and galloped toward Dunwich.

Wallace trotted his horse up to Hamish and listened while he recounted his story.

'We were both pushed,' he said breathlessly. 'There is no doubt.'

Wallace looked serious but said nothing. Hamish described how he climbed the gorge face. Holloway looked doubtful.

'Can you ride?' asked Holloway.

'Of course,' said Hamish.

He already had one foot in the stirrup and was swinging himself onto the back of Holloway's horse. The going was difficult on the way back to the gorge. The light was fading quickly, and the horses couldn't see. They had to leave them behind as Hamish and Rita had done earlier and travel the rest of the way on foot. As they made their way through the bush in the dark, Hamish was aware that he may well be leading the killers to the perfect spot for a second attempt. Still, he had to take the chance, because he had no other way to reach Rita. They scrambled onto the ledge where they had been pushed.

'What happened exactly?' asked Holloway, still struggling to comprehend how they came to fall.

'We were pushed,' said Hamish.

'Are you sure?' gasped Holloway.

The three of them stood on the ledge looking down. The blow hole was inky black in the dark.

'I can't see anything,' said Wallace.

'I know,' replied Hamish. 'You can't see the ledge from here. It's under that outcrop with the tree.'

They sat on the ledge waiting for Vissen to return. It was frustrating to have to wait, but there was nothing they could do without equipment.

'Tell me again exactly what happened,' said Holloway.

Hamish drew a deep breath. The air was cold now the sun had disappeared. The moon was almost full, so that would help them once the rescue began. Hamish felt sick with worry about Rita. He couldn't be sure she was safe from the high tide, higher than usual given the moon. He couldn't even be sure she was alive. Holloway's question echoed in his ears for a full minute before he answered.

'We were on this rock,' he began, 'Closer to the edge. All of a sudden, Rita lurched over the side and I was pushed from behind and went hurtling down as well. There was a figure, I didn't see clearly, it was out of the corner of my eye, just before I left the ground.'

Hamish paused for a moment as the memory settled in his mind. Holloway and Wallace shot one another an anxious glance.

'Who did you see?' asked Holloway?

'I don't know,' he said, staring Holloway down. 'It happened too quickly. I smashed my way down the rock face until that outcrop there broke my fall, then I slid down to the ledge below. I was lucky. I could see Rita on a ledge further down. The waves were crashing around her even then. She may have been washed into the sea by now.'

The oil lamps were sending an eerie glow into the men's faces. The energy that had sustained Hamish until this moment drained away. He was spent. If Rita had already been washed into the sea, it didn't seem possible he should be sitting on the ledge alive.

The men were silent for some time. Hamish went over in his mind his options for getting to Rita without having to wait for Vissen's return. He knew he couldn't bring her to the surface alone, but if he could just know that she was alive. Maybe he could move her away from those crashing waves. It looked to him like the tide was going out now, but he had little experience of the sea. He couldn't be sure. Wallace would know. 'Do you think the tide has turned?' he asked.

'Aye, the tide is on its way out,' said Wallace.

Hamish breathed easier, holding on to the belief that Rita had not been washed into the sea.

'You see that rock out in the sea?' Wallace pointed into the darkness. Hamish could make out a dark shadow rising from the silver-grey sea, not far from the shore. 'They say that at night you can hear the Aboriginal women wailing from that rock. They cry for the men they lost to the sea.'

Hamish and Holloway listened. The wind blew, the waves crashed, and the paper barks whispered. They all strained their ears to hear the wailing women.

The nagging fear Rita had already been swept out to sea was consuming Hamish. He was at his wit's end by the time Vissen arrived with the equipment and the horse so the rescue could begin. Hamish insisted he would be the one to be lowered to sea level to retrieve Rita. He didn't trust anyone but himself. He braced himself against his fear of falling. A few deep breaths with his eyes closed, and he stepped over the edge clinging to the rope they had tied to a sturdy tree. Several additional scratches and scrapes later and he was clinging to the ledge where he had last seen Rita. In sheer panic he lay flat, his scarred face against the rock and used only his eyes to look in every direction. There was a crumpled pile of wet clothing to his right and away from the licking waves. He crawled over to where Rita was curled up in a grotesque ball, in a foetal position. She looked a little wrong, the bones of one shoulder twisting in an unnatural direction, broken.

Hamish placed his hand on her forehead. She was unconscious but breathing. He silently thanked the Lord as he swung into action. He tugged twice on the rope to let the others know that Rita was alive. They lowered the stretcher, and Hamish tied Rita securely to it. He was as gentle as he could be with the broken shoulder and tied the bundle firmly, so she would remain secure as they raised her to the surface. Once Rita was safely back at the top of the gorge, the men helped Hamish as well. The three men secured the stretcher with Rita in her cocoon, to the spare horse. Vissen had brought a small leather case with glass vials containing morphine. Hamish administered a sufficient dose to keep Rita asleep and free from pain during the ride. The four of them set off back toward Dunwich. They travelled slowly and carefully to avoid any unnecessary stress on the cocoon carrying Rita. Hamish was beyond tired. His eyes closed several times on the journey, jolting open again as his horse shifted to find its way along the track in the dark.

3 JUNE 1883
EMILY

Emily woke to a shuffling sound in the ward. She sat up and peered through the darkness as a shape formed. One of the women was dragging something across the floor. She squinted to correct her focus, then recognised Old Margaret tugging her mattress behind her. Emily scrambled off her cot and tip toed over to her.

'What are you doing?' she whispered.

Old Margaret jumped and squealed, dropping the mattress with a thud.

'Shurrup!' cried one of the other women from her cot.

Old Margaret stared with wide eyes.

'What are you doing?' Emily whispered again.

Old Margaret looked sheepish.

'She's only gone and wet herself again,' called out one of the women. 'You feel the mattress, she'll have pissed all over it.'

Old Margaret yelled at the woman. 'Shut up, ya old witch.'

'Ah ya dusty fork,' the woman grumbled and rolled over placing the bedding on her head to shut out the noise.

Emily touched the wet mattress. She lifted it back onto the bed with the wet side down and pulled the bedding from her own cot to put on Old

Margaret's bed. She curled up on one side and went almost immediately to sleep.

Later in the night, another of the inmates, Gretchen, woke up screaming. A collective cry of 'Shurrup,' from the women followed Emily as she went to the old woman's bed. Gretchen's babbling was incoherent. She peppered German words and phrases with Australian colloquialisms and most of it was indiscernible from her sobbing. The only clear message was one of terror. Emily held the woman tight until gradually the screaming subsided. Gretchen's body relaxed into a quiet trembling. Emily traced the shape of the old woman's bones beneath her nightshirt as she rubbed her back. In the act of holding her, the terror of some long-ago experience was dispelled.

As Gretchen settled and Emily was returning to her own bed, she noticed that Mary, yet another inmate, was wide awake on her cot.

'I'm not here for long,' she whispered to Emily. 'I'll be returning to my brother and his wife at the end of the week.'

'How lovely for you,' Emily said.

'Aw, she'll tell that story to anyone who'll listen. You wanna watch out,' one of the women called out, 'She'll tell ya the same story over and over till the cows come home. Them 'ere try to avoid her eyes, to save 'emselves from 'earing it.'

Emily smiled at Mary who appeared not to have heard the outburst.

* * *

Emily asked Wallace about it that day during her kitchen shift.

Mary's brother is a newly elected member of Parliament,' Wallace explained. 'He sent her here to get her out of the way, to avoid embarrassment. Everyone at Dunwich knows he's refusing to have her back. She's not mad or dangerous as he claims. She came here a little confused. The harshness of this place has made her worse. It's a bit of a running joke in Dunwich, that she thinks she's going home. Too sad, really.'

CHAPTER TEN

In Moreton Bay, most people are familiar with the Moreton Bay Oyster Company, however they would be surprised to learn of the enormous number of oyster selections taken up, both by companies and by private individuals. In fact, the whole of the banks, both on the Islands and the Coast, are all more or less owned by people who not only take an interest in oysters but know that it is to their own advantage to cultivate and preserve them. Nevertheless, the general knowledge of oyster cultivation is still in its infancy, and the Marine Board have issued a useful little pamphlet entitled 'Remarks on Oyster Culture,' in the hope that it may prove of use to the oyster cultivators of Queensland. - The Brisbane Courier, Queensland. Monday 25 May 1885

---

5 OCTOBER 1884
HAMISH

The first twenty-four hours after the incident was the longest in Hamish's life. He kept Rita heavily sedated to be certain pain wouldn't trouble her. He also wanted her to remain as still as possible. Hamish was confident her collarbone was broken, so he wound her shoulder and arm tight with bandages to keep the broken bone firmly in place. Beyond that he could only wait.

Rita's skin was flushed and warm. He worried about damage to the blood vessels or nerves from the jagged bone. He suspected a fever, so he worried about infection. Worry became his coping mechanism. As long as he was worried, he would be alert to any sign of change in his friend. He kept himself from getting comfortable by sitting on a metal chair that was too small for him. The cold surface dug into his legs and the rails at the back were too short for him to lean back. If he fell asleep, he might miss a subtle change that could make the difference between recovery and death for Rita.

When Wallace came in to see if he could tempt the patient with soup, Hamish motioned for him to sit down. Red pattered in behind him. The existence of a dog in the hospital ward would normally have sent Hamish into the horrors. In this case, he let the dog sit by his master's legs. Hamish was exhausted.

'She is still unconscious,' he told him.

'You look dreadful,' Wallace said.

Hamish pulled his hands through his hair and pushed the lank strands back from his face. He linked his fingers behind his head to support it. 'I don't know what else to do,' he said.

'She is developing a fever, I think. I can do nothing but keep her cool and wait. If there's an infection...'

'Rita's a strong woman,' said Wallace.

'She could have died in that fall. Or she could have been washed out to sea. To get this far and have her die now...'

'She's not dead yet,' said Wallace. 'Stop looking for the worst.'

Hamish took a deep breath.

'This is not your fault,' said Wallace.

Hamish was unsure if that were true.

'It strikes me that Rita does exactly as she chooses.'

'That I can agree with,' said Hamish.

Minutes ground by at an agonising pace, but the presence of the cook comforted Hamish.

'Rita and I have recently read the works of the German theorist Karl Marx,' said Hamish. 'It makes sense when he says that the ruling class maintains its hold on power through controlling resources, exploiting the lower classes through their labour and formulating a set of institutional structures to assert authority. It makes sense in London and it makes sense here.'

'It makes the most sense here,' said Wallace. 'I think we had to see how the colonies are used to exert power and control over resources and labour to see it clearly back home.'

'It has nothing to do with evolution to a more 'fit' society.'

'They rape natural resources from this ancient country to fatten the purses of the wealthy industrialists back in England,' said Wallace.

'And in Scotland,' pointed out Hamish.

'Aye, in Scotland. Edinburgh has its own Colonialists and they're just as fat.'

Steering the conversation back to his patient, Hamish said,'Rita puts arrogant men in their place. There's one medic at the hospital, where we work. She has cut to the quick many times. She expounds more up-to-date knowledge of his cases than he has in front of the clinical consultants. He sulks for days every time.'

'What does Rita do, exactly? You said she is a qualified doctor, but she can't work as a doctor in Australia?'

'That's right. She works as a chemist instead. At the Brisbane Hospital. But she does much more than that. She has devoted her career to looking after women who've suffered from family violence. She owns homes in Melbourne and in Brisbane, which she converted for the use of women escaping violence. She pays a governess to live at each of the homes, to care for the women and to act as gatekeepers if estranged husbands try to find them. Sometimes the women heal and return to the men who beat them. Rita knows it's hard for a woman alone.'

Hamish had the thought her eulogy would speak of her selfless commitment to the welfare of others. Then he stopped himself. He mustn't think she might die.

Wallace stood to leave. 'I can bring back the soup, warmed, when she is awake.'

Red curled up on the wooden floorboards at the end of Rita's bed and indicated that he intended to stay.

Hamish was deep in thought when he noticed Rita's eyes open. She stared at him. Placing his hand on her cheek, relieved to feel her skin was cool, a little of the tension left his body.

'You are awake,' he said.

'Yes,' she said. 'I'm a bit sore.'

'I bet you are,' replied Hamish gently.

He placed a glass of water to her lips. 'Drink,' he said. 'I think you are going to recover.'

'Of course, I'll recover,' said Emily with a stifled laugh. 'Oh Lord! It hurts to laugh.'

'Stop it then.' Hamish kissed her on the forehead.

Rita's eyes closed again. 'I can't stay awake...' she whispered.

'It's as expected,' he said. 'At least you are sleeping now and not unconscious.'

Rita smiled, but her eyes didn't open.

'Sleep well,' Hamish said. He knew it was safe to end his vigil.

As he was leaving, he called for Red to follow him. The dog lifted its head and stared at him without moving.

'Come on now,' whispered Hamish, 'we'll let her sleep.'

Red stared at him with stubborn brown eyes.

'Alright then, you stay and watch over her. I have to get some rest.'

Hamish was so relieved that he slept deeply and soundly for the first time since arriving on the Island.

20 JULY 1884
EMILY

Emily had seen the strong young man who carried out odd jobs for the Superintendent many times. He erected a fence to mark off the Holloway's two-room cottage, dug drains to prevent flooding and repaired their roof after a particularly wet summer. Emily noticed his long brown legs and black curly hair. She thought he had a face that was soft and kind. But she had never been close to him, smelled his skin or noticed his cheeky smile. Not until they met at Myora on one of her visits there with Mabel.

One evening at dusk Emily was assisting Mabel with a small group of children who were dragging a kangaroo carcass across the sandy track from the bush. Emily grabbed the tail and pulled it into the fire pit while the children all took turns to let go and skip around her. She didn't see Simon approaching until he grabbed the tail over her hand and started tugging it away from her. He tried to look away when she glanced at him, but he wasn't quick enough. Their eyes met for a split second.

'Got it,' he said, looking down at the 'roo.

Emily stood where she was while the children circled him. Kangaroo was a rare meal; they were more used to eating fish. Emily watched him for a moment as he placed the 'roo on the fire.

'Emily,' called Mabel, 'In here'.

Emily knew she had to join the women, but she was unable to turn away from the man poking at the coals around the dead 'roo.

'Emily,' barked Mabel from the door.

She followed Mabel inside to prepare sweet potato. Soon the remaining hunters arrived at the fire pit and everyone stood around as they cut the meat and shared. They passed pieces around the families.

Increasingly Emily became aware of Simon's eyes on her when she was not looking his way. As soon as she dared a glance toward him, he had already turned his head. One day he followed her all the way from the asylum to Myora, walking only a few feet behind her and not saying a word. She stopped and smiled at him when she reached Mabel's hut, but he put his head down and ran away.

Summer had borne down on the Island with extraordinary force. One afternoon the air was hot and moist, and she had been yearning for the springs all day. She was dangling her feet in the cool, clear water when Simon appeared beside her. They both slipped into the water and splashed one another in the face, laughing like children. Simon took a deep dive and come up behind Emily, placing his arms around her as he rose from the water. She slipped from his grasp, turned toward him and placed both hands on his head. She pushed down with all her strength and laughed unashamedly as she forced him under the water. Simon popped back up like a cork and reached for her.

From that afternoon, Emily returned to meet Simon at the springs every evening. Their relationship seemed magical to Emily. Simon spoke very little, but she could feel warmth in his body, and she could read his eyes. The backdrop of the springs with its lush surroundings and the cool, clear water provided them with a sense of fantasy, as though the reality of their relationship in the harsh world of colonial Queensland didn't matter.

* * *

One morning, Brigid Holloway motioned to Emily to come outside and speak with her. Emily assumed there were extra tasks she wanted her to carry out.

'I notice,' the Matron began, 'that you're not hanging rags out on the line anymore.'

Emily stared at her.

'It's not difficult to work out,' she said, 'you're the only inmate who needs to do so.'

Emily was taken by surprise.

Brigid remained patient. When Emily continued to stare at her like an animal caught in a trap, Matron said, 'Emily, I think you may be with child.'

The words shot through her like a sword. The last time someone spoke those words to her, they had triggered terror. This time there was an internal hum. She was wary and desperate to protect her baby, Simon's baby, at any cost.

'I'm aware that many of the male inmates have made sexual advances toward you,' prompted the Matron. 'I'm also aware you spend a good deal of your time at Myora.'

She waited for a reaction from Emily. There was none. Emily refused to confirm or deny her condition, and she refused to reveal the identity of any potential father.

'Well,' she said, 'when your condition becomes obvious, I'll have to send you to Lady Bowen Hostel in Brisbane to see out the gestation. Once there, they'll organise an adoption. After the birth you'll return to the asylum. I only hope the father is one of the inmates,' she added. 'It'll be a lot more difficult to adopt out if it's black.'

This shattered Emily. Now that her secret was out, it was foolish to pretend that everything was going to work out the way she wanted it to. She didn't know how long Brigid would keep her secret.

She knew she needed to tell Simon as soon as possible, but she didn't know how he'd react. She stressed over the telling all that day. By evening, she'd decided to confront her fears.

Emily lay beside Simon, their bodies comfortably entwined.

'I think I'm with child,' she whispered. Simon's body stiffened alongside her and she held her breath, her eyes closed tight, praying.

Simon moved his head so that his face was close to hers. Tears formed in his eyes. He smiled and held her.

Emily was able to breathe again.

CHAPTER ELEVEN

The recent outbreak of crime in the shape of criminal assaults upon females seems to be now at its height. Society calls aloud for the instant suppression of such outrages upon humanity. The existing law is clearly insufficient. In one of the latest of these cases, the victim was a little girl, only two-and-a-half years old. In other cases which have recently occurred, the victims were drunken old women of fifty. Neither the innocence of childhood, nor the repulsiveness of degraded old age, affords any protection against the ruffians prowling about the city, in its crowded thoroughfares as well as its parks and gardens. - Evening News, Sydney. Thursday 6 March 1884.

---

6 OCTOBER 1884
HAMISH

Hamish splashed his face with water and braced himself to take care of Rita through her recovery. He was the only person on the island who knew her, understood her. When he arrived at her bedside, bright from a good night's sleep, it surprised him to find Brigid already there, wiping her skin with a damp cloth. Red was on the floor by the side of her bed.

Hamish sat in the metal chair and watched while Brigid bathed her body and slipped a clean, specially prepared nightgown over her head. The sleeves were cut out so it could be placed over her broken shoulder with the least possible movement. Hamish watched while Brigid spoke quietly to her patient. She told her what she was doing, reassured her when she grimaced from the pain and even made a little fun of her from time to time. Brigid chuckled softly at her own jokes.

Was this the same cold, officious woman he had imagined when he visited the Asiatics ward? The Brigid he worked with during the scarlatina outbreak seemed compassionate and caring, and this Brigid was similarly making a genuine connection with her patient. Perhaps he had judged her too harshly?

Brigid put a cup of water to Rita's lips and encouraged her to drink.

Hamish wondered when she was going to leave, so he could take charge of his friend's care, but concurrent with that thought came shame. He ought to be grateful that Brigid was taking good care of Rita. Then it struck him that Brigid could have an ulterior motive for staying close to Rita. She could be trying to find out if they know anything about the attempt on their lives. It was confusing that the same woman who had been responsible for the neglect he witnessed in the Asiatic ward seemed to be a skilled and caring nurse in other contexts. But this attention to Rita could well be a strategy. He'd watch her closely, and warn Rita to be wary of her, the first chance he had.

He glanced at the dog and noted that Red looked suspicious as well. A low rumble from the back of his throat told Hamish that Red was suspicious of both himself and Brigid. Red refused to leave Rita's side.

After what seemed like an age, Brigid left them alone, saying she needed to attend the other wards.

'You do have others to care for,' whispered Hamish.

Brigid indicated no sign that she heard him.

Hamish was finally alone with Rita. 'Brigid has been very attentive,' he said casually.

'Yes, I know,' sighed Rita. 'She has been heaven sent.' Her eyes were only half open.

'Hmm. I wonder,' said Hamish.

'What are you talking about?' Rita's eyes fully opened.

'I just wonder.'

'Wonder what?'

'Well, it seems out of character for her, don't you think?'

'Hamish, she is a nurse!'

'She's not that attentive to the inmates,' he pointed out.

Rita's eyes slid shut. She didn't respond.

Hamish sat back and waited.

'What are you getting at then?' she said at last.

'I just think if she had something to hide, she might want to keep us close, to find out what we know,' he said.

'Why hasn't she asked us any questions then?'

'She's biding her time. Or maybe she suspects Holloway of being involved in all this. She might feel guilty.'

Rita smiled and closed her eyes again. This time she was asleep.

Hamish couldn't think of any reason to leave her side. While he sat there watching over her, Holloway came to enquire about her progress.

'She's fine,' said Hamish. 'The fever's broken, and she's conscious, sleeping at the moment. But she'll recover.'

'The barge is due tomorrow,' said Holloway. 'I believe you should both return to Brisbane. Rita will have access to a higher quality of care.'

Hamish considered the idea for a few seconds. It was true Rita would benefit from the comfort of a real hospital. And taking her away from the dangers of a place where someone wanted them dead appealed. But the journey across the bay would be painful and dangerous with her broken collarbone.

'I won't have her moved,' he insisted.

'Nor will I be leaving her side,' he added.

Red looked up from his post. 'Nor Red.' Hamish said.

Holloway opened his mouth to argue, but the look on Hamish's face stopped him. Hamish knew there was no way the Superintendent could force them to leave the island while Rita was badly injured. Holloway puffed up his chest but turned and left them to it.

As Hamish continued to watch Rita sleep for what seemed to him like hours, the anger built up within him. It was a slow boil, an all-consuming anger that made him suspicious of everyone. When Rita's eyes finally opened, she asked him if he was feeling ill.

'Not ill,' he said.

'Go and sleep. I'm fine here. How does watching me rest help anyone?'

'I can't believe that someone tried to kill us both. Look what they've done to you. I've no idea who murdered Emily, and I'm not sure Simon was killed at all. We can't possibly be a threat to anyone. I've been skirting the edges of this situation since arriving here,' said Hamish, ignoring her question. 'I've only been half engaged in these deaths and I've done Emily May Baker a disservice.'

'What are you saying, Hamish? You've done all you can.'

'I have not done all I could do. I've allowed Holloway to present the death of Emily as suicide when I know it to be a lie. The life of Emily May Baker has value. She deserves the truth to be known. Efforts to dismiss her death because of her circumstances are unjust and I'm contributing to the injustice by remaining silent.'

'You haven't been silent, Hamish. We were both nearly killed because you haven't been silent.'

'But I haven't been effective. I have to find out who killed Emily and why. I have to have the courage of my convictions.'

At that point Brigid walked in.

'I can't help wondering,' Hamish said to her, 'If you have some ideas of your own who might be responsible for the death of Emily?'

'I cannot know more than you do yourself,' she responded, stunned.

'But you have suspicions?' asked Hamish.

Brigid didn't answer. Her skin had darkened to a deep fuchsia. She mumbled that she had forgotten something, turned the way she had come and left the ward.

'Brigid,' called out Rita. But she didn't look back.

'I can't believe you pressed her like that,' said Rita. 'She's been such a help since the...accident.'

'Why are you calling it an accident?' Hamish was at breaking point. 'Someone tried to murder us. There was no accident. It's driving me mad that the imbeciles here are referring to an accident. Now you're using that language. Call it what it is – attempted murder.'

'I'm sorry,' Rita sighed. 'You're right. But I can't believe Brigid knows anything about it.'

'I would wager my life's earnings she knows something. At the very least she suspects something.' Hamish was up, pacing from one side of her bed to the other.

Rita looked at him from below lowered eyelids. 'Do you think you might be a little jealous?' she said.

'Jealous of what?' cried Hamish.

'Jealous of Brigid,' she said.

Was she teasing him? It affronted Hamish. He stood still and summoned his most offended voice.

'Why on earth?'

Rita laughed. The rocking that came with it hurt her shoulder. 'Well, Brigid and I are forming quite a bond,' she said.

Hamish had to acknowledge, at least to himself, that he may be a little jealous. And that as a woman, Brigid could relate to Rita in a manner that seemed to exclude him in some barely susceptible way. 'Don't be ridiculous,' he said out loud.

5 AUGUST 1884
EMILY

Emily heard footsteps when she joined the sandy track just beyond the scrub that skirted the asylum. She didn't know who was following her, but she kept walking without hesitating. By the time Grimy reached her, Emily had armed herself with a tree branch. When he stumbled forward to grab her from behind, she swung the tree branch as powerfully as she could. It hit him hard across the side of the head. Grimy screamed and fell. Emily was confident the blow, in addition to the alcohol, would make it impossible for him to regain his feet again for some time. About two hours later, on her way back to the asylum, Emily walked right past Grimy, limp from too much to drink and lying in the ferns along the side of the track.

As she walked into the clearing, the shadow of the hospital ward in her sights, she noted the scent of lemon. Within seconds, Cornelius Vissen appeared before her. He was carrying a lantern, and the light sent a yellow glow upward, casting deep shadows under his eyes. Instantly, something triggered a memory within. Before she could speak Vissen had forced her with one hand against the wall of the hospital building. He placed the lantern on the ground and began to grasp at her tunic. Emily pushed him away in horror.

'Get off me,' she cried.

'What's the matter? Not black enough for you, you little tart?' He lunged toward her, and she placed her hands across her chest, ready to push him away again with all her strength. She was full of rage, not just because of the attack, but also because she remembered where she had seen him before.

'I recognise you,' she said. 'It was during that fight in Brisbane.'

Vissen stopped immediately. He seemed to instantly sober up.

'What are you talking about?' he seethed.

'I saw you in Brisbane the night that girl disappeared.'

'I have no idea what you are talking about.'

'I'm sure...' Emily began.

'Don't be ridiculous,' he spat. 'A nigger loving slut. You are nothing. Not even worth the trouble.' With that, he picked up the lantern and stumbled away toward the Stores.

Emily smoothed down her tunic and caught her breath. Maybe she had been mistaken. It was dark that night in Brisbane. And it was almost a year ago.

CHAPTER TWELVE

It is a sad reflection on human nature that either individual or collective efforts to do good, though prosecuted from purest motives, are in some degree productive of evil. One would think, for instance, that charitable institutions could only serve proper purposes. But experience has taught us to the contrary. Personal discriminate charity has been the means of creating idleness and deceit among those whom it was intended to aid and assist. By the establishment and the operation of the poor-law system in England, by which it is intended the really poor and needy should be saved from absolute want of the necessities of life, a class of hereditary paupers has been created who never have a higher aim in life than to live in the poorhouse. Dunwich Asylum. - The Capricornia, Rockhampton. Saturday 11 October 1884.

---

7 OCTOBER 1884
HAMISH

The following day, Hamish didn't get to Rita's bedside until mid-morning. Brigid was already with her, and the dog was now settled on the end of her bed, wrapped snugly around her feet. Since Rita seemed to find comfort in his warmth, Hamish didn't object. Bridget was tucking pillows under her head. Hamish thought it odd that Brigid didn't seem to be short of time when it came to providing care to Rita. Meanwhile, the inmates in the Asian ward were left to fend for themselves. Hamish was tempted to remind her that there were others in need of her attention, but he decided not to say anything.

Brigid was already chatting openly about the deaths.

'I liked Emily,' she said. 'She was a bold girl, for certain. She gave me plenty of lip. But I liked her spunk. I think she'd been through a lot in her life, to end up here at her age.'

'Did you know she was seeing Simon?' asked Rita.

'I did not,' she said. 'I knew she was running off to Myora in the evenings. I supposed there was a man behind it. But it could've been anyone. One of the inmates, or the fishermen at Amity. To tell you the truth, I hoped it was a white man for the child's sake.'

'I don't understand why Emily was here,' said Rita. 'She was young, healthy, she could've worked anywhere to earn her living.'

'I know,' said Brigid. 'She was sent here because she was declared deranged. But Emily wasn't crazy. She was still young and a bit of a wildcat, but not deranged. Circumstances just landed her here. And once you're admitted to a place like Dunwich, you don't get out easily. She certainly made herself useful around the asylum. She worked harder than any of the inmates. She looked after the older women in her ward.

As it turns out she may have been keener to join the community at Myora than to return to civilised society in Brisbane.'

'*Moongalba*,' said Hamish.

Rita and Brigid both looked at him.

'The people who live there call it *Moongalba*,' he said.

'Whatever you call it, it's not civilised is it?' said Brigid.

'That depends on what you think civilised society is,' said Hamish drily.

'I beg your pardon?'

'I suppose if you define civilisation in terms of buildings and machinery, the Australian Aboriginal culture has few of those. But they certainly have industry. I should think hunting and preparing food for an entire community is industrious.'

'Hardly production of goods to support an economy though is it?'

'I don't know. They produce goods for trade. There are several reports of artworks made in the south being traded all the way to the Cape.'

'Surely you're not suggesting a system of morals exists. Morality is an aspect of civilization, is it not?'

'If you are using the term to apply to a set of values and social rules to distinguish right from wrong, then yes. I do believe the Australian Aborigines have a strong system of morality. Their social rules may not be clear to us, but they seem to be very clear to their own members. I hear there are harsh penalties for those who step beyond them. I believe your objection may be that their belief system is not consistent with Christianity.'

Brigid was astounded.

'Do you not believe that God himself makes the laws that men live by?'

'Men make laws, not God, powerful men at that.'

Rita had been quiet throughout the exchange.

'Is this what you believe?' Brigid asked her.

Rita spoke with gentle sympathy.

'My dear Brigid, not only do men with power in our society make laws, they make them in their own name, to suit their own desires.'

Brigid went silent.

Hamish expected she was angry. Then he changed his mind. He realised she was considering what they said, trying to place it in the context of her own experience.

'Your perspective reminds me of someone I knew some years ago,' said Brigid.

'I'd almost forgotten that perceptions exist that are far outside what is considered appropriate.'

'Forgive us,' Rita said, 'but Hamish thinks of you as a bit cold and distant.'

Hamish nearly fell off his seat.

'That's a bit direct,' he said.

But he looked to Brigid, curious as to how she would respond. Red looked up warily.

Brigid straightened her back.

'I'm glad to hear it,' she said. 'It would be easy for the people who are sent here, to take advantage of the situation, if those of us in charge were weak.'

'Sometimes you sound like your husband,' said Rita.

Brigid relaxed again.

'We're trying to create a sense of order here,' she said, 'in a community that thrives on chaos and drama. These people are not just poor and ill, they are...dysfunctional. We create structure and discipline because they can't produce it for themselves.'

Rita chuckled.

Brigid swelled up again. 'What?'

'It seems to me that you believe you're creating order and structure, but the inmates really just work their lives of chaos and drama around your structures.'

Brigid looked shocked.

'Really,' said Rita, 'No one actually adheres to Holloway's rules, now do they?'

Brigid took a deep breath. 'No,' she said. 'They don't.'

'And what about the Asiatics?' asked Rita. If she was going to put Brigid offside, Hamish thought, she might as well make a good job of it, forgetting that he had also challenged her not two minutes earlier.

'Hamish says they are not receiving good care?'

'Now wait a minute,' says Hamish. 'I'm right here. I could speak for myself.'

'But you don't,' laughed Rita. She stared at Brigid.

'The Chinese are not my husband's first priority,' said Brigid.

Rita kept looking at her.

'But I admit I didn't supervise the care in that ward as closely as I should have. I hadn't been in there in some weeks when the Doctor visited.' She glanced sideways at him. 'Despite what my husband says, I am actually grateful to the Doctor for pointing out my omission.'

Hamish smiled a little. He may have been too hasty in his suspicions about Brigid. She did appear to reflect the views of her husband in public. But every now and then, when she was alone with Rita and himself, a different person emerged. Brigid left them to return to her duties, and Hamish asked Rita if she thought Brigid might be leading a life that was untrue to her real self.

Rita replied, 'It is my opinion that Brigid is no less a prisoner on the island than the inmates she cares for.'

* * *

Hamish left Rita to rest while he set off to find out where people were and what they were doing on the afternoon of the incident at the point and on the nights that Emily and Simon died. Whether it was because he needed to stretch his legs, or because he didn't trust Hamish to carry out the task alone, Red decided to accompany him.

Hamish began with Wallace because he was easier to talk to than any of the others.

'Hello Red,' called Wallace as he saw them approaching. 'Have you left your patient alone?' He scuffed the dog's ears.

'I'm asking everyone where they were on Saturday,' said Hamish.

'I was where I always am, preparing Saturday's lunchtime and evening meals. Mabel doesn't usually work Saturdays, but she was with me last week. She come in to help gut a heap of fish brought in by the fishermen from Amity. As payment, she took some of the fish home to Myora.'

Mabel nodded.

Hamish asked them both if they had seen Holloway, his wife, or Vissen during the day. Neither had. 'But,' pointed out Wallace, 'that wasn't unusual on a Saturday, you'd rarely see them about the kitchen on their days off.'

'What about the nights that Emily and Simon were hanged?' asked Hamish.

Wallace let his eyelids drop a little. 'I was drinking with my mates both nights,' he said.

Mabel said she was at home at Myora. She said she had not seen or heard anything that alarmed her on either occasion.

Neither Wallace nor Mabel seemed disturbed by the questions.

Hamish saw that Grimy was weeding the gardens behind the kitchen. He spoke to him next, Red sitting alert by his legs.

'Where were you on Saturday?' Hamish asked.

Grimy smiled his greasy smile. 'I hear there was an accident over at the Point,' he said. 'is the lady going to recover?'

'She will,' said Hamish, perhaps a little optimistically.

'Glad to hear it,' hissed Grimy between his filthy teeth.

'Although it was no accident.'

Grimy didn't respond.

'So, where were you?' repeated Hamish.

'I was at me work, sir,' said Grimy. 'In the gardens here. As is me job.'

Wallace was watching from where he now sat outside the kitchen. He heard the exchange. Hamish looked up and Wallace nodded to confirm that Grimy was speaking the truth.

'What time did you finish here?' asked Hamish.

'I worked until well after the midday meal,' he said. 'Planted all these beds,' he explained, waving across the beds of freshly tilled soil. 'Here, get out of it!' he shouted at Red, who was digging in the soil for worms.

Again, Hamish looked over to Wallace, and again he nodded. Grimy couldn't have reached the other side of the Island in time to push Hamish and Rita off the gorge. The three of them, Wallace, Mabel and Grimy, at least, could speak for one another on that day.

'Where were you when Emily was killed,' Hamish asked.

Grimy's eyes narrowed. He said in a quiet and measured voice,

'I believe the girl killed herself.'

'Just the same,' said Hamish, 'where were you that night?'

'Would've been in me bed,' he said. 'Same as every night, same as the night the Native hung.' Grimy lurched after the dog with his pitchfork in the air, crying, 'Get off!'

So much for Grimy. He might have killed Emily and Simon, but he certainly didn't make the attempt on his and Rita's lives. Hamish headed toward the Telegraph Office next. He didn't trust Holloway as far as he could kick him, but for the life of him he couldn't understand why the

Superintendent would bring the kind of negative attention to the asylum that would follow the death of a visiting doctor and his chemist friend.

He reasoned, if the murder attempt had succeeded, their deaths would have been described as an unfortunate accident. Even for the Island, such a stream of unfortunate incidents, beginning with the supposed suicide of Emily and her lover and ending with their fall from the gorge, would surely seem extreme. Or maybe not. Such was the incentive for the Government to keep the Dunwich Asylum from the public's attention.

Hamish entered the Telegraph Office after Red, who had charged ahead. Holloway stood up at his desk and shooed the dog out.

'Why can't Wallace control that bloody dog?' he cried. 'I've told him to keep the creature tied up.'

Hamish ignored the outburst, as did Red. Hamish asked the Superintendent what he was doing on Saturday. As expected, the question affronted Holloway. Still, Hamish waited for an answer.

'I was at my desk,' Holloway said. 'Completing the monthly reports in time for Tuesday's barge,' he added. 'With all the distractions of late, I've become behind in my work, I am sure you can understand,' he said looking accusingly at Hamish who he obviously blamed for the distractions.

'Did anyone come in?' asked Hamish.

'What do you mean?'

'Did anyone see you in your office?'

'How dare you...? My wife knew I was there.'

'Did she see you though?'

'We had lunch together.'

'After lunch?'

'My wife had her own business to attend to.'

'So, no one saw you in the office after lunch then?'

'Doctor, I didn't push you and your colleague from the cliff. I resent this questioning.'

Hamish considered this. Holloway said he was in his office, and he may well have been. There was no one to say..

'And the night that Emily died?'

Holloway glared at him.

'What about the night that Simon died?'

Holloway stood up to his full height and continued to glare at Hamish. Hamish turned and left him standing there. Clearly there was no more to be learned from him. He and his wife may have eaten together, but then either of them would have been free to ride to the Point.

Hamish and Red walked across the field to the Storeroom. Hamish whispered to Red, 'Everyone is going to say they were busy at the asylum on Saturday and everyone is going to say they were sleeping in their beds when Emily and Simon died.'

Red trotted along beside him.

'Someone like Holloway, for example, is unlikely to ride across the Island to push people off a cliff himself, anyway. He would have someone else do it for him. There are at least three hundred people at Dunwich who would conceivably take on such a task for sufficient reward. In the same vein, if he wanted Emily and Simon to disappear, there are plenty of people who would be prepared to make that happen as well.'

Red didn't comment.

'I'm talking to a dog, for pity's sake,' mumbled Hamish.

Hamish found Vissen in his stores, lifting rolls of grey wool onto shelves. For some reason unclear to Hamish, Red didn't follow him into the building.

'I wanted to ask where you were on Saturday afternoon,' said Hamish.

Vissen didn't look up from his task. 'I was here,' he said.

'Anyone see you here?' asked Hamish, thinking what an industrious group of employees they were at the Dunwich Asylum.

'No,' said Vissen, continuing his work.

'What about the night Emily died?'

'In my bed asleep.'

'And the night Simon died?'

Vissen didn't look up from the work.

'The Native committed suicide,' he said. 'What difference does it make where I was?' He threw a bale of wool onto the stack.

Hamish was beating a dead horse with these questions. He left Vissen to his work. Red was sitting inches from the door waiting for him. Together they walked to his tent, then Red left him.

That evening Hamish returned to check on Rita. Red was curled into a ball on her bed. Brigid was with her, as always. They were sitting quietly chatting. Hamish pulled a chair to the side of the bed and glared at Brigid, expecting her to leave. She stayed.

'Well,' he said, 'It appears that everyone was working at the asylum on Saturday. Your husband says he was in his office,' he said to Brigid.

'He was at lunchtime,' she began hesitantly.

Hamish sat up straight. He had expected wholehearted confirmation from Mrs Holloway.

'I did have lunch with him, but I don't know what happened after that,' she said. 'I didn't hear from him again until he came into the house at about five o'clock. He was asking around Dunwich if anyone had seen you return. No one had, and he looked worried. I must admit I had a bad feeling as well. The ride back in the dark could be dangerous for newcomers. He blamed himself for not instructing you to be back at the asylum by five-thirty at the latest.

He went for Vissen and Wallace and they set off to find you.' Brigid Holloway looked thoughtful. 'I saw Wallace and Mabel at lunchtime,' she said. 'And then after that – I went to the kitchen to ask about the meat for Sunday roast. Wallace said it would be mutton. I longed for the tender lamb we used to have when I was a child. Our family raised sheep.'

'Did you see Grimy in the gardens?'

Brigid crinkled her brow. 'Yes,' she said, 'He was in the garden when I went to the kitchen. Still, that was early in the afternoon. He could've made it to the Point after that.'

'What about Vissen?' asked Hamish. 'Did you see him anywhere?'

'No, I didn't see him at all,' she said. 'That doesn't necessarily mean anything,' she quickly added. 'I rarely see him through the day on a weekend. He keeps very much to himself.'

'He says he was in the Storeroom, working,' said Hamish.

'He possibly was,' replied Brigid. 'I wouldn't know.'

It all seemed useless. Rita asked if Brigid believed one of the inmates could have tried to harm them.

'I can't see why,' she began. 'Why would they bother?'

'What about the local people?' asked Rita.

'The Natives? Good Lord, why would they want to kill you? Actually,' she said, 'if they did want to kill you, you'd be dead.'

'Why would anyone want us dead?' cried Hamish. 'We have been conspicuously ineffective at finding out anything about Emily's death for certain.'

Brigid looked uncomfortable.

'In fact,' she said, 'you've stirred up quite a lot of emotion in relation to Emily Baker's death. I think it's clear that it's Emily's killer who has made the attempt on your lives.'

'Are you sure?' asked Hamish. 'We don't have any new knowledge.'

'Only that it wasn't suicide,' said Rita. 'Perhaps someone doesn't want any further investigation into why they killed Emily.'

They were all silent for some time.

Finally, Rita asked, 'Brigid, is there nothing that happened prior to Emily's death that could be relevant? I know we've all been thinking about the pregnancy and the match with Simon, but is there anything else that was out of the ordinary?'

Brigid looked as though she was about to speak, then she closed her mouth and shook her head.

'What?' cried Rita.

'Well, I don't really see how it's relevant...' began Brigid.

'It may or may not be relevant. Just tell us.'

'I overheard Simon telling Mabel that Emily had found the child, Violet, on the beach crying. She had a half-crown.'

'That's a large amount of money,' said Hamish. 'Where would the child get it?'

'I don't know, but Simon was very disturbed about it. We all surmised she had 'found' it – or stolen it, but Simon began following her after that. It happened only a couple of days before Emily's death.

'Did Simon ever tell Mabel what he found out when he followed her?' asked Rita.

'I don't know. I didn't hear anything about it. We were all grieving... in our own ways.'

They looked at one another in silence.

'What do you think?' Rita asked Hamish.

'I don't know,' he said. 'Can't see what it has to do with anything. But I do wonder.'

'Could Hamish talk to Violet?' asked Brigid.

'You would have to ask Mabel,' she said. 'She's a niece of hers, I think. It's hard to tell.'

'That would make her a cousin to Simon,' said Rita.

'They're all related in one way or another,' Brigid said.

18 SEPTEMBER 1884
EMILY

Emily left the kitchen, her hair falling stickily down her back and her skin prickling from the sweat dripping down her face. The evening meal had been prepared, delivered, and the galley cleaned out. On Sunday afternoons she usually helped Mabel in the kitchen, however this afternoon Mabel was unwell. Wallace was drinking with his friends, as he had Sundays off. Emily had worked alone through the heat of the afternoon. Now she was done, she made her way to the beach, craving the cool breeze. When she was close enough to feel its soft touch on her face, she noticed a small bundle of brown limbs and unruly black hair at the sea's edge. A little Aboriginal girl, no older than nine or ten, sat clutching her knees, her back jerking up and down as she sobbed, deep sobs of despair.

The little girl didn't notice Emily as she approached from behind. Emily sat gently beside her, and a pair of impossibly large brown eyes turned to face her. The girl's face was squashed and puffy from crying. She had a wild look, like a startled animal. Emily was afraid the child would run if she didn't remain still. She didn't move a muscle, and she said nothing. Finally, the girl relaxed a little and resumed sobbing, though less violently. They sat together for some time. Then, as the sun was sinking lower, and the mainland grew shady in the distance, Emily asked the girl if she would like to walk with her to Myora. The girl unravelled herself from the bundle she had become. Emily drew herself to her feet and reached for the little girl's hand. Her tiny fist was clenched tight around something that she seemed to have forgotten about. Emily gently touched the girl's fingers. She wanted to see what she was holding so tightly. She glimpsed silver before the girl snapped her fist shut and tried to run. Emily gripped her wrist and held her.

'I don't want to take your coin,' Emily said. The girl settled a little. 'I won't even ask where you got it. Can we walk home together? Just for the company.'

The girl relaxed, and they headed off toward the sandy track. All the way to Myora, the girl skipped and danced in and out of the bracken growing along the side of the track. Emily missed childhood, the instant switch from despair to delight, the joy derived from an intense focus on a single moment, with no regard for the past or the future.

Where had the child obtained a silver half-crown, and what had caused her to be so upset?

They reached Myora, and Violet ran between the huts until she reached her own. Emily felt no need to speak to anyone about the incident. The girl was safe, and her secrets were her own. Simon was out fishing that evening and there was nothing to keep her at Myora, so Emily made the long walk home.

The next day she knew Simon would be working on the fence behind Holloway's garden. She wandered that way after her laundry shift.

'The girl, Violet,' she said. 'She is your niece, isn't she?'

Simon nodded.

'She was sitting on the beach last evening. Terribly upset. She held what looked to be a silver half-crown in her fist.'

Simon looked up from his work on the fence, his eyes wide.

'I walked her home. I was hoping she would tell me where she obtained the coin. She seemed to cheer up. But she said nothing.'

A dark expression gripped Simon's usually gentle face. He remained silent.

Emily suspected he knew something more about the story, something she couldn't grasp, but she knew better than to press him. The one thing she had learned about Simon was that he was silent in ways that were too deep for her to comprehend. She had learned from him that Aboriginal people didn't like the way white people asked questions all the time, as though they have a right to know everything. Simon told her once that knowledge was only shared with those who had earned the right to it.

'How does one earn the right?' Emily had asked. At the time, he stared at the ground. This was another example of her always asking questions.

Emily left Simon to his work and headed to the kitchen for her afternoon shift.

Wallace was in his usual spot sitting cross-legged outside the kitchen smoking his pipe. She told him about the child, how she had found her crying and about the money. It seemed such a lot of money for the child to have in her possession. Wallace agreed. He looked worried. Then finally he said,

'I am helping with the oysters tomorrow, taking them to Moreton. You want to come?'

CHAPTER THIRTEEN

'Does the pace of modern business help to swell the lunacy rate?'
'Undoubtedly. The keenness of competition, the furious haste to be rich, the excitement of mining speculations, all leave their record in our asylums.'
'I suppose there are domestic causes which produce lunacy.'
'Undoubtedly. A scolding wife is an active agent towards filling our lunatic asylums.' - The Telegraph, Brisbane. Saturday 5 September 1885

8 OCTOBER 1884
HAMISH

Hamish knew Mabel would be busy in the kitchen until after lunch, so he decided to revisit his patient in the Asiatic ward. As he walked, he was reviewing his opinion of Brigid, perhaps she had much more humanity than he first assumed. She seemed to care about Rita. But he was less convinced that she attended the inmates sufficiently. And was she staying close to himself and Rita to find out how much they knew? He couldn't be sure. The place was full of secrets.

Hamish entered the Asiatic ward and noted that the smell had improved. He went immediately to the old man he'd cleaned on his first visit. He was sitting propped up on a hessian blanket folded into a cushion of sorts. His bandages were clean and though he was rail thin, his eyes were bright. Hamish took his frail hand in his own. It was like holding a collection of bones. His skin was cold. Hamish knew that the improvement in the man's care had happened because of his intervention. The Superintendent couldn't afford to risk a negative report to Brisbane on the level of care being provided, even to those considered undeserving of such care.

'Do you have any pain now?' Hamish asked.

The man broke into a toothless grin and squeezed his hand a little. An Aboriginal woman, much younger than Mabel, and acting as a nurse to the old Chinese man came over to his bed and began to fuss with the hessian blanket behind his head. Hamish caught her eye, which was difficult because she was avoiding that, then she whispered something.

'I beg your pardon?' said Hamish.

She tucked her chin down to her chest and scurried away. Hamish followed, catching up to her at the door.

'What did you say to me?' he asked gently.

She didn't look up. With her chin firmly pressed against her chest, she said,

'Don't trust them Sir.'

With that she pushed past him and ran toward the women's ward leaving Hamish to stare after her. Trust who? He walked quickly after her and opened the door to the women's ward. There was no one inside. The women were all out working, and the nurse was not in there. There was another door at the opposite end of the building, she must have exited through that. Hamish caught up to her at the bottom of the stairs. He held her gently by the arm, afraid she would run away from him again.

'What do you mean, who is it I mustn't trust?'

The woman turned to face him, but she didn't look him in the eye. 'My child is sick, Doctor,' she said. 'Will you see her?'

Hamish wasn't expecting this.

'Of course,' he said. 'Is she at Myora?'

'She's near,' she said.

Hamish followed the woman to the back of the asylum grounds. Violet was sitting in the shade, leaning against a tree trunk. Hamish placed his hand on her forehead and found it warm.

'Has she been coughing?' he asked her mother.

'Yes.'

Hamish pulled out the cotton dress at least two sizes too big for the child and examined her skin. A rash. Hamish caught his breath.

'Take her home,' he said. 'You need to take her home now and keep her from any of the other children. Do you understand? Stay home yourself and don't let anyone else in the house.'

'I haven't finished my shift, Doctor.'

'I said go home now and keep to yourselves. I'll tell Holloway. Your daughter may have Scarlet Fever, which means you may have it too. Go now. Stay inside so no one else is exposed. Good Lord, the whole community at Myora could have the disease by now. Go.'

Hamish hurried across the grounds to his tent. He washed himself thoroughly and changed his clothing. Then he returned the way he had come to Holloway's office.

'What is it now?' asked Holloway, his patience sorely tested.

'An Aboriginal child is showing signs of fever,' he said. 'And a skin rash. It's possible she has scarlatina.'

'For pity's sake, doctor, an Aboriginal child with a fever and skin rash is not uncommon in this climate. How would the child be exposed to scarlatina?'

'I don't know, but I want to quarantine the people of Myora. If they remain within their community, we may contain the infection...if it's not too late.'

'Doctor, the asylum can't run without the labour from Myora. You're over- reacting again.'

'Scarlet Fever will kill the largest proportion of your inmates Holloway, if it's left to spread through the asylum. You must listen to me or be held responsible for multiple deaths through negligence.'

Holloway considered his options.

'Very well,' he said. 'How long must we keep the community contained at Myora?'

'If there are no more cases showing symptoms within four days, we can relax,' said Hamish.

Holloway sent him from the office so he could make the arrangements.

'And Vissen must stay in his quarters,' Hamish said while leaving.

'Vissen has no sign of illness,' Holloway called to him.

'He might be carrying the disease,' said Hamish.

Holloway had messages delivered to the people of Myora that they were not to come into Dunwich until further notice and to Vissen to remain in his quarters. Hamish set off to pass the message to each of the wards, ensuring anyone from Myora already working, was sent home.

As he was leaving the inebriates ward, Hamish's eye turned to the smaller building beyond the Asiatic ward. It was right at the back of the cluster nestled into the scrub at the bottom of a steep upward slope that formed the backdrop to the settlement. This was the building that both Holloway and Wallace had referred to as Ward 10. Tucked away as it was at the back of the settlement, Hamish had not yet ventured inside. In fact, when he thought about it, he had been carefully guided through the asylum the first day to avoid seeing it. When Wallace mentioned Ward 10, he indicated there was a truth about the asylum to be discovered there. If that truth was one of neglect, then he had discovered it effectively in the Asiatic Ward.

Hamish noticed Brigid Holloway struggling to open the heavy door to the building. It had an iron bolt padlocked shut on the outside. None of the other wards were as secure as that. Hamish strode across the grass toward the building, reaching the door only after Brigid was already inside. He tried pushing the door open, but there was a lock on the inside as well. He knocked loudly. After several seconds the door creaked open on its heavy hinges. Brigid stood in the opening looking shocked at Hamish's presence.

'May I come in?' asked Hamish.

Brigid hesitated at the door, then she stepped aside allowing Hamish to pass. He blinked to gain focus. The room was much darker than the other wards. Before his eyes could make out the shadows within the room someone gripped his arm. He looked down and the sliver of light from the space where the door remained slightly ajar, fell on a claw like hand. Quickly, Brigid pushed the door shut and bolted it. The sliver of light disappeared, but Hamish could see the image of the claw in his mind, and the tightness of the grip was undeniable. The pressure of the claw around his wrist kept him still.

Hamish could just make out the shadow of the man who held him. He was taller than Hamish and he was wearing a filthy nightshirt. Hamish could see the line of his shoulders beneath the fabric. The shirt was unbuttoned at the front and the man's collarbone was protruding through translucent skin. Hamish found the courage to look into the man's eyes. They stood out from his skull, too wide, too keen. They captured Hamish for a moment by the dark wrench of despair. The man's lips were slack as though muscles and tendons no longer connected them to his intentions. A long line of saliva dripped from one corner of his mouth down his chin and into his spidery beard.

'Come now,' Brigid said calmly. She took the man's hand and slowly unleashed his hold, one clawed finger at a time. Hamish remained still. As Brigid forced him to release his grip, the man laughed loudly. It was a deep, cackling laugh that sent shivers down Hamish's spine. Brigid walked into the depths of the room, leading the man away from Hamish.

As Hamish became accustomed to the darkness, he could see that the few small windows on one side of the building were heavily barred. He made out several beds down one side of the room. Men and women lay curled up in them, no more than skin on bone and hopelessly strangled by dirty sheets. Their eyes stared blankly ahead. In one corner there was a shadow. Hamish didn't trust his eyes at first. Surely not! He crept carefully toward the shape to have a better look. A man, in a wooden cage, stared at him from under his eyelids. He was crouched on his haunches and he growled when Hamish came close. The man was sitting in his own faeces. A mixture of urine and faeces covered his legs and the odour, now that he was close, was unbearable.

Hamish instinctively looked around for Brigid. She was maintaining her hold on the man with the claw like grip. She was preventing him from approaching Hamish again. In doing so, she noticed too late that Hamish had ventured close to the cage. At the last moment she called,

'Doctor, no!' But at the same time the caged man's hand shot out through the bars and his nails scraped down Hamish's face. The skin on his face was tender near his scar and a chain of fat, red bubbles began to appear down the left side of his cheek almost immediately. Hamish jumped back. The man with the claw started bobbing up and down excitedly.

Brigid let go of him so she could come to Hamish's aid, but he followed her. He circled around Hamish, trying to get a good look at him.

'Should I get you a gun?' he said. 'Caw, you'll be needing one for those Natives.'

His eyes widened more than Hamish imagined possible.

'I shot a dozen of 'em myself,' he added, and laughed. Then he leaned in close, 'Get me a gun and I'll shoot 'em for ya,' he grinned.

He revealed a set of swollen and weeping gums.

'This is the Doctor,' Brigid said loudly and sternly.

The man looked away.

'Naught use for a Doctor 'ere,' he said.

While backing away from the man, Hamish tripped over a rusty wheelchair, stumbled to regain his footing, and reached out for a nearby bed. He ended up further losing his balance and falling onto it. A bundle of bones moved in the sheets.

'Come here my sweetie,' the bones said. 'Want a fuck do ya?'

Hamish scrambled off the bed and to his feet just before the man grasped hold of his waist. The man made an effort to sit up, but it was too much for him and he slumped onto his back. His eyes were instantly blank again and it was hard to believe he had ever moved.

'Come,' said Brigid. 'We'll get you out of here.'

Hamish gathered his senses.

'No,' he said, not believing his own voice. 'No.'

He breathed deeply until his composure returned. He noticed, in a dark corner at the back of the room, a wooden chair with iron clamps at the head and leather straps on the arms. An iron clamp was also attached to each of the two front legs. The contraption was fashioned so the sitter could be restrained at the head, arms and feet.

Hamish looked at Brigid.

'So, this is where the lunatics are kept?' he said.

'The moral treatment methods of work and fresh air are not sufficient for all our inmates,' Brigid answered him quietly. 'They need to be restrained because they are a danger to themselves and to others. If they come to Dunwich demonstrating violent and aggressive behaviours, we first try calming them with the use of opium and morphine. For some, like this fellow, the medicines make them worse. We use the isolation box and the chair as a last resort. We used to put Samuel in the chair for a few hours at a time whenever he was aggressive, but he would scream so much it disturbed the other inmates. Then he was in the chair more often than he was out of it, so we decided to try the box. It was a job getting him in there. It took five of our strongest inmates. He bit Grimy, took a piece out of his ear.'

'The cage is inhumane,' gasped Hamish.

'What would you have us do, Doctor?' asked Brigid. 'He'd kill everyone in their sleep if he were free of the cage. The medicines don't work on him, as I said.'

Hamish didn't know what he would have them do. He looked at the poor soulless bodies on the beds. They were kept permanently sedated until death spread its merciful cloak over them. The asylum had indeed revealed itself as a much darker place than he'd first experienced.

'Why are these people here at all?' he asked. 'Shouldn't they be at the asylum at Woogaroo if they are violent?'

'Of course they should,' said Brigid. 'We don't have the means to manage them here. But here they are. And Woogaroo won't accept them, they're beyond capacity themselves.'

As Hamish was struggling with his personal ethics in relation to Ward 10, there was a loud knock on the door. Brigid opened it to allow Grimy to enter with a heavy enamelled basin full of water. Grimy looked as shocked as Brigid had to see Hamish standing there.

'I'm 'ere to clean Samuel's box,' he said to Hamish, willing him to leave. It fascinated Hamish despite his revulsion. He stood his ground.

Brigid took the basin from Grimy and set it by the wooden box. Grimy reached through the slats and took hold of both Samuel's hands. He resisted only a little. He obviously wanted his space cleaned. Grimy held his wrists tight and pulled him to a position where he was bent at the knees, but his buttocks were off the bottom of the cage. On her hands and knees, Brigid scrubbed the floor beneath him with a large sea sponge and rinsed out the mess in the water. When the floor was cleaned of excrement, she scrubbed the man's buttocks and legs. He took exception to this and bellowed and pulled, straining at Grimy's grip. Grimy didn't let go. When the task was complete, Brigid handed the filthy basin back to Grimy, and he took it outside.

Brigid walked to the door and stood there waiting for Hamish to join her. They both left the building, Brigid locking the heavy bolt behind them. She secured the padlock.

'Grimy seems to have many roles here at the asylum,' said Hamish.

'He's unpleasant. But a necessary evil,' said Brigid. 'He's always available for the dirty jobs that no one else wants to do.'

'This level of physical restraint has long been phased out in Britain,' Hamish said. 'It's no longer an acceptable treatment in mental illness.'

'It may not be in well-appointed facilities with sufficient qualified staff,' said Brigid. 'But here, I've no accommodation in which to isolate the violent, and I've no skilled staff to supervise them. The only options remain sedation and restraint.'

Hamish walked alongside the Matron silently until they passed the kitchen block. There he turned off while she continued on to the telegraph station. He desperately needed to wash.

Hamish found Mabel outside the kitchen. She had just finished her shift.

'Weren't you told to go home earlier?' cried Hamish.

'What are you talking about?'

'The child, Violet, she has symptoms that suggest scarlatina. Holloway has ordered everyone from Myora to return home and stay there.'

'I didn't get any such message,' said Mabel. 'So, you want the disease to spread through the Aboriginal population but keep your own mob safe?' she quipped.

Hamish had nothing to say.

'It's a disease that belongs to you lot,' she pointed out.

'Actually, I wanted to ask you about Violet,' Hamish said.

Mabel's fierce eyes glared at him.

'You white cunts leave nothing alone – leave it Doctor!' She pushed past him and strode off toward the top huts and the sandy track.

Hamish was as shocked as if she had slapped him in the face. Mabel had not been exactly welcoming before now, but she had always tolerated his questions. He stared at her back as she marched away from him, defiant even in her walk. What to do next? It flashed across his mind that maybe he should collect Rita and return to the mainland on the next barge. But even as he rolled it around in his mind, he knew it was not going to happen.

* * *

Hamish washed up and changed his clothes to join the Holloways for dinner. When he received the invitation, he hesitated. He didn't relish the Superintendent's company, but he hoped he might find something out that would help him understand what was happening in this place. When Hamish arrived, Holloway and Brigid were already in conversation. Brigid was perfumed and dressed in her best. She didn't appear to be the same woman who had bathed Samuel earlier that day.

'Ah – join us, please,' said Holloway.

Holloway handed Hamish a glass of wine.

Mr and Mrs Holloway were in good humour as they sat down at the dinner table, yet Hamish found it impossible to relax. Not even two more glasses of expensive red wine settled his anxiety. The meal had been prepared in the asylum kitchen and transported to the Superintendent's cottage on a trolley. Brigid only had to serve it.

Although he was seething about what he had witnessed that day, Hamish didn't want to alert Holloway to his concerns about Ward 10 before he had properly considered what he wanted to do. He needed to relay his observations to Brisbane without leaving Holloway any opportunity for further concealment. In regard to the possibility of scarlatina travelling through the community, he hoped he had done enough to contain a potential outbreak. It was possible Violet didn't have the disease, but in light of the proximity of the ship, and Vissen's exposure, he wanted to be sure. He did wonder what contact Vissen could have had with a girl from the Aboriginal community.

Hoping to begin with a comment that would set the conversation on a positive tone, and to keep himself as far from the topic of Ward 10 or scarlatina as he could manage, Hamish said,

'I am impressed with the amount of production the inmates at Dunwich realise. It has been no small achievement to establish this settlement as close to self-sufficiency as it is.'

'I take credit for the industry of the inmates at Dunwich,' said Holloway. 'It's my steadfast opinion that personal, indiscriminate charity has been the means of creating idleness and deceit among those whom it was intended to aid and assist in the benevolent institutions, both in England and the Colonies. Mine will not be among those institutions that create a class of hereditary paupers who never have any higher aim in life than to live in a poorhouse.'

Brigid said, 'It is deplorable to think of the existence of people so utterly devoid of a spirit of independence.'

'Surely, though, the primary purpose of asylums such as Dunwich is to provide the common necessities of life to those who cannot do so for themselves,' said Hamish.

'Indeed,' replied Holloway, 'I agree the purpose is sound; however, reality is another matter entirely. The majority of people sent to Dunwich are as capable as anyone of productive work. There are many sent every year who should never have entered at all. Persons who have private means of support find their way into Dunwich and think it no disgrace to live off the public purse.' Holloway poured himself another glass of wine. 'Indeed, we had one case, an inmate who was left a legacy of six hundred pounds by a relative. He went home to England and had a merry time by all reports. Then he returned to Brisbane without a penny to his name. They immediately despatched him back to Dunwich.'

Brigid nodded. 'Some of them have military pensions which they allow to accumulate for a few months. They take their savings to Brisbane for a spree and return to the Island when cleaned out.'

'You can see,' Holloway said, 'that an institution supported as a charity can be easily abused by the avaricious, selfish and unscrupulous.'

Brigid served a hearty fish soup to each of them.

'My first concern here is how to punish bad behaviour and consequently maintain a sense of order and discipline,' said Holloway. 'I have no official authority. The only punishment for misconduct, that of discharge, is no punishment at all. The one time I resorted to expulsion, the fellow lay about in his own filth on the streets of Brisbane for a week and then they sent him back to Dunwich. I often wonder if a good beating is the only recourse.'

Hamish shot him a warning glance,

'Surely you have no authority to use corporal punishment here.'

'Absolutely not,' confirmed Holloway quickly. 'There are times, however, when it's necessary to restrain an inmate physically when they are threatening the safety of others.'

An awkward silence followed while Hamish grappled with his observations of restraint that day.

'I read today there have been protests about the conditions of the workhouses in London,' said Holloway, in an attempt to shift the subject to somewhere other than Dunwich.

'Of course, this lot here don't know how well they have things,' he added.

'I doubt they would survive in a London workhouse,' agreed Brigid.

'What say you doctor?' Holloway looked directly at Hamish as he asked.

'I do agree conditions would be far worse for the poor and weak in London, for the most part,' he replied. 'They have the opportunity for sun and warmth here...'

'Too many of them,' said Holloway. 'That's the problem.' The other two stared at him.

'I think the architects of the Reforms had it right,' he went on. 'The consequence of bringing easy relief to the poor, is that there'll always be too many of them.'

He thrust a spoonful of fish soup into his mouth.

'The workhouses get them off the streets and force them into useful labour. Out of sight of decent Christian citizens.'

Hamish said, 'You are not in accord with those who argue that the plight of the poor is a circumstance thrust upon them by those with wealth and power then?'

Holloway laughed. 'Surely it is God's plan that there are those of lesser intelligence to serve His favoured, so they may enjoy the abundance our world provides.'

'The Chartists say those times are behind us,' said Hamish. He was certain he sensed Brigid stiffen as he spoke. 'The working classes are no longer prepared to carry the burden of the rich and their insatiable appetite for abundance.'

'The Chartists?' cried Holloway. 'They've all but died out. It's true they transported a few radicals to Tasmania, but they're naught but criminals.'

'Working-class men have the vote in Victoria,' said Hamish. 'It won't be long before it is so throughout the Colony. And in England too, before the decade ends.'

It seemed to Hamish Holloway was amused by his ideas, no doubt finding them naïve. Brigid, on the other hand, appeared to be deeply affected. She excused herself from the table and stacked the dirty plates on the sideboard. Hamish noted that her hands were trembling.

'Fresh air is what we need after such a wholesome meal,' declared Holloway. He picked up his pipe and looked to Hamish to join him. Hamish was tempted to stay behind with Brigid. He wanted to ask her why she was suddenly anxious. He watched her back for a moment and then decided it would be too awkward to speak to her with her husband hovering outside. Instead, he joined Holloway. It was a clear night. The Southern Cross looked down over them as brightly as Hamish had ever seen it.

'I expect your views raise eyebrows in Brisbane,' Holloway said.

'Actually,' replied Hamish, 'Brisbane is less conservative than you might think.'

'It's true,' said Holloway, 'that the real wealth is in New South Wales.'

He was staring out over the settlement, quietly puffing on his pipe. He had an air of superiority far beyond that justified by his station. In fact, both Holloway and Vissen did. At least Hamish was spared the arrogance of

Vissen throughout this evening. He would have been present if it were not for the quarantine. Hamish found Vissen, a storeman at a backwater asylum, far too sure of himself. He and the Superintendent fed one another's delusions of grandeur. Hamish noted to himself that as Storeman, Vissen had keys to all the buildings at the asylum and he had access to all the registers and files.

21 SEPTEMBER 1884
EMILY

At sunrise, Emily, Wallace and two men from the Moreton Bay Oyster Company set off in a fishing boat skirting the shore beyond Dunwich, past the mangroves at One Mile and Two Mile and on toward Amity. Emily was excited about the prospect of a day off the Island. She needed a distraction from the oppressive feeling that everyone was watching her, waiting for the truth to come out. Perhaps it would feel like less of a burden if she told Wallace, somewhere safe, somewhere away from Dunwich or Myora.

On the shore and on the mud flats there were curlews, sea snipe, divers and gulls. The smell of the mud was strong and full of salt. Emily took long, slow breaths to drink it in. There was a soft breeze that touched her skin like cool fingers brushing against her face. She was free of the asylum, the closeness of the inmates, the weight of her secret. She knew that people at Dunwich had seen her leave in a boat with three men, and she knew what they would be saying. She didn't care. The problems of Dunwich belonged to the land. They had no consequence on the water. She trusted Wallace completely, and she knew the fishermen respected him as well. The men showed no interest in her as they were intent on the day's work.

They arrived at Amity with the tide at its lowest point and secured the boat at the edge of the vast mud flat. The tree line that marked the shore was at least a half a mile away. They picked their way through the mud, collecting small oysters in baskets. Emily was anxious to do her fair share of the work. She worked quickly, establishing a basket brimming with twisted, gnarled shells glistening in the sun.

Once they had their baskets full, they transferred them from the fishing boat to a cutter. Once loaded with blinking oyster shells they boarded and set off across the South Passage toward Moreton. The passage was deep and tumultuous. It was the sea road into the Bay for the ships travelling from Britain. It was also the path the steamers took coming up from Sydney or coming down from the North. It was where the sea currents poured into the Bay and where they were dragged back out again by the tides.

As the cutter pulled up in the shallows of Moreton Island, Emily looked back toward Amity, drinking in the beauty of Stradbroke Island. Looking forward the dazzling white sand of Moreton awaited. They climbed off the boat and splashed their way through the clear waters. Emily's tunic was wet to her waist. She gathered it up and held it to her thighs. Her legs were free to experience the cool air against her skin. She had removed her boots and the warm sand gripped her bare feet. They walked across a sand ridge to the margins of an aqua lagoon, perfectly protected from the keen westerly wind by cypress and honeysuckle.

'The Lagoon is connected with the water of the Bay by a break in the sand hills,' said Wallace, pointing to the break. 'Saltwater washes into the lagoon only at Spring Tides. At the head of the lagoon there is a permanent stream of fresh water running into the lower stretches. That sheet of water has a firm sandy bottom that is constantly changing. It's sometimes more, and sometimes less, salty.'

Emily's gaze followed his pointed finger.

'At some point, generations past, the Aboriginal people shared their secret with the white fishermen, that the oysters that grow in this lagoon, grow preternatural in size, have extraordinary thick shells and are more luscious than any that grow anywhere else in the region. The fishermen soon realised that these oysters were, in fact, the best in the world, both for size and for their delicious flavour.'

'Don't the oysters in this particular lagoon run out?' asked Emily.

'The Moreton Bay Oyster Company uses the lagoon as the perfect spot for fattening oysters. They pick the oysters from the mud flats at Amity, transport them across Moreton Bay by cutter and place them in the lagoon to grow.'

Emily worked alongside the men carrying the baskets of oysters across the sand ridge to the lagoon and spreading them across the sandy floor with a shovel. It was heavy work, but Emily was able to keep pace with the fishermen and she easily outpaced Wallace, who was older and the worse for a lifetime of drinking. The fishermen appeared grateful for the extra hand. The day went quickly. They were all tired, sore and sunburned as they travelled back to Amity.

Emily sat close to Wallace. Her right arm rested against his left.

'You are a strong girl,' he said. Emily smiled. Her own father had never paid her a compliment. It sent a warm flush down her spine to have the old man's respect.

'I couldn't help but notice you are expanding at the waist' said Wallace quietly. 'Do you want to tell me about it?'

Emily looked him in the eyes. She was terrified. She froze. All her intentions to share her secret with him dissolved in that instant.

'I'll not say another word,' soothed Wallace. 'But you'll not be able to hide it for much longer.'

That evening Emily met Simon at the end of the causeway at Dunwich, as they had arranged. Simon was working on the Superintendent's roof during the day while she was out collecting oysters. They were both tired. Emily noticed a small figure walking from the asylum buildings down toward the shore. The figure made its way along the sand toward the causeway, head down, unaware there was anyone watching. As the figure came closer, it was obvious it was a child, and then it was clear that it was Violet. Emily and Simon both recognised her at the same time, and a cold expression came across Simon's face. Emily called out to the child. Violet stopped suddenly at the sound of her name and looked up with a face immobilised by shock. She turned and ran as fast as she could back down the causeway and through the scattered buildings toward the track. Simon's face went to stone.

'Why did she run?' asked Emily.

Simon stood up and began to stride away from her.

Emily scrambled to her feet and followed him.

'Simon,' she called, 'what's the matter? Where are you going?'

Simon kept walking. 'Go home,' he said.

The following evening Emily joined Simon at Myora, determined to find out what was going on. They sat together in his hut with the rusted corrugated iron walls. Tree branches gently scraped along the sides of the building. Simon told Emily that he had followed his niece Violet and found out why she was crying. Later that evening they visited the home Simon grew up in. His sister lived there now with their mother and Violet. Emily sat on the dirt floor alongside Violet, who was playing with pig knuckles.

Violet told Emily why she had been crying and where she found the half-crown.

Emily was deep in thought as she plodded through the soft sand toward home. The news she had from Simon and from Violet was deeply troubling. Surely, it would shake the Island. Or would it? How many people already knew? How many people turned away? How much did Holloway know? Emily was glad she wrote the letter to the Colonial Secretary, but it would have been better if Violet's mother had not taken it from her. It mattered little. She would write it again.

CHAPTER FOURTEEN

Events are transpiring in Brisbane, which should remind men from the old country of the time when the chartists massed themselves in Lancashire and Yorkshire. We have before us, in a young colony, in a colony whose undeveloped riches are far beyond counting, in a colony the labour resources of which are inexhaustible, the humiliating spectacle of hundreds of well-meaning, hard-working men marching in procession to the doors of the Houses of Parliament to ask for means to earn their bread. This seems a gross anomaly, but it is, to the disgrace of the colony, a stern and stubborn fact. The question naturally arises – Why does this state of affairs exist? The answer comes as readily – owing to an indiscriminate system of immigration. Extraordinary facilities have been given for people to come to Queensland, and their influx has been far in excess of the development of the natural resources of the colony. - Toowoomba Chronicle and Darling Downs General Advertiser, Queensland.

---

9 OCTOBER 1884
HAMISH

The following morning Hamish sat by Rita's bed. He told her about his suspicions that Violet had contracted Scarlet Fever, how Mabel had abused him when he approached her and how the dinner conversation had a strange effect on Brigid. He decided not to burden her with the revelations of Ward 10. He was still processing what he had observed and deciding what he could do about it. Whatever that was, he didn't want Holloway to hear about his plans in advance. Rita listened carefully. She enjoyed the intrigue, while Hamish found it exhausting.

'Hmmm,' she said when he finished talking. 'Why do you look like you've been in a fight?' she asked.

Hamish's hand went straight to his cheek where the inmate had scratched him. 'Oh this,' he said. 'An inmate. He was quite mad. I got too close. Should have known better.'

Rita eyed him carefully. She looked as though she might request more detail, but she didn't. She appeared to refocus on the information he brought her.

Unsure of where Rita would begin, Hamish was still surprised when she chose to focus on the story about Violet.

'Violet will have stolen the coin,' she said. 'It is unlikely that someone would lose as valuable a sum without mentioning it.'

Hamish replied, 'It's also unlikely that someone would remain silent if such a sum was stolen from them.'

Rita frowned. 'Unless the person should not have had the money in the first place...'

'So, Violet stole the crown from a thief who stole it from the rightful owner?'

Rita slumped back on her pillow. 'It does seem a bit absurd,' she agreed.

'And there's no real reason to believe the event is connected to the murder, other than timing.'

'What about the infection? Why would Violet be infected if Vissen was the carrier?'

Just as they were pondering the possibilities, Brigid joined them. There was an awkward tension between them for a moment, then Rita was the first to speak.

'We were trying to make sense of the story Emily told you about Violet,' she said.

'I spoke to Mabel,' began Hamish, 'but she was very angry. She told me to leave it alone.'

Brigid didn't speak, so Rita went on.

'We can't see how it's connected to the murders,' she said.

'It may not be,' Brigid said at last. 'But we will never know unless all the secrets come out.'

Hamish and Rita tensed up.

'What secrets?' they said together.

'You see,' Brigid continued, 'I have secrets of my own, to do with my past.'

Hamish and Rita kept watching her, afraid that if they spoke, she might stop.

'When you talked of the Chartists last night, I felt ill,' she said quietly toward Hamish.

'You did go pale,' he said.

'I know. There's something about me that my husband doesn't know. Vissen is aware of it and he threatens to tell my husband. That's the only reason I tolerate his presence in my home. He has ingratiated himself to my husband and believes he wields power over others in this place because of it. They are unbearably pathetic, both of them.'

Hamish and Rita's eyes widened, in spite of their efforts to remain unmoved.

'No one in Brisbane cares about this handful of drunks and derelicts, the scrapings of Hell.' Brigid scoffed. 'My husband and his friend are in control of nothing. Yet the fools believe they are important because they pretend to exert power over a community of people no one else wants or cares about.' She gave an ironic chuckle.

'What could Vissen possibly hold over you that your husband doesn't know?' Rita asked gently.

Brigid took a deep breath. She looked around, but there was no one else in the ward.

'When I was nineteen,' she said, 'I fell deeply in love with a man I believed to be the one true companion to my soul. He was handsome and passionate. He talked for hours and I absorbed every word he said. I was drunk on ideas I'd never heard expressed before. I could have lived forever on the sustenance of his words. I experienced feelings I'd never imagined, sensations that have not been invoked since his passing.'

'What did he talk about?' asked Rita.

'He was a Chartist. He believed that all men are equal. He believed that this country is at a moment in time when the grievances of the working man can be put to rest at last.'

'That's not a bad thing,' cried Rita, 'the Doctor and I believe so ourselves.'

'I know,' replied Brigid. 'As soon as you and I began talking, the chains around my soul loosened. You've reminded me of my first husband. My great love.'

'But surely that's no secret to fear,' Rita said incredulously.

'My first husband did more than talk. He was a true radical, a political agitator. Before we met, he lived in Tasmania. He had a friend, William Caffey, a man he considered a mentor. He was not young, a coloured man, the son of a freed slave. He was transported to Hobart as a leader of what they call, the Orange Tree Conspiracy in London. He and his supporters were arrested with pistols, knives, swords and gunpowder. They were angry that the House of Commons had rejected their partition for suffrage for all men, for a second time.'

Rita's eyes were as wide as saucers. Hamish squirmed a little restlessly.

'My husband's mentor received a pardon after only three years in Hobart and he began agitating again. He and my first husband were stirring up a protest movement against the *Master and Servant Act*. A spy from within their numbers told the local authorities, and all were arrested, except my husband. He heard of the betrayal and managed to avoid charges by travelling to Ballarat. There he became actively involved in protests with the Gold Miners. Again, he avoided arrest by moving on to Brisbane. When I met him, he was mobilising the working men, forming a committee to demand the progress of the Chartists' remaining demands throughout the Colony. There'd already been some success in Victoria. Apparently, Vissen came across my husband in Victoria and found out about his connections to William Caffey. We ran into Vissen again in Brisbane not long before the accident that killed my first husband.'

When Rita was certain Brigid had finished talking, she said, 'I still don't think....'

Brigid didn't let her continue.

'You must understand, my current husband is poorly educated and has ambitions way beyond his station. I fear that my past associations would be intolerable to him. He is eternally anxious about the appearance of things.'

'Do you love your husband?' asked Rita quietly.

Hamish had been restless all this time, but he jumped at this question.

'It's all right,' Brigid said. 'It's a relief to be open about these things. I don't know if I love my husband. I believe he thinks he loves me,' she said. 'Ours was a marriage of convenience: I needed somewhere to go; he needed a nurse. My first husband died from a ridiculous accident. He was trampled when he fell from his horse. Such a simple way for a complex man to die. I was left with nothing, so I moved in with my sister and her husband. Holloway was an acquaintance of my brother-in-law. He came to stay for a few weeks' respite. It was not twelve months since the death of his young wife at Dunwich. I do wonder now whether his appearance at my brother-in-law's home was coincidental, as suggested at the time, or part of a scheme to marry me off. My sister and her husband wanted to be rid of me. Anyway, I wanted a home of my own and a purpose. I've never yearned for a grand house or life. I prefer to feel that I am useful. The work here seemed an ideal solution.'

Brigid bid them good morning and returned to her work, leaving Rita and Hamish to consider all she had said.

'I'm struggling with the contradiction between my impression of Brigid when I first arrived at Dunwich and the woman who was speaking just now,' Hamish said. 'I thought her cold and hard, but she does not seem to be without compassion.'

Rita suggested that the appearance of coldness would come of a loveless marriage to a man such as Holloway.

'Yes, but if she was genuine about her commitment to the work, why was she so lacking in compassion in her treatment of the Chinese for example?' Hamish was still avoiding a discussion of Ward 10.

'Perhaps her enlightened first husband's views of equality didn't extend to the Asiatic races?' said Rita.

'I guess people become complacent under difficult circumstances, and besides, she was expressing the views of her first husband. She was in love with him, in love with his passion and his tenaciousness, but she didn't say that she actually shared his views.'

'True,' agreed Rita. 'It's probable that she only understands them at a superficial level. She was clearly deeply in love. Still, what does it add to what we know about Emily's murder?'

Hamish thought for a moment.

'It explains why Brigid is nervous around Vissen. We now have some context around the odd relationship between Vissen and Holloway. But what it has to do with the murder? I don't know.'

* * *

That afternoon Hamish and Brigid were approaching Holloway's office at the same time. Hamish wanted to ask the Superintendent if he knew anything of the child called Violet, who was seen so often hanging around the asylum and who now had the symptoms of scarlatina. Brigid was returning to join her husband for afternoon tea after her rounds. As they approached, they could hear the voices of Holloway and Vissen.

'I've spoken to him about the fences,' Vissen was saying. 'We can't have cattle wandering all over the Point and disturbing the tracks.'

'Quite so,' agreed Holloway. 'The motley beasts are full of ticks. I don't know why he was granted the land in the first place. It's entirely unsuited to cattle.'

Brigid stopped.

'What is it?' asked Hamish.

Brigid was pale.

'I...I've left something in the wards,' she said and turned back the way she had come. Hamish watched as she backtracked her steps rather than going into the office as planned. He pushed on alone, wondering what had disturbed her. As soon as he entered the Telegraph Office, Vissen and

Holloway stopped talking. Vissen gave Hamish a slight bow of acknowledgement and left.

'What is he doing out of quarantine?' demanded Hamish.

'What can I help you with?' asked Holloway wearily.

'I wanted to ask what you know of the Aboriginal girl called Violet, the one with the infection,' asked Hamish. 'She is often seen around the grounds of the asylum'

Holloway frowned. 'I don't know anything of her,' he said. 'I would assume she is the offspring of one of the workers. What of it?'

'I'm not sure,' said Hamish. 'It's just that she was observed to have quite a lot of money in her possession. Half a crown, in fact.'

Holloway's frown deepened. 'Good Lord, where would a native child get that kind of money?'

Hamish shook his head. 'Has anyone lost such a sum?'

Holloway coughed. 'I would be surprised if anyone here had such a sum,' he said. 'Who observed this?'

Hamish didn't answer. 'It's not important,' he said instead.

* * *

After a quick dinner of beans warmed on his own campfire, Hamish joined Brigid at Rita's bedside. Red was perched on the bottom of her bed. Brigid was sitting beside her, holding her hand.

'Does that woman have anything else to do?' thought Hamish.

'I wondered,' Brigid began, if you spotted any cattle on Saturday on your ride to the Point?'

'Yes, we did,' they said in unison.

'They were all over the track,' went on Hamish. 'We had to dismount. Why do you ask?'

'I heard Vissen telling my husband that he spoke with Frank and told him to fix his fences to contain the cattle,' she said.

Hamish and Rita stared at her, not sure what this meant.

'Yes, I heard that too, said Hamish. 'I am concerned by the fact that Vissen was not in his quarters as ordered. He may well be spreading Scarlet Fever throughout the asylum.'

'I would imagine that if Vissen is infectious, he has already done considerable damage, Doctor. I would suggest that the horse has already bolted, as they say.'

'What of the cattle then?'

Brigid explained, 'I don't know when Vissen could've seen the cattle, other than the day of your... accident. I know he hasn't been over the other side of the Island for months, he said so himself at dinner only a week ago.'

Hamish felt his skin prickle.

Rita was cautious. 'Could they have seen the cattle when they came to find us?' She was looking at Hamish.

'The cattle were not there on our way back,' he said.

'Vissen was missing all that afternoon,' added Brigid.

'He told me he was in the stores,' said Hamish. 'You said yourself you wouldn't normally expect to see him on Saturdays.'

'It does seem interesting though,' said Rita.

Brigid looked thoughtful. 'I can't help thinking it was him,' she said.

'Who? Vissen?' asked Hamish. 'Why would he want to kill Rita and me?'

'What if he killed Emily?' asked Rita.

'Why would he want to kill Emily?'

'Perhaps because she rejected him and fell pregnant to a Black man?' suggested Brigid.

'That would seem like the ultimate insult to a man like Vissen,' agreed Rita.

Hamish said, 'Surely he wouldn't murder a woman and risk everything over that?'

'What risk?' said Rita. 'If you hadn't interfered, the death would've been reported as suicide.'

'But Vissen knew the Inspector was coming that day.'

'Even better, a credible witness to the suicide. No one was going to look into it. He didn't know you were coming.'

Hamish still couldn't believe it.

'There must be more to it than that,' he said.

Hamish didn't sleep well that evening. He knew he'd have to write to the Colonial Secretary to relay recent events. The fall he and Rita had suffered, and Rita's injury had already been communicated by Holloway, who referred to the incident as an unfortunate accident. Hamish wanted to have something definitive to say before he contacted the Colonial Office with stories of attempted murder. He was sure they were less than convinced that Emily's death was anything other than suicide. In addition, he needed to describe the scene he had witnessed in Ward 10. He was certain that Callahan had never visited that ward during his inspections. He was not sure what could be done for the men and women in Ward 10, but there needed to be a better solution than the one he witnessed. Asylums in other parts of the world were already addressing these kinds of conditions.

Conversations replayed in his mind all night. He was still troubled by the story of Violet, and Mabel's aggression toward him. He was anxious about the possibility of an outbreak of scarlatina. But what could any of it have to do with Emily's death?

Hamish remained awake to see the dawn light creep into his tent. He heard the cawing of crows and held his hand against a pounding ache that was building in his forehead. He stroked the rough skin of his scar and winced at the soreness of the scratch made by Samuel in Ward 10. Hamish made up his mind to confront Holloway about the cattle on the track. He was more and more convinced daily, that both Emily and Simon had been murdered. Once he spoke to Holloway, he would draft a letter to the Colonial Secretary relaying his concerns. He dressed purposefully and made his way to the Telegraph Office early, expecting to find Holloway alone.

His expectation was unfounded. Not only were Holloway, Brigid and Vissen together, their conversation sounded tense and they didn't look impressed at his intrusion.

'What could you possibly understand of such things,' Holloway was saying to his wife. 'Wallace lived at sea all his life. Who knows what depravity he has seen... or worse? I am telling you he had a relationship with Emily Baker.'

Vissen added, 'If there is an investigation into her death, they will hold him accountable.'

'Accountable for what?' cried Brigid. 'For being kind to her? Wallace is a homosexual, for pity's sake.' Holloway and Vissen stared at her. She might as well have said he came from another planet.

'What the devil do you want?' Holloway noticed Hamish at the door.

Hamish glanced from Vissen to Holloway to Brigid. They were all staring at him. It was immediately obvious it was a mistake to confront Holloway with his questions in the audience of his wife and colleague. He didn't know who he could trust, if anyone.

'I can see you are busy,' muttered Hamish, 'I will return later.' He turned on his heels and left as quickly as he could.

Hamish returned to his tent to write the letter to the Colonial Secretary. His new plan was to tell Holloway about it once the letter was safely on its way to Brisbane. As soon as he arrived at his tent, he could see that someone had already entered. He edged in carefully, unsure of what to expect. When he recognised the person standing there, his eyebrows lifted in surprise. It was Violet's mother. The girl-woman held out a greasy piece of paper, folded and refolded. Hamish took it from her slim brown fingers and unfolded the paper without speaking.

'Emily gave me this,' she said. 'She was going to send it to Brisbane. I kept it and asked her not to tell. I was shame. The next day Emily was dead.'

Hamish began reading. When he looked up, Violet's mother had gone.

The letter read:

Dear Secretary,

I write to you in the utmost confidence about a circumstance here in Dunwich so monstrous that it seems too evil to exist even in this place.

I have recently discovered that an Aboriginal girl known as Violet, who says she is ten years of age, has been forced by the Storeman here, Cornelius Vissen to perform unspeakable acts of an intimate nature. While in his quarters the child has stolen money, which she believes is compensation for the horrors she had endured by his hand. I am certain of these facts because the child has relayed them to me herself. In case you think she must be lying, I can tell you that her Mother's brother, a man called Simon, followed the child and saw with his own eyes that she entered the Storeman's quarters. It is unclear what this monster, Vissen, has over the child, but she is clearly terrified of him.

In addition to this information I am concerned about another child who went missing in Roma Street in May of this year. I saw a man who I believe to have been Vissen, leading a child away from this very same place, on the evening the girl was reported as missing. While I may be mistaken about this latter incident, I have only a vague recollection, I am certain of the incidents that have taken place in Dunwich in respect to the child.

I expect you will respond to this account with the necessary urgency and the full force of the law.

Emily May Baker.

The letter was never sent. Emily was killed and then Simon was dead.

Hamish rushed to the hospital ward. It was still early and there were two women in beds who had been ill overnight with fever. They were placed at the furthest end of the ward from Rita so as not to risk infecting her. Hamish checked them over carefully, trying not to wake them. He was relieved to find no sign of a rash on either woman. They were both in a feverish sleep and he was satisfied that if he spoke quietly, they wouldn't hear him. Hamish told Rita about his visitor and finally handed her the folded letter.

'This is it,' she cried when she had finished reading. In an exaggerated whisper she said, 'Vissen killed Emily and then he killed Simon.'

'He can't have done it alone,' said Hamish. 'Even if he killed Simon, or knocked him unconscious, he couldn't have raised a man that size up to put a noose around his head and hang him from a tree.'

'Two men could do it,' said Rita. 'Holloway? Do you think?'

'It was Holloway's idea to send us to the Point,' said Hamish. 'He could've sent Vissen to push us off the gorge.'

'They obviously don't know about this letter,' said Rita, handing it back to Hamish.

'I'm going to send it on the barge today,' said Hamish, 'with an outline of my own.'

'What barge Hamish? The barge came yesterday – there won't be another until Tuesday.'

'There's a choir coming over to entertain the inmates,' said Hamish. 'They're expected at midday. I'll get a message to the Skipper before they leave. Then I need to speak with Violet. There is something she is afraid of.'

'I want to come,' said Rita.

'You need to stay in bed,' cried Hamish. 'You can't walk to Myora.'

Rita flopped back on her pillow in frustration. She knew he was right.

Hamish left her and returned to his tent, where he penned a summary of events for the Colonial Secretary. He placed his own account, and the letter written by Emily, into an envelope and sealed it. He took it to the causeway himself and waited for the barge. He passed the envelope from his hand to the Boat Master with instructions that he take it personally to the Colonial Office.

He greeted the members of the choir one at a time and slipped away an instant before Holloway arrived for the official welcome. Hamish set off along the shoreline and around the side of the asylum to join the sandy track with the least chance of being seen. Holloway was sufficiently occupied with the guests not to notice him.

Hamish set off on the long, familiar walk to Myora. He found Violet sitting on the front step of one of the Myora houses. She didn't look at Hamish when he greeted her. He sat on the step below. 'Do you know who I am, Violet?' he asked gently.

She nodded.

'Can you tell me about the white man who runs the stores?'

Violet shook her head.

'Has he hurt you?' asked Hamish.

Violet didn't look up. She was turning a rock over in her hands.

Hamish asked, 'Can I see?' as he gently took the rock. 'It's pumice,' he said. He threw it up and caught it. 'See how light it is?'

Violet also had a small collection of bleached coral and shells. Hamish picked them up one at a time and examined them.

He started a little when he noticed two bare feet appear on the step above Violet. He looked up to see Violet's mother staring down at them.

'Tell him, girl,' she said.

Violet shuffled her thin frame on the stair.

'What happened?' Hamish encouraged her.

'He said the white people would take me away if I didn't do it,' she murmured.

'Do what?' Hamish asked nervously.

'They took 'em before,' she said. 'Ma knows. The missionaries took the *jarjums* away and no one ever saw 'em again.'

'Why did you think they would take you away?'

'Coz I was bad. I shouldn't have been in that place. I took a coin. I gave it to Ma. But that man caught me and 'e said they would take me away. He said if I told, they would take me away. I didn't want to go back there, but I didn't want to get sent away. He let me keep the coin then, for what he made me do.'

'What did he make you do?'

She shuffled again. 'He shoved his *budu* in my mouth' Her face was screwed up as she said it.

Hamish couldn't believe what he was hearing. 'Does anyone else know?' he said, trying to keep his voice calm. 'Apart from Ma?'

'Uncle Simon and Emily,' she said. 'Uncle Simon saw me come out of the Stores and made me tell. After Emily died, Uncle Simon said he was gonna kill that man.'

Hamish looked up at Violet's mother. 'I am so sorry this happened,' he said, his voice cracking. 'Make sure Violet does not go near the Stores again. This man will be punished.'

He looked directly at Violet. 'You will not be taken away, I promise.'

Violet's mother just looked down at him, her dark eyes unconvinced.

On his way back from Myora, emotion swamped Hamish.. There was revulsion, there was indignation. How much did Holloway know of this? Was it a cover up to protect the reputation of his bloody asylum? Hamish's resolve set like steel. There was no way he would back away from his responsibility to Emily now. She had the courage to act, and it led to her death. There was no doubt in his mind that the same intention led to Simon's death. But who could he trust? He had no idea how long it would take the Colonial Office to act once they received his letter. He knew himself to be entirely ill-equipped for any kind of confrontation with Cornelius Vissen, or with Holloway for that matter.

Hamish was so pre-occupied with his thoughts that it came as a surprise when he noticed a shadow descend on the track ahead of him. The shadow grew larger until it almost completely blocked out the sun. Hamish strode on. A rush of wind lurched him backwards, causing him to stumble. He looked up to see the underside of an enormous Sea Eagle. It was so close he could make out the individual feathers, snow white on its belly. The bird's wingspan seemed unnaturally wide, feathers of tan and black with white tips that stretched away toward the clouds. It flew close enough for Hamish to see its beak, ivory and brown, hooked for snatching prey, talons, long and sharp for carrying stolen creatures high into the cliffs or across the sea.

The eagle swooped and soared above Hamish all the way along the sandy track. It made him even more irritable. The sound of voices was all around him again. What were these damned voices? As he pushed on, the sound of chatter in the trees, each side of him, became deafening. He looked from left to right expecting to see crowds of people gathered in the bushes. The chattering became louder and louder as he made his way toward the asylum. As he passed the hanging tree, the noise reached a crescendo, then stopped flat.

He forged on through thick silence, a sensation just as unnatural. Where were the birds? There was no cawing of crows, no screeching of white cockatoos, no laughing kookaburras. Even the crickets had stopped their incessant clicking. Still, the eagle swooped above him, diving every so often deep enough for him to feel the rush of air from its wings on his face.

Not for the first time since arriving on the Island, Hamish could imagine himself losing his grip on reality. There was something eerie in the air, in the constant voices when no one was there. What were the voices telling him? Then there was the eagle that seemed to follow his every move. The dizziness returned. The sand moved beneath him. The ground was shifting again. Still, he strode on.

Out of the corner of his eye, Hamish glimpsed the fleeting image of a figure running between the trees to the left of the track. When he tried to focus directly on the figure, he could see no one there. He told himself he was imagining things again, then a little further on he caught a glimpse of the same figure. It was moving faster than him. But it must have waited ahead, because he kept passing it again and again. For a fleeting moment, the figure seemed to gesture toward him. He stopped to get a better look, but as was always the case, when he looked directly at the figure, it was gone. Again, the figure appeared to be covered in long brown hair. But that was ridiculous.

Hamish was relieved when the bush dwindled to low scrub and the familiar shape of the asylum appeared before him. As he came out onto open grass, he stopped short. Grimy was in front of him. Grimy grinned his seedy grin.

'Just clearing the weeds,' he said.

He was holding a scythe and working away at a vine that had tangled itself through the fence line at the back of the grounds. Hamish hesitated a moment and then on a whim he said to Grimy,

'I saw someone in the bush, just now. Actually it, or they, followed me from Myora.'

Grimy kept at his work.

'It ...was about three feet tall,' Hamish said, realising how ridiculous that sounded. It was 'stocky.'

Grimy stopped. His scythe was suspended in mid-air. He let it fall to the ground at his feet. Grimy shuffled close to Hamish, he was so close Hamish could smell the foulness of his breath.

'Was the creature covered in brown hair?' he whispered.

'I... think so,' replied Hamish. 'Aye, but that's a little hairy man ya seen,' he said. 'A *Junjudee*, as the Natives call it.'

Uncomfortable, Hamish said, 'A what?'

''Tis a creature that roams the forests,' said Grimy. 'They can be mightily mischievous, the *Junjudee*. Naught to be afraid of, as a rule. But beware, there are ancestral spirits about as well. They're not as harmless as the little hairy man.'

Hamish was at a loss. Was Grimy telling him the figure he had seen in the bushes was a mythical being? Furthermore, was he warning him to be wary of ghosts? Or eagles? Did the ancestors come back in animal form? He shook himself to release the sensation of spiders crawling up his neck. Nonsense. He walked away from Grimy and his tales.

Nonetheless, in the back of his mind was the incessant image of the small stocky figure, the sound of the chattering voices when no one was present and the eagle that seemed to be everywhere he went. It struck him for an instant that these images appeared when he was feeling beleaguered by his self-appointed quest to give Emily a voice. Would the Aboriginal ancestors care that much about the murder of a white woman? 'No,' the idea came with sudden clarity. 'But they would care about the murder of Simon's child.'

Hamish forced himself to focus on what was real. Emily and Simon had been murdered. So had their unborn child. The certainty that Vissen had killed them to cover up his abuse of the girl formed a knot in his stomach. It followed then, that Vissen had been the one to push Rita and him off the cliff. There was no proof that Vissen tried to kill them, but no one had seen him at the asylum that afternoon either. It was possible. And then there was the question of the cattle on the track. As Brigid pointed out, he couldn't have known the fences were down unless he had been there that afternoon.

Still, Vissen couldn't have acted alone. How much of this did Holloway know? How much was he involved? Did Holloway set them up by sending them to the Point?

Hamish wanted to confront them both, but he needed time to think things through. What could he do if he did confront them? He needed to have a plan. He burst through the door of the hospital ward where Rita was resting and slumped into the chair beside her cot.

'What has happened?' she asked.

Hamish was red in the face and beads of sweat clung to the hair that flopped onto his forehead. He was out of breath.

'I have spoken to Violet,' he said.

Rita sat upright.

He repeated every word of the interaction with Violet and her mother.

'My Lord!' cried Rita. 'So, it is Vissen. And you are right, we don't know how deeply Holloway is involved. Poor Brigid!'

'What should we do?' cried Hamish.

Rita looked alert. 'You sent the letter on the choir boat?' she asked.

'Yes,' Hamish confirmed.

'The Colonial Secretary will receive Emily's letter this afternoon. What we have now is confirmation from the girl. But no one here knows about the letter, so that gives us some time.'

'Did you tell Brigid about the letter?' Hamish asked suddenly.

'No, of course not.' Then she added, 'I doubt Brigid knows anything about any of this.'

'I want to question Holloway about this business between Vissen and the girl,' Hamish said. 'At least we will get some impression as to whether he has been covering that up.'

'It could be dangerous,' cautioned Rita. 'He'll deny any knowledge either way, but it alerts him to the fact that we know. If he and Vissen are working together, it puts our lives at risk again.'

Hamish glanced at his hands. They were shaking.

'I don't care,' he said. 'I have to confront him and see his reaction. I believe I'll be able to tell if he is lying. In any case, what is he going to do? Shoot me in cold blood? How will he explain that to Brisbane in light of everything that has happened?'

'I don't know,' replied Rita, but you won't know either, when you're dead.'

They stared at one another for a moment, then Rita said, 'I am coming with you.' She swung her legs onto the floor.

'No!' cried Hamish.

'Stop blubbering,' Rita said. 'I'm sick of being stuck here, and you said yourself I should start getting up and about.'

'Yes, a little at a time – but not now. Not this.'

'I am coming,' she said. Red was tossed off the end of the bed as she swung her legs around to get up.

Hamish knew he had lost the argument.

22 SEPTEMBER 1884
EMILY

It was a particularly light evening. There was a silver glow where the moon peaked from behind the clouds. Because she was deep in thought, Emily didn't hear the sound of someone coming up close behind her. At the last moment she became aware of a presence, a breath at the back of her neck, then suddenly a dark, powerful shape engulfed her and there was something cold held tight against her neck. The assailant smelled familiar. She reached up intuitively to grasp at the wire that was being pulled tighter and tighter against her throat. She was gasping for air. The strength of the hands tugging hard on the wire was terrifying. The realisation came slowly that she was dying. Her tongue unbearably dry and swollen filled the inside of her throat. Her lungs began to burn. Emily grabbed at hair and skin, but her strength soon left her. She became vaguely aware of a second presence, someone other than the monster squeezing the life from her throat. She felt her body supported, just when she expected to fall. Emily slipped into unconsciousness.

The following evening, she was found hanging from the Moreton Bay Fig.

CHAPTER FIFTEEN

The Chartists were the cause of considerable fear among the middle classes in England. And yet among them were men of sense – hard headed men who were worthy of better treatment than they received. Of the six points covered by the Peoples' Charter, vote by ballot has been secured; and England is fast drifting down towards another – manhood suffrage. The other four points – equal electoral districts, annual Parliaments, no property qualification for members of Parliament and payments of members; and none but an unwise man would venture the assertion that these would not become the law of England in less than, say, ten years. – The Brisbane Courier, Queensland. Thursday 16 July 1885

---

10 OCTOBER 1884
HAMISH

When they reached the Superintendent's cottage, they could see through the open door that Brigid was sitting with her head held high and a look of determination on her face.

'I need to tell you something,' she said as her husband poured himself a drink.

Holloway spotted Hamish and Rita in the doorway and nodded in their direction.

They entered quietly.

'What is it then?' Holloway said to his wife. 'Vissen will be here soon and we'll need the table to go over the accounts. There's been a mistake in the supply of medicinal alcohol from Brisbane.'

Brigid took a deep breath, in readiness to speak.

'Damn them,' went on Holloway. 'They're determined to find me at fault. I'm certain of it.'

'It's about my first marriage,' began Brigid. She didn't dare look at Hamish and Rita directly, fearing she would lose her nerve if she did.

Holloway put down the wine flask and his glass. 'What of it?' he said.

'My first husband, he was ... something of a... well ... he lived outside the law.'

'What are you saying? He was a criminal?' Holloway's face distorted into a distasteful grimace.

'No. Well, in fact, yes. He was a political agitator. A Chartist. Wanted for radical agitation.'

Hamish and Rita glanced at one another. 'We should leave,' whispered Hamish. But they remained where they were.

Holloway's eyebrows shot up and his jaw dropped. 'What? Why have you never told me?'

'Because I knew how you'd react.'

'Why tell me now?'

'Because Vissen knew my first husband and is threatening to tell you about him.'

'Vissen knows?'

'Yes. And Dr Hart and Miss Cartwright.'

'Hamish and Rita know?' Holloway shrieked.

Hamish and Rita were rooted to the spot. They were aware of the intrusion, but they couldn't move.

'This isn't the catastrophe you think it,' Brigid was saying.

'It's catastrophe enough. Once word reaches Brisbane, my reputation will be ruined.'

'I doubt the powers in Brisbane care two figs for your wife's past dalliances. How could my past husband's activities impact on your reputation?'

'A radical?' sniffed Holloway. His face took on the effect of a man deeply hurt, but it seemed anything but convincing to Hamish.

'It's the deceit that moves me so deeply,' he said.

'I intended no deceit,' cried Brigid. 'I didn't want to trouble you unnecessarily. That part of my life is in the past.'

'What you have left unsaid amounts to deceit, dear wife.' Holloway turned his attention to Hamish and Rita. 'I'm sure you will respect the privacy of my wife and myself while we discuss this personal matter.'

Hamish watched Brigid carefully. She nodded to them almost imperceptibly.

'We will... return later,' stuttered Hamish.

'So, they've not yet come to terms with that,' Rita said as they left.

'It would seem not,' agreed Hamish.

'We will confront him in the morning,' said Rita.

'Right,' said Hamish.

Hamish tucked Rita back into her bed and sat in the chair beside her. He told her he would stay until she went to sleep. Less than half an hour passed before Brigid came in. She made her way up to the bed cautiously.

'Do you mind if I sit with you for a while?' she asked.

Hamish looked surly, but Rita said, 'Of course. Sit down.' She motioned for Hamish to vacate his seat for Brigid. He did so reluctantly and then glanced around the ward for another to sit in. Hamish found a chair and dragged it over to the bedside. Then he and Rita both looked at Brigid, waiting for her to speak.

'My husband is not taking the news well,' she said.

'Oh dear.'

'Really?'

Hamish and Rita spoke at once.

'He's upset,' said Brigid. 'I think it may wear off. It's not really my past marriage he's disturbed about. It's the current situation. He's worried about Dunwich. He thinks that after Hamish submits his report on the asylum, the authorities will replace him with a medical superintendent.' Brigid glanced at Hamish and then bowed her head.

Neither Hamish nor Rita spoke but their silence was just as telling as if they had.

'I know it would be for the best,' Brigid said. 'I try to pretend otherwise, but I'm aware of his... our... shortcomings. I've not been effective here. I have so few skilled staff to help with the genuinely ill inmates. We need regular visits from a medical officer, more medical supplies, trained nurses... and there are some,' she shot a knowing glance at Hamish, 'who shouldn't be here at all.'

Hamish and Rita were silent. There was nothing to say. She was right; the place needed people with medical qualifications to lead the asylum toward the twentieth century.

'It's always about money, isn't it?' Brigid asked. 'Everyone must agree that more of everything is needed at places such as this, but who is prepared to pay? Many of the wealthy believe that in supporting the asylum they'd be supporting people's natural proclivity to laziness.'

'I believe your husband is also of that view. He'd rather maintain the conditions as they are, to dissuade shirkers from thinking they might have an easy time of it at Dunwich.'

'I have to admit,' said Brigid, 'I do agree with him in some respects. I too, believe that the people here should work for their keep. However, there are many who can't. The nurse in me worries that the ill are not receiving proper treatment, merely subsistence until they die.'

Rita's brow was furrowed in a way that made Hamish's heart skip a beat – she was so beautiful even when she was frowning.

'I suppose the greatest proportion of people think families should take responsibility for the care of their elderly or ill relatives,' she said. 'And if people have no relatives or their families are too poor to care for them, it shouldn't be the State's responsibility to do so. The trouble with that argument is – who is responsible then?'

Hamish said, 'Surely the modern state, now that we are coming close to the turn of a new century, has a responsibility to its citizenry. The payback for being good citizens, working all one's life to contribute to the economy of the nation, would be the expectation that the State would provide the means to health and care in one's old age.'

'I'm not sure I have the answers to these questions,' said Brigid. 'I find my thoughts are a jumble of contradictions these days. I thought life was simple here at Dunwich. I convinced myself I was doing good work. God's work. But when I listen to you two, you sound like my ex-husband and I begin to question everything again. It isn't always a healthy way to live, I think. A life of questions. I think I may prefer the simple structures set out for us by others, by the Church and the State, as you call it.'

Hamish felt sorry for her. He knew enough about the confusion and inertia that can be caused by contradictory thoughts to last him a lifetime.

'Enough of this talk,' he said.

'What about your husband's mood with you?' asked Rita. 'Will he forgive you for deceiving him? Will he accept that you have a right to your own political views?'

Brigid laughed. 'I don't even know what my own political views are,' she said. 'I loved my first husband with such passion, I believed everything he believed. Then when I married again, I lost all faith in anything of that kind. It didn't occur to me that a woman should have her own views on politics.'

Rita was beside herself, 'Oh Brigid!' she cried.

Hamish put his hand on Rita's shoulder. 'Leave it,' he said.

'You know,' began Brigid slowly, 'I actually think the events of recent weeks have had a positive impact in the long term. I believe I may care more for my husband than I knew. I only hope he discovers feelings for me that will allow him to see past my previous marriage.'

'I hope so Brigid,' said Rita. 'I hope we find that he is a man of more character than we've given him credit for.'

Hamish looked doubtful.

Brigid hugged them both and left them to return to her cottage.

'There is so much more to come,' said Rita. 'What if Holloway was complicit in the murder of Emily?'

'And Simon,' added Hamish.

'And the attempt to kill us,' said Rita.

CHAPTER SIXTEEN

At that time, about eleven o'clock in the morning, a sailing boat was observed cruising about between Stradbroke Island and Peel Island, Mr Hamilton passing it at some distance. Just as he had got across the strong tide current, that runs about one mile off the latter Island, there was a sudden, though by no means severe gust of wind, and one of the men in the Superintendent's boat saw to his intense surprise, the sailing boat lurch over to leeward, and instantaneously disappear below the water. Mr Hamilton at once put about, and after a struggle with the oars through the strong flowing tide, managed to get up to the spot where the accident took place, and picked up the unfortunate crew. Three of the men who could swim, were making desperate efforts against the tide and the fourth, who could not swim, was hanging on to an oilcan while just at the time of their rescue, a shark was observed approaching the scene of the disaster. - The Week, Brisbane. Saturday 27 March 1880

10 OCTOBER 1884
HAMISH

Hamish left Rita falling asleep and returned to his tent. He was outside brewing a pot of tea and thinking on the events of the day when Wallace stumbled up to him. He had been drinking with his mates. Red was with him, as always. The dog jumped onto the seat next to Hamish.

'It's the Dunwich Lightning', Wallace said by way of explanation. 'I can't drink too much of it – it makes me sick. I left them early with their bloody home brew.' He laughed.

'Join me?' offered Hamish, shifting the dog so that Wallace could sit down.

Wallace looked eager to fall into bed and sleep, but he lowered himself carefully onto the seat and drew his mug from his coat.

'What do you know about the child, Violet?' asked Hamish.

'The child is related to Mabel, I think,' he said. 'Though they are all related one way or another so that's not saying much.'

'Have you noticed her around the asylum?' asked Hamish.

Wallace looked thoughtful. 'From time to time,' he said. 'What's bothering you, my friend?'

Hamish told Wallace what he knew. Wallace went pale.

'The filthy scum,' he said quietly.

'Do you think Holloway knows?' asked Hamish.

'Hard to say. I couldn't imagine him condoning such a thing,' he said, 'he's so bloody righteous. But he wouldn't want it public knowledge either. It might reflect badly on him.' Wallace thought further. 'No-one would give a toss about the girl,' he went on slowly, 'but the whole thing would be sufficiently distasteful to mark his reputation. My guess is that Holloway would have Vissen sent somewhere else. Just get rid of him quietly.'

'Do you think Vissen would kill to keep it quiet?' asked Hamish.

'Vissen would do anything to protect his reputation,' he answered immediately. 'While a native girl matters naught to the society of Brisbane, his carrying out lewd acts with a native child would be tantamount to bestiality in the eyes of the genteel.' Wallace was quiet for a moment, then he added, 'God help us all if the girl has Scarlet Fever.'

'I need to know if Holloway is involved. I'm going to confront him in the morning. No more putting it off. Will you come with me?'

Wallace nodded. He rose to leave. 'This is going to cause a shake-up,' he said.

'I hope so,' said Hamish.

Wallace seemed a good deal more sober as he made his way toward the row of huts on the hill where his bed was waiting for him, Red skipping happily about between his legs. Every now and then Hamish saw Wallace trip over his dog.

Hamish went over the past two weeks in his mind. He'd come to Dunwich to write a paper on poverty and illness in the asylum and had ended up conducting a murder enquiry, albeit clumsily. He had uncovered a vile account of abuse of an Aboriginal child at the hands of one of the asylum's staff, and someone had tried to kill himself and Rita. He felt certain it was Vissen who had murdered Emily, and he was just as sure, although there was no evidence, that he killed Simon as well. But it was also clear he couldn't have carried out either murder alone. Holloway was the obvious accomplice, but it didn't seem probable that Holloway would involve himself in such a scheme. If he knew about Vissen's abuse of the girl, why wouldn't he just remove him from the Island, as Wallace suggested.

Hamish worried about what should be his next move. He and Rita were still in danger while they stayed on the Island. Rita had recovered sufficiently that she could manage the trip on the barge with the help of pain medication. Perhaps he should take her home. But in doing that, he must abandon Emily. Vissen and Holloway would be released from any level of accountability, for surely it must be Holloway who is his partner in this.

Hamish was startled from his contemplations when Red appeared beside him again, barking enthusiastically.

'What are you doing, mate? Where is your master?'

The dog continued jumping up and down, barking at him.

'What is it, Red?' Hamish placed his hand on the dog's head to try and calm him.

Red showed his white teeth and growled. Hamish pulled his hand back. He tried to imagine what was troubling the dog, then Grimy appeared behind him. 'Come quickly,' he said, 'Your lady friend's in trouble.'

'What? I left her in the hospital not twenty minutes ago. She's fine.'

Red was tearing around Grimy's legs, barking madly. Grimy kicked him and the dog was sent tumbling across the grass.

'Hey, wait a minute,' cried Hamish. 'What's going on?'

'She's in the Stores,' Grimy cried. 'There's been an accident.'

'How did she get there?' said Hamish, still unable to equate his memory of leaving her safely in her bed only twenty minutes earlier with this new information.

He picked up the dog to save it from any further abuse. Red was still growling at Grimy.

'I don't know but you need to come, sir.'

Fear overtook confusion. Hamish ran toward the Stores, still clutching the dog, with Grimy running behind him.

As Hamish burst through the door of the stores everything inside disappeared into darkness. Red went quiet at last and Hamish set him down. Hamish stood still to allow his eyes to adjust.

The storehouse was a long narrow building with stocks of goods and produce required by the asylum stacked high in every direction. There were stacks of woollen blankets and bedding on one side of him, and sacks of flour, sugar and tea on the other. Beyond that it was difficult to make out any discernible shape in the dark. There was a musty odour to the place, the sweet smell of rotting fruit, mixed with the dry, sour smell of grain. Hamish looked back toward the door and noticed that the moon was shining on the asylum outside, but within the Stores there was only darkness and shadows. He moved forward warily. He could no longer see Grimy behind him. Red had already run back out the way they had come.

'Rita?' he called out. He heard a noise toward the back of the building. His mind was ticking over at an alarming pace. What the devil was going on? His mind was telling him there was no way Rita would be in this place in the middle of the night. But a troubling mixture of trepidation and curiosity propelled him forward. He put one foot in front of the other carefully, his senses alert to any sound or movement.

A rattling noise caught his attention. Was there something moving at the end of the building? He glanced behind, expecting to see Grimy coming in, but there was nothing. He moved toward the rattling sound. A figure became apparent, no more than a shadow at first. He stepped forward and made out the rough shape of someone seated in a chair.

Hamish approached the figure slowly. The chair was rocking from side to side.

'What the devil...?'

Hamish drew close to the chair. A rush of nausea engulfed him.

It was Rita!

She was tied up with a cloth wrapped around her mouth. His first reaction was one of panic.

Nothing made any sense. He lurched toward the figure on the chair, knowing only that he had to release her. Then he felt a sharp blow fall on the back of his head and his consciousness was reduced to a tiny white dot, and then nothing.

Hamish regained consciousness to feel someone tying his hands behind his back on the floor. Cornelius Vissen was glaring down at him. Hamish immediately scanned the area for Rita.

Ah! There she was, still tied to the chair.

'Are you alright?' he asked, realising instantly the stupidity of the question. Rita told him with her eyes that she was terrified, but intact.

'You two have been surprisingly difficult,' said Vissen. 'If you'd only fallen into the sea at the gorge as you were supposed to, everything would have worked out. As it turns out now, I have to leave the Island and dispose of you two as well.'

'It was you who killed Emily and Simon,' said Hamish. For some reason there was some satisfaction in the accusation, even though he had no expectation that he would be escaping this situation alive.

'Yes, it was me,' Vissen hissed between his teeth. 'The little slut was easy. I knew I only had to wait for her to come stumbling back after fucking that native. I was easily able to strangle the breath from her. With Grimy's help, I strung her from the tree.'

Grimy stepped into Hamish's line of sight. He was smiling from ear to ear.

'Simon wasn't as easy', Vissen went on. 'We had to silence him before we could string him up. Grimy took morphine from the dispensary.' Grimy was grinning proudly. 'He has been well paid for his help,' said Vissen.

'And I get off this bloody island,' Grimy chimed in.

'Is Holloway in this with you?' asked Hamish, struggling to get to his feet. He had to know.

Vissen laughed. 'Holloway? Good Lord, no,' he cried. 'That fool doesn't know what is going on right under his nose. In fact, it was my idea to send you to the Point. He won't even remember that I put the idea into his head.'

Grimy forced Hamish back down onto his back. He pushed his knee into his chest while he tied a piece of calico tight around Hamish's mouth. His lips burned, and his tongue was forced back into his head.

Hamish could see that Rita was being dragged up out of the chair where she had been bound and her hands were being tied behind her back by Vissen.

Grimy produced a gun from a nearby table and forced it into the small of Hamish's back, yelling at him to get up on his feet. With the gun pressed tightly against his skin, he and Rita were pushed out of the stores into the night. Their mouths remained gagged. Hamish coughed and spluttered. His tongue was too far back, and the cloth stretched the corners of his mouth so that they bled. He was struggling to move his tongue, even a little, to release the pressure. But his concentration had to remain on moving forward. It was difficult to breathe and they were being forced through the bracken quickly.

Hamish and Rita struggled as they skirted the edge of the settlement south past the causeway and into the mangroves along the shore. They both stumbled numerous times. The brush scratched against his legs and he twisted his ankle as they made their way across a shallow creek depression.

All the while, Vissen and Grimy pushed them forward. Rita was struggling just ahead of him. He was distraught, thinking about the pain she must be experiencing in her healing shoulder. His heart was beating so hard in his chest and he was breathing so heavily he imagined his lungs would explode. At the same time, his ankle was throbbing and refusing to hold the weight of his body. He stumbled along, dragging one leg and trying to keep all his weight balanced on the other.

When they reached the mangroves, Hamish's good ankle sunk deep into the mud and it was difficult to pull one foot after another. He was sucked down into the soft swirling pools of seawater. Hamish could see that Rita was also struggling to remain upright. Vissen and Grimy continued to force them through the sticky mud.

Finally, they saw an old fishing boat at the edge of the tidal swamp, perched precariously, half on the mud and half in the waters of the Bay. The boat was too heavy for the men to drag it out into deeper water. The tide was on its way in. It was going to be at least half an hour before the boat would be afloat. They scrambled onto the vessel with Grimy and Vissen still thrusting the guns into their backs. The muscles in Hamish's back seized. He tried to rotate his shoulder to release the tension, but Vissen forced the tip of the gun deep into his skin. Hamish stumbled and fell on the deck.

'Why don't we shoot them now?' said Grimy. 'We got 'em on the boat.'

'The sound would echo back to the asylum, you idiot,' snapped Vissen. 'We'll send them off in the Bay. They'll drown without making a sound. Tie their feet so they can't get up.'

There was a tense wait for the tide to come in sufficiently for the fishing boat to move.

'That savage threatened to kill me, when he worked out I had strangled his slut,' gloated Vissen

Hamish and Rita glared at him.

'Disgusting Black had no idea what happened when Grimy came up behind him. He was sitting under the hanging tree moaning about his lost love. Grimy knocked him down, and I pumped him full of morphine. Might not have been enough to kill him, but he was quiet. Hey Grimy?'

Grimy chuckled.

'Heavy load he was though. No easy task to get him hauled up on that rope. But we did. And there he swung.'

'With his missus now,' snarled Grimy.

Eventually, they were afloat and rowing across the Bay. Grimy rowed while Vissen kept his gun pointed at them. Hamish and Rita kept their eyes on each other. Hamish tried to express his sincere apologies for getting her involved in this. Rita's eyes remained bright and alert.

Hamish worked furiously to loosen the knot that kept his hands tied. He could see the second gun at Grimy's feet as he rowed. If he could just release his hands, he could grab the gun and take them by surprise. He had to loosen the rope without Vissen noticing. He remained as still as possible as he worked at the ropes behind his back. He wound his wrists first one way then the other, feeling the knot slacken with each movement. It was taking too long, and he could feel the ropes sticky with blood. He was terrified, but he kept his face blank. From where she was bundled in her own terror, Rita could see what he was doing. Hamish appreciated that her eyes remained steady. She gave nothing away.

When they were about halfway across the Bay, and Hamish could just make out the grey line of the mainland in the darkness, Vissen nodded and Grimy stopped rowing. Vissen moved to hold Hamish's head off the deck and Grimy lifted his legs. They rolled Hamish toward the side of the boat. Grunting, they lifted his struggling body, ready to roll him over the side. The edge of the boat was holding his full weight and his face was inches from the black water when the ropes finally loosened sufficiently for him to release his hands. He grabbed Vissen around the head and he stumbled. At the same time, a shout sounded across the Bay. 'You there!'

Startled, Vissen and Grimy dropped Hamish back onto the deck and peered across the water. Hamish took the opportunity to grab Grimy's gun.

Slowly and silently, a cutter had drawn out of the dark alongside them. Three men jumped from the cutter onto their boat. Two of the men overpowered Grimy while Vissen held tight to his own gun with one hand while he drew Rita to him with the other. Her eyes were wide, and her head was shaking violently. She was using every ounce of energy she had to attempt to wriggle free of Vissen's grasp. He managed to manipulate the gun to her head, holding the weapon's muzzle to her temple. Everyone was instantly still.

'Back off,' shouted Vissen. Hamish let the hand holding Grimy's gun fall to his side. The two men holding Grimy remained stationary, but they didn't let go of him. One of the men was Wallace, the other was the Aboriginal man who had told Hamish to fuck off at Myora. Harvey.

'Let him go,' snarled Vissen as he shoved the gun into Rita's temple. She dared not breath. But Wallace and Harvey did not let go. They were looking past Vissen at something behind him. He turned his head in time to see a tall, wiry Aboriginal man slip up out of the water and tower over him. It was Simon's brother, Ned.

Ned grabbed Vissen around the neck and pulled him over the side of the boat into the water before he could register what was happening. Rita lost her balance and fell toward the centre of the boat. Just before she hit her head on the deck, one of the men who had boarded from the cutter slipped his arm beneath her and gathered her up. She looked up at his face. It was James Holloway. He carefully untied her and removed the gag from her mouth.

Harvey was releasing the binding around Hamish's mouth. Hamish let out a loud gasp as the tension on his tongue was released. Wallace used the same ropes to secure Grimy's hands and feet. He was cursing loudly when one of the men shouted, 'Shut up or we'll stuff ya mouth with that cloth.' Grimy shut up.

Ned climbed up the side of the boat, splashing water onto Grimy as he did so. Everyone noted that Vissen was no longer with him. They scoured the water for a sign of movement, but there was none. They all looked at the Aboriginal man. He looked away.

'For my brother,' he said to the wind, not looking any of them in the eye.

The water was calm. There was no sign of a ripple as far as they could see in any direction. Moonlight skipped and danced on the waters of the Bay, but there was no disturbance beyond the boat. No one spoke.

At last Holloway said, 'We are more than halfway to the mainland. We will continue that way. We had the Pilot station caretaker telegraph the authorities from Amity and they should be there waiting for us.'

With Vissen lost in the Bay and Grimy tied up, everyone relaxed a little.

'I noticed the boat on the mud flats earlier this evening,' Wallace said. 'I thought it was odd at the time. But I didn't realise what was going on until Red came bounding up to my tent creating a racket. He wouldn't stop barking until I followed him back to the Stores. I saw Vissen and Grimy force you two across the mudflat and into the boat with guns. I knew I couldn't stop them alone, so I woke up Holloway. We rode out to Amity for the cutter and picked up Ned and Harvey from Myora on the way. I knew we had time before the tide came in. We just hoped we could cut them off before they shot you or dumped you in the Bay. It was touch and go. We waited in the shadows of Peel before we made our run.'

The authorities were waiting for the boat when they landed at the mouth of the Brisbane River. Later Hamish, Rita, Holloway and Wallace sat in the office of the local constabulary. Ned and Harvey had declined the invitation to join them at the police station. Rita was bundled in a blanket, holding her injured arm against her chest. Hamish knew that her shoulder would be throbbing.

'Can we have morphine sent over from the hospital?' he said. The incident involved far too much activity for her healing bones. The Police Sergeant nodded to a constable to see to it. Hamish was wet through, his shirt was hanging out, his hair was dishevelled, and his face was pale. But he was alert. He was explaining to the police the series of events that had occurred that evening. The story made little sense though, until the Colonial Secretary himself arrived. The policemen all stood to attention when he entered the office.

He put out his hand to shake that of Hamish. 'Hamish Hart,' he said, 'it is a pleasure to meet you at last.'

'At last?' asked Hamish.

'Callahan has kept me informed of your suspicions,' he said.

Holloway was cowering in the background. It was a soggy and undignified way to meet the Colonial Secretary. Hamish knew he would be disappointed in the circumstances.

'And you must be James Holloway,' said the Colonial Secretary, holding out his hand to Holloway.

'An honour to meet you, Sir,' said Holloway.

Hamish explained that Holloway, Wallace and two Aboriginal men, had rescued them just in time, before Cornelius Vissen and Jim Grimes tipped them into the Bay.

Everyone turned their eyes toward Grimy, who was no longer tied-up but was instead sitting on a bench in a cell.

'So, you believe that Cornelius Vissen killed the inmate to prevent her from sending this letter?' asked the Colonial Secretary holding out the soiled paper.

'I do,' confirmed Hamish. 'He valued his reputation above all else,' he added.

'And you knew nothing of this?' He directed the question toward Holloway.

'Of course, I didn't!'

'It is true,' said Hamish. 'Vissen admitted he'd been manipulating the Superintendent. Mr Holloway knew nothing.'

'A native child...' began the Colonial Secretary, his face contorted in disgust.

'Where is Vissen now then?'

'The small group glanced at one another. 'Fell overboard,' said Hamish. 'In the tussle that followed when these men came aboard.'

Holloway opened his mouth to speak but no sound came out. He closed it again under the acid gaze of Rita.

'That's right,' he said at last.

'That's it then,' said the Colonial Secretary. He handed Emily's letter along with Hamish's report to the constable. Take statements and charge this devil with assisting in the murders of Emily Baker and the Native known as Simon.'

Jim Grimes snarled and shivered in his cell. It was impossible to tell whether it was fear that made him tremble or that he was wet through to the skin in a cold cell. No one cared much.

CHAPTER SEVENTEEN

While the asylum at Dunwich began with a small group of inebriates and paupers it has grown considerably over the years to become one of the most significant institutions in the colony. Consequently, an entire change in administration is necessary. -The Brisbane Courier, Queensland 8 January 1885

---

23 NOVEMBER 1884
HAMISH

Six weeks later, Hamish and Rita sat in one of the two rooms that made up Hamish's newly established general practice on Wickham Terrace in Brisbane. The terrace house was a handsome building with four separate dwellings, each with two storeys. Hamish would live in the rooms upstairs, while he had the two rooms on the ground floor refurbished for his waiting and treatment rooms. The rooms on the lower floor and the beautifully crafted spiral staircase, he had painted in pale mint with white trim. There was a decorative white rose at the centre of the ceiling in each room. The doctor planned to see patients there three days per week and work at the Brisbane Hospital a further three days.

Hamish and Rita sat upstairs in his private lodgings. The weeks since their adventures on Stradbroke Island had been busy. There was the purchase of the house, decorating and setting up the practice, and there was the article that Hamish had promised *The Brisbane Courier*. Rita had her own work to attend, the two safe houses for women and her pharmaceutical practice.

The sun shone through large glass windows this November morning and warmed the room. Rita leaned back in the window seat with one leg resting comfortably on the cushioned seat, and the other touching the floor. It was a position that reflected complete comfort in her surroundings. Her skirt was pulled up over the raised leg, exposing her petticoat and an inch of pearly skin above her boot. Hamish was in his favourite chair, trying desperately not to be distracted from his newspaper by Rita's perfectly smooth leg.

Reading aloud from his newspaper, Hamish said, 'There is a piece in here in response to my article.'

Rita looked up from her book.

'They have conducted their inquiry into the management of the asylum,' said Hamish. 'Here it says, *The Committee have investigated the visiting Justice, Mr. Roy Callahan, the asylum Superintendent Mr James Holloway and the Matron Mrs Brigid Holloway. The Officer in charge of the Stores, and Assistant Superintendent, Mr Cornelius Vissen has been declared missing, presumed drowned.*'

'I hope he has been eaten by sharks,' interjected Rita.

Hamish read on. '*It has been shown that the institution has carried on without any code of regulations for the guidance of the officials or the observance of the inmates. It will not be a surprise to anyone that grave and serious abuses have crept into the Administration which demands the serious attention of the government. There are certain criminal matters now with the courts.*'

'Bravo to that,' cried Rita.

'Agreed,' said Hamish. 'This is the part where they get to the point, *While the visiting Justice has inspected the asylum at least once a year, no reports were ever submitted to the Colonial Secretary to indicate issues of concern at Dunwich. No reports at all were received from the visiting surgeon and only vague reports, of no particular value, were received from the Superintendent.*'

Rita laughed out loud at this.

Hamish continued. '*Nonetheless, without attaching undue weight to the complaints which have been made, there is sufficient evidence to show that the treatment of the inmates has not been as humane or as effective as their condition and their dependency demanded.*'

'Well, that is an understatement,' said Hamish. 'Here there is a list of recommendations. *The following changes are urgently demanded. One: Removal of all female inmates to a location on the mainland.*'

Rita screwed up her face. 'So, exactly where will that be?'

'Lady Bowen Hostel, I suppose,' said Hamish.

'Yes, she has room for thirty more women,' said Rita in her most sarcastic tone.

'Do these men intend to budget additional funds to accommodate these women properly?'

Hamish assumed the question was rhetorical and continued on. '*Two: That the management of the asylum be placed in the hands of an experienced medical practitioner.*'

'That's a good thing,' said Rita.

'Absolutely,' agreed Hamish.

'Exactly what Holloway was afraid of.'

'I think he knew it was inevitable, don't you?'

Rita smiled nodding.

'*Three: the recovery from inmates or their relatives of some contribution towards the expense of their maintenance.*'

'Hmm,' Rita pursed her lips. 'What of those who cannot contribute?'

'I expect they will be required to work, contribute their labour to sustaining the community,' said Hamish.

'It seems to me that those who can already do so,' replied Rita.

'Apparently, they're demanding that inmates sign a paper binding them to obey the rules of the institution and agree to pay a portion of the costs of their upkeep. Those who receive pensions are being required to sign them over. I've heard that some have refused and have been turned out.'

'Good Lord! Where will they go?

'I suppose they will be on the streets in Brisbane.'

'Surely, places like the asylum exist primarily to support those who cannot support themselves.'

'Yes, but many opinion pieces in this very paper say that those with any income at all should be contributing to the cost of their support. I imagine the fellows who have refused to sign and have been turned out as a consequence, will either drink themselves to death on the streets, or reconsider their decision and return to Dunwich under the new requirements.'

Rita was not so easily silenced.

'It's not about the money for these men. It's about retaining some control over their lives. They are to be cowered into submission to government rules, even their meagre pensions stripped from them, and they're left with no independence at all, no dignity. This is the price of age and poverty.'

Hamish understood what she was saying. Rita was far more radical in her ideas than Hamish. He admired her for that.

He said, 'Of course they will need a code of regulations for Dunwich. I believe the Legislative Assembly is preparing such a code now. The Premier here in this paper, is reported as saying, *'there are several benevolent institutions in the Colony, the principle of which is Dunwich, yet there has been no law for regulating such institutions and no power for asserting authority. In relation to Dunwich, there was an old Act covering the Benevolent Asylum wards of the Brisbane Hospital, but the legislation does not translate across to the asylum that has grown up on Stradbroke Island. A new Act is being drafted.*'

'I wonder how much difference the new Act will make?' said Rita. 'I wonder if the new medical superintendent will close Ward 10?'

'I can't believe you bottled up that experience and kept it to yourself. I know how deeply it would have affected you.'

'There was no reason to burden you while you were ill,' said Hamish. 'As it happens, there was enough to deal with in the hours following my visit to Ward 10.'

They both reflected for a moment.

'What happened to Violet after we left, Hamish?' Rita was ashamed she hadn't asked about the girl sooner.

'Violet recovered after a few days. It's unlikely she had Scarlet Fever. There were no more cases. Nonetheless I'm not sorry I at least tried to impose restrictions. If it had been scarlatina, the results could've been catastrophic for the asylum.'

'I can't imagine that any medical practitioner would allow a place so out of touch with contemporary practice to continue,' Rita said.

'Have you heard anything of Holloway and Brigid?' she asked.

'Oh yes,' said Hamish. 'They moved to Roma where Holloway is managing the rail service. He has his own railway station.'

Rita laughed. 'How grand is the Roma railway station?'

'It has one platform. The train runs between Brisbane and Charleville twice weekly. And I hear that the station house is a handsome timber building, larger than his cottage on the Island.'

'What will Brigid do?'

'It seems there's a great need of nurses out that way. Brigid is providing health care to the wives of the homesteaders and farmhands.'

Rita said, 'Something has been troubling me. I understand that Vissen murdered Emily to stop her from sending that letter, and he murdered Simon because he was threatening to take his revenge. But why did he try to kill us?'

'Vissen hoped that both deaths would be accepted as suicide. That would've been the case if we hadn't been on the Island. It suited Holloway, because a double suicide would have been far less difficult to explain to the authorities than two murders.'

'So,' began Rita, 'when Holloway held the funeral at Dunwich and publicly announced that both of them committed suicide over their grief, it suited both Holloway and Vissen. Why not leave it at that? What prompted him to try to get rid of us?'

'I think the spur may have been when you joined me. Vissen expected I'd be ignored, but then there was two of us. He knew you came to the Island for the explicit purpose of helping with the investigation.'

'You don't think my ruse was convincing?' laughed Rita.

'And then there was the letter. Vissen must have known about the letter, or at least, suspected that Emily was about to write one. But he didn't know for sure if she had, or where it was. I guess he was afraid if we kept asking questions, we would come across the truth eventually.'

'He wanted us to die,' said Rita.

'But we didn't die. We found out what a vile creature he really was. As it became more obvious that his secret was unravelling, he became desperate. He decided to kill us both once and for all, then disappear to another part of the country.'

'Do you think Holloway would have covered up for him if he had known?' asked Rita.

'Yes. I do. I think he would have covered it up. He would probably have sent him away, but that's all.'

'Thank God for Wallace,' said Rita.

At that moment, a scruffy man of indefinite age with wispy red hair entered the room carrying a tray of tea and freshly baked scones.

'I thought you might be hungry,' he said, 'so I prepared a tray.' He placed it before his new boss. A red-haired terrier that looked remarkably like his owner trotted in behind him.

'Good,' said Rita, clearing a space for Wallace on the settee. 'Join us for tea. We were just talking about you.'

23 NOVEMBER 1884
WALLACE

At that moment there was a knock on the door downstairs. Wallace put down the tray and went to the door immediately. Red took the opportunity to jump into his seat. Wallace was still a little unsteady on the stairs, not having had to climb stairs for such a long time. He breathed in the smell of fresh paint and reminded himself how lucky he was that Hamish had retained him as his cook and personal assistant. It was a far more luxurious life than he was accustomed to. He had too much time on his hands, truth be told. Still, at his age he was grateful for a bit of easy living.

A young constable stood at the door, cap in hand.

'I wonder if I could speak with the doctor,' he said.

'May I ask the nature of your inquiry? asked Wallace.

'It's an official matter,' he replied.

Then when Wallace continued to stare at him unmoved, he went on. 'Look here, there was a meeting of the workers at the Wickham Hotel last night. Some kind of fight, and one of them was killed. The Police Sergeant doesn't think it's as clear cut as all that though. The man killed in the fight – the sergeant thinks it may have been murder.'

Wallace reflected once more on his easy life, then a smile passed across his lips, so slight it was imperceptible to the eager young constable.

'You had better come through,' said Wallace.

AUTHOR NOTES

The characters and the storyline in *Murder at the Dunwich Asylum* are fictional. While the Dunwich Benevolent Society operated in Dunwich from 1865 until 1946, there is no indication that a murder of one of the inmates took place, or that any of the inmates had an intimate relationship with anyone from the Myora community. This book is a series of imagined events that take place within a setting that is *partly* real. By this I mean that while much of the portrayal of the asylum and surrounds on the Island are based on descriptions of the place documented at the time, there are also aspects that are entirely fictional. For example, there is no evidence that Ward 10, as it is portrayed in this story, existed at Dunwich. Although such wards existed elsewhere in Australian asylums.

The actual Benevolent Society first operated through the Brisbane Hospital, housing a number of paupers who were not acutely ill, but with chronic conditions or disabilities that meant they were unable to work and sustain themselves. By 1865 the hospital was becoming dangerously overcrowded so the paupers were transferred to the Quarantine Station at Dunwich and so began the Dunwich Benevolent Asylum. The asylum was funded under *the Benevolent Asylum Ward Act* of 1861. All the initial supplies for the asylum came from the Brisbane Hospital.

In the earliest days of the asylum there were between sixty and seventy inmates, mostly men. This number grew rapidly over the decades and by 1884 when Hamish visits, there were over 400 inmates and reports of severe over-crowding. Up to 45 inmates were packed into wards designed to hold thirty. There were both men's and women's wards, as well as wards for inebriates, Chinese (or Asiatics as they were known at the time) and the blind.

Historical records relating to the asylum survive and indicate that most inmates were over 60, however, there were some under that age who were listed as paralysed, crippled, maimed, imbecile, diabetic, blind and epileptic. People from all over the colony were sent to Dunwich, ostensibly for being poor and unable to support themselves. The newspapers of the time were full of editorials about the 'undeserving poor', describing them as 'burdens to the State' and 'idlers and drunks.' There was a lively debate about whether the State should be carrying this burden. There was a very high mortality rate with over one third of inmates dying within the first year of admission to the asylum.

The asylum was run according to the theory that inmates should contribute to the society within which they live. Doing so was believed to contribute to a sense of well-being and health. Inmates worked as wardsmen, clerks, woodcutters, nightsoil-men, floor sweepers, gardeners, candle-makers, tailors, mattress makers and managers of livestock. The asylum by the 1880's was largely self-sufficient with large tracts of land under cultivation, stables, cow sheds, piggeries, poultry yards and milk supply. Swamps had been drained to claim land for cultivation and for running cattle and sheep. Inmates also supplied the community with fresh fish.

The Aboriginal people of Stradbroke Island lived at Myora (*Moongalba*) during the period of the story. There had already been three generations of contact with Europeans, beginning with the convicts in 1827. They had assisted in the building of the quarantine station, worked with the fishermen and oyster farmers, and had been a significant part of the labour force for the asylum since its earliest days. Through the circumstance of close proximity, they were arguably more connected to the non-Indigenous people on Stradbroke Island than were their contemporaries on the mainland.

I have imagined myself within the setting of 1884, at the Dunwich Asylum and developed a work of fiction within that setting. I hope there is sufficient historical detail that the story *rings* true to the reader.

Murder at the Dunwich Asylum

Shawline Publishing Group Pty Ltd
www.shawlinepublishing.com.au